Finally Time to Dance

A Novel

Mamie Thompson

Bloomington, IN   Milton Keynes, UK
authorHOUSE®

AuthorHouse™
1663 Liberty Drive, Suite 200
Bloomington, IN 47403
www.authorhouse.com
Phone: 1-800-839-8640

AuthorHouse™ UK Ltd.
500 Avebury Boulevard
Central Milton Keynes, MK9 2BE
www.authorhouse.co.uk
Phone: 08001974150

© 2007 Mamie Thompson. All rights reserved.

No part of this book may be reproduced, stored in a retrieval system, or transmitted by any means without the written permission of the author.

First published by AuthorHouse 8/29/2007

ISBN: 978-1-4343-0516-9 (sc)

Printed in the United States of America
Bloomington, Indiana

This book is printed on acid-free paper.

The Oak Hill Preservation Association 2007

Photo credit: Rob Phillips

To my dear, patient Richie.
Thank you for showing me
how to live, and love, again.

Acknowledgments

Thank you to every woman who inspired the growth these pages represent: Sisy, Benita, Donna, Kimberly, Christi, Alicia, Dorothy, Karri, Sharon, Dana, Dee, Fay, Jerri, Jane, and The Girls of TBC. You may see yourselves in these pages. Forgive me, laugh with me, praise God the grieving is behind and the next dance is ahead.

Pamela, you cheered me every step of the way. How could I have had the courage to tell this story without your enthusiasm? You're my hero.

Thank you to Adeline, Amanda, Andrew, Adam, and Alicia, the five finest editors in the world. You gave me the faces, the expressions, the words, and the feelings to write a book about a family that loves each other enough to forgive the bad parts, enjoy the good parts, and live out loud in between. I adore you. You are the five best gifts God has ever given me. Thank you for your input while I wrote this and for being excited when you saw yourselves come to life on the pages.

Betty and C.A., thank you for making us part of your life. We're blessed to be Thompsons and we love you.

Rich, thanks for telling me I could do this. Neither of us realized how much healing would come from it, but we're on the winning end now.

And finally, thank you to God. For the healing, for the book, for the family…for all the dances we all receive.

Blessings,
Mamie

Prologue

Megan bounced the tiny infant lightly in her arms. Her three middle children had already made their way to the waiting limousine. She looked down at Ali.

"It's time to go, sweetie." Megan offered her oldest daughter her hand.

Instead of taking her mother's hand, however, Ali said, "I'll be right back."

Confused, Megan watched Ali's red curls bounce as she quickly made her way back to the front of the sanctuary. Ali stopped and tugged on the dark sleeve of a man Megan had seen before the service started. He bent down so that his eyes were level with Ali's. The two exchanged a few words and then he stood and took Ali's hand. They walked together to the front of the church. He left the small girl standing there for a moment then returned with a metal folding chair. He opened the chair and stood it where Ali was pointing.

Megan watched her six-year-old daughter, wise beyond her years, climb onto the chair and wait for the man to open the casket for her. She tugged the pink carnation corsage off her tiny wrist and tenderly placed it on her daddy's chest. She spoke again to the man. He nodded and then leaned forward and pulled something out and handed it to Ali. Megan saw Ali thank the man before she climbed down from the chair and made her way back down the aisle, Chris's necktie hanging almost to her knees on either side of Ali's small frame. When she reached Megan, she said, "I wanted to keep this."

"Daddy would love that." Megan stooped down, quickly made a loose loop in the tie, and touched Ali's cheek. "You're such a brave girl." Megan straightened and looked back one last time at the front of the sanctuary. The flowers and posters had been taken out already. Chris's body was flanked by the pallbearers, all his brothers or brothers in Christ, waiting to load the funeral coach for the short trip to the cemetery. Megan motioned to the man holding the door open. He let the door go and walked toward Megan.

"Ali, you and Krissy go with this nice man to the car." Megan handed the baby to the funeral director and smiled at his clumsiness with Krissy. When the trio had made their way out the door, Megan turned and walked to the front of the church. She stopped about ten feet from Chris's body and paused. The man who had helped Ali stepped back and opened the sanctuary's side door. Silently, the pallbearers filed into the hall.

Alone with her best friend for the last time, Megan walked slowly to his side. She choked back sobs as she looked down at the crayon drawings and wadded tissues that his children had laid on their father's chest. Chris had requested a closed casket so that the sight of such treasures could remain locked in the hearts of Megan and his children forever.

Megan stood trembling for several moments before she tenderly bent over and kissed Chris one last time.

"Catch you on the flip side, Bud."

Chapter 1

"Thanks." Megan breathed in the scent of the steaming caramel latte Dee set in front of her. She sank into a deep leather chair and relaxed. Even in the crowded café, Megan enjoyed these quiet moments with her friend. Usually their conversations were over the phone and punctuated with the demands and activity of a combined nine children. The young mothers looked forward to these Tuesday afternoon rendezvous where they could actually complete their sentences. Megan stretched her legs across the rustic table and sighed.

Dee asked, "What was that for?" Megan looked at her friend quizzically.

"What was what for?"

"The sigh. It sounded important." Dee set her cup on the table and turned to her friend. "Anything you want to talk about?"

Megan should have known that she couldn't hide her mood from Dee. Still, she wasn't ready to divulge her feelings. Truth be told, Megan had not yet put her own finger on her current swirl of emotions.

Maybe it was the weather. Chris had died in late fall last year, and the changing leaves and cooler days were reminiscent of their final days. That was it. More of the grief stuff. Well, it had not brought her down, yet, and Megan Hardin wasn't about to let it get the best of her, now. God had blessed her with a long and happy marriage, five healthy children, and a roof over her head. She had no room to whine or complain.

"I'm fine. I guess I've just been a little, I don't know, restless, lately. This, too, shall pass," Megan said more to herself than to her friend.

Dee seemed accepting of this summation and changed the subject. Megan was relieved to spend the next half-hour discussing which boutiques of south Oklahoma City might hold the perfect purse for fall. After their cups were empty, the women left the café and spent the remainder of their afternoon shopping, laughing, and visiting about nothing in particular.

Megan closed the door to the boys' bedroom softly and made her way down the carpeted stairs. Randy and Chad had been particularly rambunctious at bedtime, causing Megan to doubt whether they would settle down without argument. Thankfully, the evening's ritual of stories, prayers, and softly sung hymns had gone smoothly and Megan found herself contently snuggling into her large armchair before nine o'clock. She picked up her worn Bible and was about to open it when she thought about the moment of uneasiness during her conversation with Dee this afternoon.

The notion that anything was wrong seemed ludicrous to Megan, but still, the sensation that something was missing would not subside. Megan tried the exercise she suggested to her nine-year-old daughter, Ali, when the pre-adolescent experienced bouts of mal-contentment. Megan tore a slip of paper from last week's church bulletin and began a list of things she was thankful for.

Health, home, happiness, being cherished by my husband. Children, ability and resources to teach them at home, friends, coffee (smiley face next to that one), reliable vehicle, cooler weather. The list went on until Megan had filled the scrap of paper. Megan read the list twice and sighed. Ali was right. This system was not foolproof. There was still an empty, restless place in Megan's heart.

Megan had just flipped her pillow over for what seemed like the fortieth time when the phone rang. Not wanting the shrill sound to wake her sleeping children, Megan snatched up the receiver quickly, knocking over a small glass of water in the process.

"Hello," Megan almost growled as she tried to rescue a soggy parenting magazine and flip the lamp on at the same time.

"Hello, yourself. What's wrong?"

Megan relaxed only a little at the sound of Julie's voice. "Hang on." Megan retrieved a dry towel from the master bathroom and returned to her bedside. She picked up the phone and quipped, "Just spilled a glass of water when I picked up. How goes it?" Megan had to work at sounding cheerful.

"You sound distracted. Should I call back later?"

"It's OK. Have you made plans for Natasha's birthday?"

"That's why I called. Sorry for the short notice, but we're having the party this Saturday. Think you can make it?"

This cheered Megan considerably. "We wouldn't miss it. What time?" Megan and Julie had met at work when they were both pregnant with their first children. Born only five days apart, Natasha and Ali were inseparable, even after Julie and Todd had moved an hour and a half away. Missing Natasha's birthday was out of the question. They would clear the calendar and be there. In fact, when Julie told her that the party would be before lunchtime Megan had a wonderful idea. "How about we come late Thursday or early Friday and we can gad about downtown a few hours while I'm down there."

"Ooooohhh…now you're talking. I have to work Friday, but only for a couple of hours. If you come to town with me, we can have lunch on Main Street."

The thought of spending a few days in Julie's sleepy little college town thrilled Megan to no end. Some peace and quiet might be just what her restless heart needed. "We'll be there around suppertime on Thursday. What can I bring?"

"Just you and those kiddos. See you then."

"Great. Call if plans change."

"OK. Love you."

"You, too, Jules. Bye."

Ah, a road trip. A distraction. Just what Megan needed to pull out of her slump. She tossed the damp towel into the hamper and walked to the kitchen to refill her water glass. On the way back through the living room, the sight of her abandoned Bible on the ottoman caught Megan's eye. Guilt crept in as she realized she'd not opened it tonight. Instead, she had slumped off to bed in frustration. Knowing she'd rest better after a little quiet time with her Father, Megan settled into her chair a second time and set the small glass on the table beside her. She prayed silently for direction. *It's been a year since Chris died, Lord. What am I supposed to do with the rest of my life here on earth until I can be with him again?*

Absentmindedly, she opened the front cover of her Bible and thumbed through the bulletins and notes she kept tucked inside. A bright yellow bookmark caught her eye. She cringed at the memory of Pastor Dave challenging the congregation to follow the daily Bible readings outlined on the bookmark. Megan had fallen behind the "read the Bible through in a year" schedule months ago. With a resigned sigh, she picked up the bookmark and found today's date. "Better now than never."

Megan opened her Bible to the forty-first chapter of Isaiah and began to read, intent on absorbing the history in the story. She rarely expected to find God's direction in an "assigned" reading, so Megan was confused when her heart began pounding at the nineteenth verse.

I will put in the desert the cedar and the acacia, the myrtle and the olive, I will set pines in the wasteland, the fir and the cypress together, so that people may see and know, may consider and understand, that the hand of the LORD had done this, that the Holy One of Israel has created it.

Megan paused and read the verses again. Was God speaking to her about trees? It seemed plausible. Not that she and Chris had ever gotten one to grow here. The soil in their suburban neighborhood had not been kind to the few they had planted on the small lot. In fact, this past spring Megan had dug out the last carcass and vowed to stop killing trees by planting them in her yard. Megan's thoughts wandered to her own childhood home in the Deep South with oaks so massive you could climb on the roots and be several feet off the ground.

"Enough musing for tonight," Megan chided herself out loud. She and her children were exactly where God wanted them. Until *He* moved her, Megan wouldn't budge. She spent the next few minutes praying for her children and for her mother. Megan ended her prayer with a plea for direction. *You're trying to show me something, God. I know that.*

Make it clear so I don't miss it.

Chapter 2

It was already dark when Megan pulled into the Sheldon's driveway. The children had gotten burgers along the way, but Megan's stomach growled. She focused on getting the children inside in an orderly manner, if such a thing existed.

Megan issued an order before opening the door to her SUV. "Big guys help the little guys find toothbrushes when we get inside." This directive was met with a series of groans and sleepy yawns. "If you want to play with Natasha, Heston, and Jake, I suggest you look more lively." This woke the crowd some and Megan heard seatbelts unbuckle and doors begin to open. She walked around to the back of her vehicle, popped open the liftgate, and began unloading pillows and teddy bears. Megan felt a small hand on her back and she turned to see Randy rubbing his eyes.

"Am I a big guy or a little guy?"

Megan's heart melted every time her four-year-old son asked such innocent questions. Her middle child lived with an uncertain identity at times. Megan put down the pillow she was holding and stooped so that she could look Randy in the eye. She fixed the collar of his lop-sided jacket while she explained, "You're the most special kind. You're medium. That means you can get your own toothbrush out and then help Lily find hers."

His face brightened. "Yeah. I'm medium! Cool." Randy picked up his pillow and ran to find Lily. Once Megan could see that all five children were on the porch and on their way inside, she began unpacking in earnest. As she dug a few more items out, Megan saw Todd Sheldon coming around the back of her truck.

"Need some help there, ma'am?" Megan laughed at Todd's exaggerated drawl as she hugged him.

"You're still a mess, I see?"

"Always." He tipped his baseball cap in her direction and began loading his back with the gear Megan had unloaded.

"Poor Julie."

Todd winked. "She loves it."

Megan was still laughing when a figure came up behind Todd. "Hey! Thanks for the invitation. I can't wait for our lunch date tomorrow."

Instead of a reply, Megan was met with the frame of Todd's oldest friend, Ron Wellbourne, stepping around to help Todd with the bags. Embarrassed by her remark that had obviously been intended for Julie, Megan tried to explain.

"Oh, Ron. I'm sorry. I thought you were Julie."

Without saying a word, Ron picked up two pillows and a small suitcase and turned back toward the house. Megan wrinkled her nose in his direction and commented to Todd, "Wellbourne's as outgoing as ever, I see." Why that man couldn't at least be civil to people was beyond Megan's comprehension and she said as much to Todd.

Todd shrugged, "I know. Seems to get worse with each passing year, too. Not much you're going to do about, though." Todd nudged Megan and smiled, "Come on. My wife's got a slumber party planned for the big girls." Megan let out a small whoop before she closed the liftgate and followed Todd inside.

Megan slipped under the covers of her makeshift bed on the Sheldon's family room floor. The full moon outside the picture window afforded enough light for Megan to see her Bible next to her on top of her suitcase. She picked up the thick volume and closed her eyes to recount the day and thank God for seeing her through it. Traveling with five children was exhausting, but being in the safe confines of close friends was always worth it.

A twinge of guilt crept into Megan's heart. Why had she made such ugly comments about Ron? Just this week before prayer service, Pastor Dave had outlined the ingredients of an effective witness. Megan sat up and opened to the notes she had made in her Bible. She pondered what she had written: *compassion, we have to be willing to see past people's actions to their need for a Savior.* Megan let that soak in. She furrowed her brow.

It wasn't that Ron needed a Savior. He had claimed that long ago. Ron had, however, forsaken his Lord. He didn't depend on a God that made promises. He depended on a job that made money. Witnessing was not what Ron needed. What he needed was to quit whining.

Even in her frustration, however, Megan saw the weakness in her line of reasoning. Obviously, Ron was hurting. Why else would he brood endlessly? Megan prayed for compassion for this dark, lonely man. Then she prayed that God would intervene and send someone to show Ron how God could fill his empty life. So that she'd remember to pray for Ron Wellbourne, Megan reached for her prayer journal.

Chris had given Megan the journal for her birthday during their senior year of high school. The minute she saw what the gift was, Megan had opened it up and written "Mom, salvation" on the very first page. Megan had prayed for Aimee Harris's salvation every day since. Aimee was always hostile when Megan approached anything remotely related to church, so Megan also prayed faithfully for God to send someone to whom her mother might listen more openly. Pushing thoughts of her family aside, Megan took a deep breath and flipped pages under she found an empty space to add, "Ron, a good, swift kick back in the right direction."

The crackle of the gravel in his small driveway was a welcome sound to Ron. He couldn't wait to get inside and find something to soothe his pounding head. Ron put his Jeep in park and looked out the windshield at his small cottage that Stan and Mabel had built for him shortly after he'd graduated from college.

Ron drew a deep breath and closed his eyes in shame. He had punished them for almost twenty years for asking a simple question. *What's got you so upset, son?*

Ron's reaction had been so severe that they never pried again. Instead, The Wellbournes had built him a home where he could have more privacy and still be loved unconditionally. He knew his parents had prayed for him all these years even though Ron had pushed them as far away as the few yards between their homes would allow.

Feeling older than his forty-two years, Ron grabbed his briefcase and lowered himself out of the Jeep. He walked up the cobblestone path to his front door, lifted the day's mail from the small black box, and tucked it under his arm so that he could juggle his briefcase and keys while he unlocked the door. Ron walked through the tiled living room and set his belongings on the breakfast bar before pressing 'play' on his blinking answering machine. He shook two aspirin from a bottle on the counter then surveyed his refrigerator while he listened to Mable's dinner invitation. He had successfully avoided going to the main house for dinner by staying at Todd's house until after dark. And just to be certain his parents wouldn't seek out his company, Ron had gone by his office and worked on a report he didn't need until next week. It was well after midnight and Stan and Mabel's lights were out.

Ron pulled three cups of yogurt out before finding one with a valid expiration date. With yogurt and a plastic spoon in hand, Ron meandered out the front door and back down the cobblestone path, past his Jeep. Not really caring if he soiled a good work shirt, Ron raised the garage door and walked inside. He walked slowly to the middle of the hollow room and eased down into a dusty vinyl chair.

Though he knew it was time to stop avoiding the past, Ron still tried to hold back the memories that threatened to flood his mind. He opened the container of yogurt and took his time emptying the cup. When he was done, Ron tossed his trash into a small wire wastebasket and stood. He walked over to the figure under the heavy canvas.

Working slowly in an effort stir as little dust as possible, he started at the hood and pulled the canvas back over the tiny windshield with three wipers and continued to peel the cover back until the trunk was exposed. Laying the tarp behind the small car, Ron returned to his seat. For the first time in twenty years, he didn't stop the memory of his last drive in the treasured MGB.

The first time Ron ever laid eyes on Clare Donavan, he knew his heart was gone. He was on a short break from his senior studies and taking in some fresh air outside the Business College. Clare was sitting under a magnolia tree in the quad. The October breeze was blowing through her long, thick locks and one sleeve of her battered sweatshirt was over her left hand. She was bent over her journal, writing poetry she would later read to Ron as they spent countless evenings together.

Convinced he had met his soul mate, Ron began restoring the 1971 British classic, imagining how Clare would look with her long hair billowing as they drove. An only child of parents who'd had him when they were in their late thirties, Ron had had little experience with sharing. The longer he worked on the car, the easier it was to imagine sharing it and so much more with Clare Donavan.

Ron drove the car to Clare's dorm on a bright April afternoon. Clare asked him to take a walk with her before they went for a drive. Happy just to be near her, Ron readily agreed and they slowly made their way to the center of campus. As he held Clare's hand under the magnolia tree where they'd met, Ron waited for an opportunity to pull out the small promise ring he'd bought the week before. The urgency in Clare's voice snapped him back to reality.

"Did you hear me? I got accepted! *Penn State.*" Clare was beaming.

Ron's world had spun out of control in the days that followed as he realized that she had not been planning the same future as he. Clare had planned all along to attend law school. Alone.

Ron owned up to some of the blame in not communicating better with Clare, but he licked his wounds by vowing to never enter another relationship. He threw himself into his work after graduation. Ron had guarded his heart all these years, not willing to take another chance on being hurt.

Funny how it all seemed so simple and far away, now. He'd been afraid to remember what had happened, but, truth be told, there were far worse things that could have come Ron's way. His thoughts turned to Megan Hardin, who had dared to love.

She lost in a far more brutal way. Yet her faith had never wavered. Ron stopped his musings just short of calculating how long it had been since he'd been in church, or opened his Bible for that matter.

Just before pulling the overhead door down, Ron gazed

Finally Time to Dance

once more at the small car. It looked almost like a toy, still in its box, waiting for someone to come and play with it. He flipped off the lights and lowered the door. As he turned the knob that locked the door, Ron prayed, *Show me how to come back, Lord.*

Chapter 3

"I think we're done for now. I don't see how any more books are going to fit here." Julie frowned at the monumental task.

"You could just leave these in boxes until Christmas break and take your time going through them," Megan suggested. Maybe some of your graduating seniors could use the old stuff." She was trying to sympathize with her overwhelmed friend. On short notice, Julie had been asked to change offices at the university. The new office was more spacious but had fewer bookshelves.

"A task for another day." Julie glanced at her watch. "My meeting shouldn't take more than an hour. You gonna be OK?"

Megan tugged her tattered sweats. "That's why I left my pj's on. I'm going to run while you work." Megan patted her firm tummy. "It'll make room for lunch."

Julie picked up her briefcase and her mug and held open the door that led into the hall. "You know where the track is?"

"I can find it. We drove past it on our way in." It was Megan's turn to check the time. "Meet you back here in an hour?"

"Perfect. See you then."

Megan watched Julie stride off to her meeting, coffee in hand. She didn't miss the pressure of a full-time job, but sometimes Megan missed the perks. She envied Julie's sleek wardrobe and manicured nails. She missed meetings with adults and being treated like a professional.

Megan shook herself from her reverie and turned on her heel. Six years ago, God had asked her to stay home and take care of Chris and their children. That job had perks far more meaningful than professional recognition and a tailored wardrobe. Teaching her children to read and ride bikes and swim and study God's Word filled her days with activity and her heart with joy. Not to mention that God had provided generously for her to be able to raise the children without working outside the home. A tune from one of her children's videos ran through Megan's head, "A thankful heart is a happy heart." Megan laughed and stepped from the long hallway into the crisp fall air.

Taking a moment to orient herself so she could find the track, Megan was taken with the brilliant reds and yellows in the quad. No longer interested in the stark outline of a football stadium, Megan started her run under the thick magnolia trees in the courtyard.

The cool morning and bright sun energized Megan and she ran harder than she had in months. Not even the steep hill on the south edge of the campus slowed her pace. At the top of the hill, Megan took a short detour onto a residential street and began to descend the hill a block further south.

Though she had been to this part of town with Julie before, Megan had never noticed the charmingly sleepy homes that surrounded the small university. The old houses, with their wide porches and massive trees whose drooping branches almost touched the ground below, reminded Megan of her beloved south Louisiana roots. A lump caught in her throat as a stately antebellum mansion came into view. Megan slowed her pace until she stopped at the end of the long ribbon of sidewalk that led to the high porch on the majestic residence. Breathing heavily, Megan took several slow steps up the sidewalk then stopped and propped her hand on the metal sign next to her.

"Good morning." Megan started at the strange woman's cheerful greeting. "I'm sorry. I thought you saw me coming across the lawn." The sharply dressed woman held her hand out to Megan. "I'm Karen."

"Megan Hardin," Megan replied, breathing heavily, as she shook the stranger's hand. She was still catching her breath, perplexed as to why the woman had introduced herself.

"Are you ready to get started?"

Megan looked down and noticed that her hand rested on a realtor's sign. "No, no. I apologize for walking up here." Megan took a step back and looked up at full expanse of the home. "It was just so taken by the sight of this house. I think I walked up the sidewalk in a trance." Megan gave the older woman a crooked smile. "I'm not your appointment."

The realtor laughed, "Don't apologize. Lots of people like to stop and gaze at it. The setting is perfect. Almost like a scene from *Gone with the Wind*."

Finally Time to Dance

Indeed. Megan looked back up at the stately home. "Yes, it's breath-taking, really." Finally, Megan found her manners and held out her hand. "It was a nice to meet you, Karen. I'll leave you to your work. Have a wonderful weekend."

Megan was backing down to the street when Karen asked, "Would you like to see inside?"

Megan looked at the realtor sideways and whispered, "Really?"

Karen whispered back conspiratorially, "Why not?"

Megan clapped her hands with glee and followed Karen up the walk. The realtor filled Megan in on the history of the house and told her which residents of the community had called it home. The names meant little to Megan, who was not from the area, but knowing that the house had a rich history made it all the more appealing. Megan couldn't wait to see inside. Each room likely held stories about the people who had lived there. Suddenly, getting in her run before lunch was not a priority.

As she walked inside, Megan felt compelled to add, "I'm really not interested in buying the house. I live in Oklahoma City."

"It's no trouble at all," Karen assured her. "I think my appointment is running late. We can chat and look around until they get here." That was all Megan needed to hear. She relaxed and decided to enjoy the tour.

Karen told Megan about each room downstairs and showed her the bedrooms and closets upstairs. The architecture and novelty of the residence intrigued Megan. She marveled at the number of small closets and caveats she found throughout the house. Megan hadn't seen such big rooms since she had left her childhood home. She had become accustomed to tiny suburban bedrooms and storing extra clothes and towels in the plastic tubs in the garage. It was refreshing to see a home that was so easy to live in.

What struck Megan most, though, was the home's practicality. It was part of the town's history and had the potential to be regal and stuffy, but its residents had *lived* here. The soft décor and sunny rooms gave it a relaxed feeling.

"What do you think?" Karen interrupted Megan's thoughts.

Megan searched for the right words. "It's so, so... functional? Is that the right word?"

"Yes. That's exactly the right word," Karen agreed and then frowned, "and exactly why it hasn't sold." Karen set her notepad down and folded her arms. "I show this house three times a week. Everyone who comes in here expects it to look like the outside. But inside, it's a home, not a showpiece."

"That's good, though. Isn't it?"

Karen's expression was dry. "Not if you want something to show off. This place needs a family. That's what it's served all its life." Karen quoted the asking price. "That's more than most families can afford."

"How much are they asking?" Megan asked, thinking she had misunderstood.

Karen repeated the number and laughed, "I know it sounds low, Mrs. Hardin, but real estate is different here in the more rural parts of the state."

Megan realized that. But this house was huge! And beautiful. And it was also selling for what Megan's current house would sell for in the city. Not to mention the hardwood floors and glass doorknobs and long windows... *This is crazy! Get out of here before you're late for lunch with Julie.*

Megan held out her hand to Karen again, this time resolved to be on her way. "Thank you so much. It's been incredible," Megan laughed. "I loved seeing the inside."

"Maybe you should bring *Mr.* Hardin back and let him see it, too. Would his line of work allow him to move here? Or he'd be willing to commute?"

This line of questioning snapped Megan fully back to reality. "No, thank you," she answered firmly. Megan tapped her watch. "I'm meeting a friend who works on campus. I'd better be on my way."

Karen quickly pressed her business card into Megan's hand and motioned to the back door. "You can get back to campus through the backyard. And you can see the gardens back there on your way."

Gardens? Oh my. Megan thanked the realtor and reached for the back doorknob. She stepped outside looking for the path back to the university but stopped cold in her tracks. Tears welled up in Megan's eyes as she took in the sights and smells of the massive garden. It looked like something out of a movie.

Oh, who was she kidding? It looked like *home.*

With only a slight glance backward, Megan bid Karen goodbye. "Thank you again." With that, the realtor closed the back door and left Megan alone with her thoughts. She spotted the break on the trees that would lead back to campus and slowly headed in that direction.

Megan absently flipped the realtor's business card against her fingers and strolled through the trees and plants. The magnolias outside Julie's office had reminded her of Louisiana, but the variety of things growing here almost made Megan feel like she had actually traveled twelve hours south and east. She tried to identify the trees as she passed them. Crepe myrtles were just beginning to lose their blooms. Tall cedars lined the east property line. Thick pines marked the north edge. "Incredible," Megan sighed.

Megan was only a few steps from Julie's office when it hit her. Her mind raced back to the late night earlier this week when she had cried out to God and asked for direction. *Make it clear so I don't miss it.* The passage in Isaiah rang in her mind. Megan looked at the pine trees that lined the property and said the promise out loud, "That the hand of the LORD has done this, that the Holy One of Israel has created it."

Chapter 4

"I know you feel led of God to do this, but Megan, please think about what you're doing. This is such a *big* thing."

Megan's heart did a little flip-flop as she watched Dee take another picture off the wall. Closing was scheduled for next week, and Dee had offered to help pack. But reality was proving to be too much for Megan's dear friend. She walked over to Dee and brushed a stray hair back behind her ear. "God didn't promise this was going to be easy. But He did promise me He'd be with me every step of the way."

Dee began sobbing, "I'm so sick and tired of you being the strong one while the rest of us fall to pieces over what's happened to you." Dee took a long breath and tried to rephrase her thoughts. She faced Megan and said hoarsely, "I just want to be happy for you." Dee stroked Megan's cheek softly. "Are you sure God said to sell your house and buy the Taj Mahal?"

Megan chuckled at Dee's quip and kissed her on the nose. "Yes. I'm certain." Megan pressed her forehead against Dee's and narrowed her eyes. "And I'm trying not to be scared." Megan swallowed hard and whispered, "Help me not be scared." When her upper lip quivered, Megan backed away from Dee. She opened an empty carton and held it out. Dee carefully wrapped the picture she had been holding and gently placed it inside.

"I honestly didn't think I had enough stuff to fill this place. Where did I keep it all in that small house?" Dee and Marty were collapsed on the office floor next to Megan. The Mitchell and Hardin children were playing house in the basement room, while the adults tried to recover from unloading *both* of Megan's rented trucks. They felt fortunate to have found an empty space to flop. Stacks of boxes filled almost every inch of space in the Hardin's new school room.

"Most of *this* was in your dining area alone, Meg." Dee sighed. "I guess I'm going to have to start admitting that God sent you here. You and the kids needed more space." Dee sat up and nudged Megan's foot with her own. "I'm happy for you."

Tears sprang instantly into Megan's eyes and she squeezed Dee's foot affectionately. "I would have understood if you weren't ok with all of this, but your blessing means so much to me."

Dee swallowed hard and excused herself to check on the children, muttering something about dinner on her way into the hall. Marty sat up and groaned as he stretched his long legs. "Sorry. I guess I worked you guys pretty hard," Megan lamented.

Marty chuckled, "Actually, it's an honor, Mrs. Hardin."

Megan hooted with laughter, "An *honor*? Since when is working like a dog from dawn 'til dark an honor?"

Marty's face became serious as he replied, "Since you chose obedience over comfort." Megan looked down at the carpet and rubbed her left temple with one finger. Marty waited for her to reply. When she did not, he continued, "Noah's friends and neighbors thought he was a nut."

Tears pooled in Megan's eyes. She motioned around the massive room lined with empty bookshelves and said, "One could argue that I'm nuts. This is a big responsibility."

"But you've done what God asked. Now, take your family inside and thank God for the protection from the rains." Marty ruffled Megan's sweaty hair.

Megan shut both her eyes and tears squeezed out. "Thank you."

The two adults started at the loud chime. Marty's eyes were comical. "I guess that's your doorbell."

"Oh my!" Megan was shocked at its volume as it resonated through the large house. She waded through stacks of boxes as she made her way to the front door. Megan was relieved to see Julie standing on her new front porch. Her friend was hiding something behind her back. Megan was almost too tired to be curious.

"Three little words," Julie whispered in mock seduction.

Megan leaned on the door. "Yes?"

Julie pulled three large, flat boxes out from behind her back and crooned, "I brought pizza."

Megan turned in the direction of the basement stairs and bellowed, "Pizza!" Julie made her way into the foyer, followed by Todd and their children, who were loaded with pop, paper plates, and homebaked cookies.

"Sorry we missed the festivities, today," Julie apologized. The Sheldons had a prior commitment to attend a family reunion on Megan's moving day.

"Not to worry," Megan reassured her. "There's plenty unpacking to do." She motioned to the boxes stacked haphazardly throughout the hallway and in every room on their way to the kitchen.

"Where did all this come from?"

"Beats me." Megan tried to sound nonchalant, but inside she was beginning to wonder how long it might take to settle in. She had planned to stow things away and be ready for school by Monday, but that wasn't sounding realistic at this point.

Just as Megan was ready to admit defeat, Dee chimed in, "We'll get the office settled before we go to bed tonight. That way, she'll be able to at least get things together tomorrow night for school on Monday." Megan looked at Dee to see that she was not talking to Megan but to the other adults in the room. Marty, Todd, and Julie agreed with her plan and made a game plan for after dinner.

Megan silently thanked God for her circle of friends and tried to relax and enjoy her family's first meal in their new home.

"I don't have time to go all the way there, Mom," Ron Wellbourne snapped at his mother. Mabel Wellbourne was holding a heavy basket of fruit, snacks, and children's movies and for some insane reason expected him to drive an hour and a half one way to deliver it to someone he did not even know. Mabel could ship the gift if she took the perishable stuff out, and Ron said as much to his mother.

"Why on earth would I pay to have something shipped when you could drive over there in a few minutes?" Mabel gave her son an exasperated sigh and set the basket on the table. "I'd bring it myself if Suzie was here to watch after your dad..." Mabel's voice trailed off as Ron wondered at what had come over his mother. Why was this basket so important? He watched with relief as she seemed to put aside the idea of Ron making a quick trip to the city to deliver a *fruit basket*. Mabel settled into her chaise in the sunroom and sighed.

"Ron?"

"Hmm?" Ron's head was bent over the stereo Mabel had asked him to fix and he was desperately trying to tune her out so he could retreat to his cottage and gain some peace for the evening.

"Why won't you drive five miles to do this for me?"

Ron raised his head at Mabel's comment. "What are you talking about? The last time I clocked the miles to Oklahoma City from here, it was more like sixty-five miles. And I haven't been to the Hardin's house in years."

"Do you think Megan and her children are in the city?"

"Well, unless I've missed something, that's where they live." Ron went back to his work and added in a condescending tone, "Julie and Todd live five miles away, not the Hardins."

Mabel's eyebrow went up in amusement at her son's implication that her "feeble" old mind was keeping Mabel from recalling details of people's lives. She watched her son's face carefully as she mused, "Well, now I could have sworn Todd and Julie said Megan and her children took the old Kipling mansion near the college. Must be my mistake."

Ron's heart pounded in his chest as what Mabel had just said hit him. The lovely Megan Hardin lived five miles away. He had gotten only a glimpse of that chestnut hair and her radiant smile a few weeks ago at the Sheldon's, but the picture in his mind was still vivid. Ron savored the memory a few more heartbeats before he reined his emotions back in. *Get a grip, old man. She moved to town. So what?*

Ron composed himself and nonchalantly told his mother, "Well, Todd and Julie would know if that was the case." "I would certainly hope so." Mabel was puzzled. "They never mentioned this to you?"

Ron cringed inwardly as he remembered the stack of messages from Todd and Julie he chose not to return. Business had been phenomenal in recent weeks, which kept Ron busy. And picky. If you weren't going to generate revenue, he didn't return your call. Ron blew off the guilt and shrugged at Mabel. "Not that I can recall." Ron wiped a bit of sweat off his brow. "Is it hot in here?"

"Not really," Mabel answered as she did a poor job of hiding a smile. She picked up her Bible and turned to the book of Proverbs. No need to worry about that basket. It would be delivered before sundown.

Chapter 5

"I think that takes care of everything, Mrs. Hardin." Megan watched with relief as the sharply dressed man unrolled his sleeves and stood to shrug back into the coat of his suit.

"Thank you, Mr. Bradshaw. That wasn't as painful as I remember it being the first time my husband and I bought a house." Megan scooped up the folder of real estate papers the closing agent had placed in front of her. She was amazed that she was already done.

The young man gave her a wry smile and commented, "You're lucky enough to be able to do this without a mortgage company. Their paperwork makes the process a lot longer."

Megan turned to him with a smile and a handshake as he came around to her side of the table and corrected him. "I am indeed very *blessed*." Megan saw the thirty-something-year-old man almost roll his eyes at her comment. Surely he didn't believe that Megan's home ownership was a chance stroke of "luck." She had met Carl Bradshaw in Sunday school the first week she attended church after her move. He always greeted her warmly, welcomed her to the class, and encouraged Megan to participate. Why was he acting indifferent about giving God credit for a material possession? She pushed the matter aside and bid Mr. Bradshaw and his staff a good afternoon before stepping into the crisp November air.

Megan headed to her vehicle more slowly than necessary, soaking in the sights and smells of autumn on Main Street in her new town. Most of the shop owners had put out hoards of pumpkins atop bales of straw and accented their fall decorations with items from their stores. Megan silently thanked God for a place where she could easily bring her children to shop without worry of being confronted with the frightening images that businesses seemed so compelled to use to celebrate fall in the city. Megan worked hard to teach her children the real significance behind holidays and God's plan for the way families should celebrate. She smiled as she wondered what incredible blessings God had in store for her family here in the future.

"Penny for your thoughts." Megan looked up to see Ron Wellbourne eyeing her curiously and she laughed at his use of the old cliché.

Megan greeted Ron with a handshake and huge smile. "Actually, I was just marveling at all that's gone right in my life and how God's blessed me so richly as of late." Megan was pleased that Ron flustered her less and less each time she saw him. When she had her wits about her, Megan could "witness" to Ron more easily. He'd been by last week to deliver a house-warming gift from his mother, and Megan had glimpsed a side of Ron that had given her hope as she prayed that he'd find what he was searching for and renew his walk with the Lord. He'd lingered a few moments in the dining room chatting easily with her children while he helped them unpack the snacks Mabel Wellbourne had sent.

Ron glanced at his watch and surprised Megan with an invitation. "If you've got a few minutes, I'd love to buy you a cup of coffee and hear about some of these bountiful blessings of yours."

Megan lifted one corner of her mouth in apprehension and fidgeted with the silver cross at her throat. She didn't want to get into a conversation with Ron that would lead to her getting frustrated with him and saying things she shouldn't. Megan prayed quickly for some wisdom. Megan decided that a short visit over coffee might do more good than harm. She opened her mouth to say as much when Ron interrupted her, "I'm sorry. You probably have to get home to your children."

Megan shook her head. "Actually I have a few minutes before the sitter expects me home. I just came from an appointment that took far less time than I expected."

Ron smiled widely, "Then a few minutes we shall have." He fell into step beside Megan and began to point out landmarks of interest on Main Street. Megan was enjoying her tour so much she was surprised when Ron stopped and opened the door to the Alderson. The historic Main Street hotel was still beautiful, and the owners had wisely turned part of the lobby into a hip, cozy coffee shop that appealed to the young and old in town.

"We're here already?" Megan queried.

"Time flies when you're having fun," Ron said in jest and

punctuated his teasing with a wink and a smile.

Inside, Megan ordered her favorite, a caramel latte topped with whipped cream and drizzled with caramel. Ron ordered a soft drink. They found a table near the window and Megan let out a long sigh.

"Wow. I haven't done this since I moved here. Thanks." Megan set her drink carefully on her beverage napkin and scraped a generous spoonful of whipped cream off the top.

"Why not?"

"I'm not sure. Busy, I guess." Megan held the spoon in mid-air and gazed out the window while she reflected back on her afternoons with Dee. "In the city, I had a friend with a daughter old enough to watch my children and hers, so we'd sneak off once a week or so. I guess here I have to call in a babysitter and I just haven't gone to the trouble." Megan let out a small giggle. "Not to mention that I haven't found someone willing to meet me once a week for coffee, yet. I might need to hit Julie up for that job. Maybe she has a break between classes somewhere."

Megan looked back at Ron to see his thoughtful expression. He looked very serious when he asked, "Weren't you going to tell me about how much you've been blessed of late?"

Megan's expression was that of mock shame. She told Ron, "Yes, I was. And instead I started to complain about not getting out for coffee."

Ron was quick to correct her, "You were hardly complaining, Megan."

"Well, I almost was." Megan picked up her latte in both hands and rested her arms on the table. "I did something big, today. I closed on my house."

"Congratulations. I guess I thought you'd already crossed that hurdle."

"I should have, but there were a few snags here and there. So, against my better judgement, I moved in before I closed. I really didn't want to, but God just lined everything up so neatly and the former owners were so gracious about it all." Megan's eyes danced with excitement. "Anyway, it's all ours, now. I'm so thankful."

"I'm happy for you. It's a wonderful old house. It seems in good repair. Discover any major flaws, yet?"

"No. And I had an inspector put it through a pretty extensive test drive. He listed some things that will likely have to be dealt with, but there's nothing pressing." Megan mentioned the name of the inspector she had hired and Ron said he was familiar with the man's work.

"I'm sure Ricky did a thorough job. But please call me if you have anything you're concerned about."

Megan blinked in confusion. She had honestly never imagined Ron Wellbourne with a wrench or hammer in his hand. In the decade or so she'd known him, Ron had been deeply submersed in his business, which required little or no physical exertion. "Really?" Megan asked skeptically.

Ron chuckled, "Don't look so surprised. I'm actually pretty handy." He flashed Megan a devious grin. "I try not to let anyone know, of course."

"Of course," Megan laughed at his playful tone. "Your secret's safe with me."

Ron sat his cup on the table and folded his arms on the

table in front of him. "So, what else? You look like you have more on your mind."

Megan saw this as God opening a door for her to share more of her faith with Ron, so she prayed for the right words as she elaborated. "Yes, it's more than just the house. It's the new life here in general." Megan looked out the window again and motioned to the shop across the street. "I'm thankful for things as simple as the decorations in front of that store." She looked back at Ron and said in a serious tone, "I don't feel like I'm fighting an uphill battle here. It's not exactly Mayberry, but it comes close. God's given me a safe place to do this enormous job for Him." Megan breathed deeply. "For the first time in years, I feel good about where we are." Megan held up a hand and quickly recanted, "Don't get me wrong. We had a beautiful home and an incredible circle of friends in the city. But sometimes I felt like I was working without a net. I couldn't even let the kids skate on the sidewalk alone. Of course, we have more space here, but I also just feel safer."

"Do you enjoy being so close to the college?"

"Oh, my, yes!" The location of her home was likely Megan's favorite part of living here. "Julie can, and does, pop in for lunch when she's pressed for time, which I love. And having a university library within walking distance makes for great field trips. I'm even considering enrolling the kids in some of their continuing education courses for the community, like gymnastics and tae kwon-do."

"Will they be doing that next semester?"

Megan shook her head. "No." She put her cup down

and folded her hands. "I think this is a very rare season God has put us in. We're not really plugged in at church yet and I haven't made any commitments to the homeschool group. It's a good opportunity to rest."

"And you feel comfortable with whomever you've found to babysit?"

"Yes. One of the many perks of homeschooling is you can tap into a network of like-minded families. I got some referrals from other moms I met at the library and found three high school girls whose mothers let them baby sit after their school work is done. That's a huge blessing to those of us with younger children." Megan listed a few of the families she had met. Ron knew some of them; others were new to the community, like Megan's family. "There's another blessing. This small community embraces newcomers. That's probably rare."

A cell phone tone interrupted their conversation and Megan and Ron both reached for their cells. They laughed as Megan conceded, "I think it's yours." Ron answered his phone and had a brief conversation. Megan peeked at her watch and saw she was nearing the time she told her sitter she'd be home. It was time to get back and wrap up the school day. She picked up her wide mug and went to the counter for a to-go cup. Ron walked up behind her.

"Looks like afternoon coffee break is over."

Megan nodded, "Yes, but I'm so glad I ran into you." She held out hand and said, "I enjoyed the break. And the company." Megan smiled warmly and shook Ron's hand. "Thank you."

Ron paid the cashier and turned to Megan. "You are most welcome. I'll walk you to your car." Megan tried to tell him it wasn't necessary but they were on the sidewalk and headed to her SUV before she could put up much of an argument.

When they reached her vehicle, Megan unlocked the door and Ron opened and held it for her while she got in. She gave Ron a small wave as she backed out of her parking spot. *Thank you, God, for a wonderful encounter with an impossible man.*

Ron was still staring at the license plate that read MEGAN as he began plotting how he could manage to bump into Megan Hardin again.

Chapter 6

"Great job, Sweet Pea!" Megan scooped Lily up in her arms and swung her around as Chad, Randy, and Ali gathered around their mother to give their younger sister a hug.

"That was fun!" Lily beamed.

Chad was ecstatic. "You were the best angel ever! Maybe we can all be in the pageant next year."

The Hardins had joined their new church too late in the game to be fully involved in the Christmas program. Lily had happened into the role of an angel when her Sunday school teacher's daughter had come down with chicken pox. "That's right," Megan assured him. She was relieved to see Chad's positive attitude while they adjusted.

By the time Megan had gathered her crew, the crowd had thinned significantly. She hurried them along so that the nursery workers would not be waiting on them. By the time they made their way down the long hall to the children's area, Krissy was the only toddler left in the nursery. Megan gathered Krissy's things quickly and bid the workers goodnight. The Hardins were about halfway to the exit when she heard someone call her name. She looked back toward the nursery to see Carl Bradshaw waving at her. Megan balanced Krissy on one hip and held Lily's hand on the opposite side and managed an awkward wave and a quick smile before turning to continue toward the door. Megan was actually relieved to have the distraction of her five children to prevent her from paying more attention to Carl.

Mr. Bradshaw had been unnecessarily attentive to her during Sunday school lately, escorting her to her seat and sitting next to her during class. Though Megan could not put her finger on why, his attention made her uncomfortable. Each Sunday, she could feel the looks and smiles of their classmates as Megan and Carl sat together.

Even more troubling was the odd feeling she'd had when Carl helped her with the closing on her home. Right there in the hall, Megan resolved to put some distance between them starting next Sunday. She was thinking of how she could discreetly ask Liz Fairbanks, an older woman in their class whom Megan trusted, to help her avoid Carl when someone sidled up next to her as she reached to push open the door to leave. Megan let out a small scream when she saw a man's hand land on hers.

She heard Carl Bradshaw chuckle, "Wow, you scare easily."

Megan flushed with anger but tried to keep her tone in check. "Actually, I don't. I didn't think there was anyone else in the hall."

"Can I walk you to your car?"

It did not escape Megan's notice that Carl did not offer to walk *them* to *their* car. She guessed that, if asked, Carl could not tell her how many children were in their presence. Megan did not bother to quiz him. She opted, instead, to make her exit as quickly as possible *without* Carl Bradshaw as their escort.

"That's quite all right, Mr. Bradshaw. But thank you."

She saw Carl back away from the door, his expression gone cold. "No need to get snippy. Just trying to help, *Mrs. Hardin*."

Knowing her children would sense the tenseness in Carl's voice, Megan quickly asked Chad, "Would you open the door for Mommy, honey?" Chad obliged his mother and Megan quickly ushered her children to their SUV parked only a few spaces from the door.

She heard steps behind them and knew Carl had followed her out. He stepped in front of her and held out his hand, "If you give me your key, I can get the door for you."

Still unsure that she wanted to accept Carl's offer for help, Megan turned to Ali, "Unlock the door, please." While Ali pressed in the combination, Megan explained, "I can't keep track of car keys, so we just lock the keys in it." When Carl laughed at her explanation, Megan's mood brightened a little. "Thank you for walking us out."

"I was, well, wondering, um." Carl ran his fingers through his hair and shoved his hands into the pockets of his leather jacket. "Would you like to get some ice cream?"

Megan was amused by his awkwardness but happy to have an excuse to decline the invitation. She thanked Carl warmly and explained, "Tomorrow's a school day for us." She glanced at her watch. "And it's already half an hour past bedtime."

Megan saw Carl watch the Hardin children get into Megan's SUV as though he had not noticed them before, staring as Randy buckled his seat belt. Once the door was shut and the children were safely out of earshot, he motioned to the vehicle with his thumb and asked, "So, you ever get a sitter for them?"

Though he had said nothing overtly wrong or insulting, Carl's question, and the seedy tone with which he asked it, made Megan queasy. She suddenly wanted to get away from this man as quickly as possible. In an effort to discourage Carl from asking any more personal questions without making a scene, Megan laughed and said as nonchalantly as possible, "Rarely. We stick together most of the time."

Thinking there would be no more comment from Carl, Megan turned to get into her vehicle but was mortified when she felt his breath on the back of her neck. His toes were almost touching her heels when he whispered, "If you ever decide to get a sitter..."

Megan tugged on the driver's side door just hard enough to catch Carl off guard with a slight blow to his left shoulder. When he winced and stepped aside, Megan slipped into her truck, started the ignition, and locked the doors. She pressed the button to lower the window and spoke to Carl Bradshaw in a definitive tone. "I won't."

Carl was rubbing his shoulder and glancing around as he muttered, "Yeah, well, goodnight."

Megan checked the front door once more before heading

to the master bedroom. She could feel the heat in her cheeks as tears finally spilled onto them. Megan had wanted to be certain that all of the children were tucked in for the night before she recounted the episode in the church parking lot. She was seething with anger as she thought of the way this seemingly upstanding man had, at the very least, invaded her personal space.

She had done nothing to lead Carl to believe she would welcome any advances from him. Megan was reminding herself of this and searching her mind for some Scripture on controlling her anger when the phone rang. She saw it was Liz Fairbanks on the caller I.D. but let it ring and listened as the answering machine picked it up. Megan did not trust herself to talk to Liz right now without blurting out what had happened. She wanted to be thinking more clearly and let her anger subside before deciding if she even needed to bring Carl's behavior to anyone's attention.

"Hello, Megan. I need to talk to you. Please call me as soon as possible."

Despite her mood, Megan smiled. She loved hearing the older woman's voice. Megan's relationship with her own mother had been strained for years, so Liz's motherly demeanor was always a great comfort to her. Relieved to have an excuse to return the call right away, Megan dried her eyes and dialed the Fairbanks' number. Liz picked up after the first ring.

"Hello."

"Hi, Liz."

"Megan, hello." Liz's voice sounded strained.

"Is everything all right?"

"You tell me."

With that, she knew that Liz knew about Megan's exchange with Carl Bradshaw. Megan licked her dry lips and struggled to speak, "It will be." The tears were threatened to spill over again.

"Are the children in bed?"

"Yes," Megan almost whispered.

"Tell you what, then," Liz chirped in a cheerful tone. "You put on a kettle and I'll bring the tea."

Comforted by the thought of an impromptu tea party with someone who could offer a godly ear, Megan gladly agreed. "Will do. Tap on the back door when you get here. I'll turn on the back porch light."

Megan watched Liz's headlights grow bigger against the back fence. She turned off the burner under the kettle and walked across the large kitchen to open the back door. Liz held up a small tin of tea bags for Megan to see. "Thank you," Megan managed. Liz settled down at the large rustic table in the breakfast room while Megan fetched the steaming kettle. Liz chose tea bags from the tin and placed them in the cups already on the table.

When Megan returned to pour water into their cups, Liz began gently, "Tom had a talk with Carl Bradshaw about an hour ago."

Relieved but still unclear, Megan asked, "So Carl went to Tom...?"

Liz shook her head. "No." She steeped her tea bag in

the steaming water. "Tom and I were walking out of church when we saw Carl walking toward his car, brooding. Tom's known Bradshaw since he taught Carl's third-grade Sunday school class. Tom figured if he was mad about something, it was likely of his own making. They talked for a few minutes and Tom finally figured out that you and Carl had exchanged words."

When Liz paused, Megan hurried to clarify, "He didn't touch me." She swallowed hard before adding, "But he was inappropriate."

Liz put her hand on Megan's. "That's not your fault, nor should it be overlooked." When Megan's eyes widen and she began to shake her head, Liz continued. "Now, don't worry. We're not going to make a big deal out of this. Tom did, however, let Carl know he was way out of line if he had upset you with his words or actions."

Megan let that sink in. Oh, good grief! This was all so foreign to her. She and Chris had fallen madly in love in high school and had married after their sophomore year of college. He was the only man she ever had feelings for, ever been approached by. Megan had absolutely no experience with dating or courting, though she had read articles in Christian parenting magazines that she thought she'd apply to her daughters when they were old enough. Suddenly, Megan had a horrifying thought.

"Oh, Liz, but I did do something wrong. I shouldn't have been alone with any man!"

Liz held up her hand and argued, "I know what you are saying, but you should be able to trust a fellow church member to walk you to your car. Don't blame yourself for Carl's bad behavior."

Megan gave that some thought. She was still not entirely convinced that she couldn't have acted differently and avoided the encounter altogether. "I think I can learn from this, though. I need a better plan for avoiding that kind of situation." Megan felt a strange kind of sadness sink in. She was trying to put her finger on the source of her sadness when Liz interrupted her thoughts.

"Megan? You okay?" Megan felt Liz's hand cover hers. Realization was beginning to dawn and Megan did not like where all of this was heading.

Finally, reality hit Megan like a lightning bolt. "Oh, Liz. I'm *single*."

Liz chuckled softly, "Well, that's not a sin!"

Megan smiled at her friend's incredulous tone and swatted playfully at Liz's hand. "I know that. But I have been friendly to Carl and let him get me coffee on Sunday mornings. Maybe he took my friendliness the wrong way."

Liz took a sip of tea and shrugged. "Like you said, you need a plan."

"For Sunday school?"

"For everything. For when the time comes when someone sincerely expresses a romantic interest in you. What's your plan?"

Megan shrugged and honestly said, "I don't plan to worry about that for another twenty years, Liz. I have five children to raise."

Megan saw Liz regard her carefully. "That's your plan?"

"That's my plan."

"Avoidance?"

"No! Reality."

Liz leaned in closely, looked Megan squarely in the eye and asked, "You don't honestly think God moved you all the way out of your comfort zone into this exciting new life so that you could live it all by yourself, do you?"

"No, I don't. I believe He brought me here because it was the best place for me to raise my children. I'm *not* alone," Megan answered honestly. "I have them."

"What if God wants you to have more?"

Had Liz lost her mind? "I was loved and cherished by an incredible Christian man. We had five beautiful, healthy children together. He was completely and totally devoted to God and to us until he drew his last breath. Chris left us with a godly heritage and provided the resources I'd need to take care of things until they were grown." Megan leaned back in her chair and threw her palms up. "I'm good. I don't want any more than I have right now."

"It's really not about what *you* want."

Megan watched a smile play at the corners of the older woman's mouth. She countered with logic. "I have loved and been loved. I'm *still* loved, Liz. I still feel Chris here with me, helping me, through God's grace, raise these children."

"Okay." Megan saw Liz concede her point and nod as she sipped her tea. "But you still need a plan."

"True." Megan took a long sip of tea and set the cup back on its saucer. She had never had any intention of dating Carl, yet she had gotten into a sticky situation with him. In general, a single woman, if that's what she was, needed a plan. "So, what's the plan?"

Megan watched Liz cross the kitchen and find a small notepad on the counter. "Just some simple, logical things should get you started." Liz took notes while the women brainstormed for the next hour, making "rules" for Megan to follow regarding single, and married, men. It was good to have Liz's perspective and giggle about the silly way men and women react. It was enlightening to be reminded of the sinful nature that so easily leads both men and women off course and into temptation. By the time they had drained their second cups of tea, both women felt satisfied that they had a good plan for Megan.

Megan asked Liz to be her accountability partner and check on her periodically to be certain she was following "the plan." Megan knew she'd be teaching her sons and daughters valuable lessons by subtly demonstrating appropriate Biblical behavior between men and women.

Liz prayed before she left. She asked God to give Megan wisdom and discernment. Liz also asked God to give herself strength to be a godly mentor for Megan. By the time they parted ways, Megan was exhausted but thankful that God had turned an unpleasant evening into an opportunity for growth.

Megan slipped into bed and relaxed into her pillow. She could hear Krissy and Lily snoring softly on the monitor next to her bed. As Megan reached to turn off the light, she let her fingers rest on the picture of Chris under the lamp. She remembered a conversation they had shortly after he'd entered hospice care in their home.

"You'll get married again. I was raised by a stepfather. Remind the kids of that. They love Pops."

Megan was aghast. "I'll hardly have time for romance while I'm raising five children. I'll be in my fifties before I give another man a second glance."

Chris rose from the bed and took Megan's hand. "Come with me." He led Megan into the master bathroom and had her face the large mirror. "Look at yourself, Meg. You're a young, beautiful woman. Someone, the right one, is going to fall in love with you, and I don't want you holding out just because you told me you wouldn't get married again." Their eyes met in the mirror. "You will get married again. I know that. I want that."

Tears fell onto Megan's pillow as she kissed her index finger and tenderly touched Chris's picture. "I really hope you're wrong. I don't *want* to love anyone else."

Chapter 7

When the small brook came into view, Megan slowed her pace. Thankful for a sunny January afternoon, she walked over to the edge of the water. At least a dozen turtles plunged in from their sunbathing spots on a moss-covered log. Megan was sorry she had disturbed them but sat down to enjoy the peaceful time alone.

College wasn't back in session yet, so Julie had offered to take the kids for an afternoon of cookie baking and stretching out in her sunroom. Megan had plans to catch a movie with Julie later while Todd rode herd on all eight kids. Megan smiled at the thought of Todd readily agreeing to such a task. She marveled at the wisdom of God for bringing the Sheldons into her and Chris's life almost a decade ago.

Megan had met Julie when both women began teaching at Oklahoma City's large community college the same year. Megan was introduced to Julie at freshman faculty orientation. They got to know one another very quickly, as their departments shared close relations. Julie was in social work; Megan taught nursing. Consequently, many of their students took classes in both departments, giving the like-minded instructors ample opportunity to interact and get to know one another.

During their third year of teaching together, they discovered the same week that they were both pregnant with their first children. The young mothers-to-be enjoyed their pregnancies together as they plotted and planned nurseries over brown bag lunches or dozed in front of movies on Saturday afternoons while Chris and Todd assembled cribs and installed safety latches on drawers and cabinet doors. The Hardins and the Sheldons bonded deeply as they watched each other's marriages grow into families.

Shortly after Ali and Natasha were born, however, the world went topsy-turvy. Out of nowhere the diagnosis came: Chris had brain cancer. Within a few weeks, the shock of it wore off and Chris and Megan decided to beat the odds or glorify God trying. For five years, Megan had, as gracefully as she knew how, taken the role of Chris's private-duty nurse through brain surgeries, radiation, intravenous therapy for infections, and rehabilitation. She willingly left her full-time job as an instructor to care for her family, and had three more children within the next four years. Megan made ends meet by running an in-home day care while Chris returned to his job teaching at the large suburban high school he loved.

Shortly after the treatments ended, she and Chris had been told the prognosis: it'll either come back in five years and kill you or you'll live to be an old man. Chris and Megan had opted to believe the latter and live like Chris was completely healed. They never shared the first part of the prognosis with anyone else, not even their families. Megan had told Chris,

"If you're dying, we're all dying. Life will go on."

By the time they reached the five-year anniversary of Chris's diagnosis, everyone except Chris and Megan had all but forgotten about the cancer. Megan had a lump in her throat as she tried to break the news to Todd and Julie. They'd moved to Todd's hometown to run his family's business after the older Mr. Sheldon passed away.

Megan tucked the kids into bed and then went out to the patio and dialed the Sheldon's number. "Hey, Jule," Megan sounded solemn.

"Let me guess. You're pregnant?" Megan laughed at her friend's candor. That was usually the reason Megan called late at night.

Megan took a deep breath before she spoke bluntly, "The tumor's back."

"Why? What happened? I thought they said it would never come back," Megan could tell that Julie was reeling from the shock and the questions spilled out before she could help herself.

"I know. It's a long story. Late-night version is that I had to take him to the ER this weekend and the tumor is the size of a lemon. Since he had a clear MRI five months ago, they say the cancer is growing fast. They went ahead and admitted him and will do surgery in a day or so," Megan's voice was mechanical.

"I'll be there in an hour," Megan could hear Julie rummaging in her dresser. An hour later, the two friends were swaying on Megan's porch swing wondering how they had ever come to that moment.

Amazing how those memories came flooding in when she least expected it. Megan stood and walked away from the brook. She tried to focus on her prayer of thankfulness that had slowed her pace and didn't pick up her run again until the lake was in view. Once she could see her vehicle, she charged forward and sprinted several hundred yards, moderating her pace only after she'd cleared the last hill on the track and passed her parking spot.

Megan could feel the cold breeze chill the streams of tears on her cheeks and lips. As she slowed to a walk, she wondered why it always came to this. Julie gave her an afternoon off with the best of intentions and Megan wound up crying and thinking about a past she could not change. Without her children to fuss over, she had far too much time to think. Megan often reasoned it was why God gave her and Chris five children. He knew that was how many it would take to keep Megan distracted until the grief passed. Megan rubbed a sweaty sleeve across her face and went over the facts that pulled her out of these slumps.

Chris had loved only her. He had been her only love. They had been married twelve and a half years and had gone to bed happy every single night. God had given Chris and Megan the opportunity to remind each other that they had no regrets. They had made every moment count to the best of their ability. In the end, Megan had no reason to whine or complain or even grieve. She had only blessings for which she should be thankful.

With the pep talk under her belt and a firm resolve to

stop her tears, Megan wound back up the path and found her SUV. She switched off the stereo as soon as she started the ignition.

Every disc in the player held a memory. As long as the children were with her and they could sing together or remember "when," she felt safe. Hearing the familiar songs alone was too risky. Megan only had two hours before she planned to meet Julie. If she was going to squeeze in a bath and a pedicure, she needed to keep moving forward.

Megan tried to not attack Julie the minute her friend sat down, but she was dying to know how the afternoon had gone. Megan was particularly concerned about Krissy, whose nose had been running since yesterday. Thankfully, Julie knew Megan well and pulled a sheet of paper out of her purse after she ordered her iced tea. "Lily sent you this."

Even before she unfolded the wrinkled paper, Megan knew she'd find a rainbow. Lily was fascinated with the magical array of colors she saw in rainbows and even colored them in the right order, starting with red and ending with purple. Megan brushed back a tear and looked at Julie. "I love that child."

"They sent cookies, too, but I left them in my van. We'll nibble on those on the way to the movie."

"If we have room. I love the food here." Megan had been to the small, elegant Italian eatery at least half a dozen times since she moved here. At noon, they served pizza by the slice, which let her feed the children something they liked while she enjoyed a 'big girl' meal. Megan knew from experience she'd likely fill up on dinner and not have room for dessert.

"You come here by yourself?" Julie queried.

"I take the kids with me." Megan wondered at the furrow in Julie's brow. "What's wrong?"

"Nothing. I just can't imagine taking my kids here." Julie lowered her menu and gazed past Megan. "I guess I see this place as 'special.' You know, somewhere you go when there's a special occasion or someone special to share it with."

Megan lifted in glass in a mock toast. "And taking my motley little brood out to lunch is always a special treat." Julie's expression was transparent. Megan stopped her in her tracks. "I'm fine, Jule. I take my children on dates. I'm okay with that."

Megan saw Julie lower her eyes. She looked back at Megan and continued in a contrite tone, "I know you are. I just can't help thinking about…"

Megan put her menu down. "What?"

"Never mind." Julie laid her menu on the table and focused on poring over it.

Megan pretended to look at her menu as well. The silence lasted less than a minute. "Don't start with me," Megan warned without looking up. She could feel Julie's eyes on her, so Megan conceded and looked up to give her friend her full attention.

Julie sighed deeply. "Don't read anything into this."

"But?"

"No 'but.' I just keep thinking about how much fun it would be for the four of us to go out to dinner sometime. Not a 'double date' or anything. Just four friends going out to dinner, maybe a movie."

Megan was mystified. "The *four* of us?"

Julie's smile was now wide. "Yeah. Wouldn't that be fun? You could get out with adults." Julie laughed, "Who am I kidding? It'd be a treat for us all to get out with adults."

"*What* are you talking about?"

"About Todd and I taking you and Ron out to dinner." Julie's expression showed that she summed it all up. "It would give both of you a chance to get out."

Megan closed her menu and held up her hand with her palm facing Julie. "Stop right there. Just because you know two single adults…"

"I'm not talking about *romance*. I'm talking about friendship."

"Ron and I have coffee. In the light of day. Occasionally."

"And you've seen how he's changed. You've done more to reach him in ten weeks than Todd and I have in ten years. It's like he's alive, again. You *know* what I'm talking about." Julie picked up her menu and looked at the list of sandwiches on the back.

"Hopefully you're talking about Ron's relationship with the Lord, which, I might point out, can be dealt with *before* six p.m.*"

Julie gave Megan an exaggerated roll of her eyes. "Oh, lighten up."

Megan shot Julie a look of disdain. "But you're talking about pairing up people so that we're two couples. I'm just not comfortable with that."

"So what is it when you're alone with Ron? One couple. That's okay?"

"I'm not *alone* with Ron when we meet for coffee. We're sitting at a window table on Main Street. Sometimes, we're on the sidewalk. Then we part ways and go about our lives."

Julie looked contrite. "I'm sorry. I'm pushing too hard. I guess I've just waited for so many years to have you live close by again. I think I just want to be able to see you enjoy a nice dinner out with a great guy. Nothing more."

Megan rested her chin on her hand and shrugged. "I know, but it's not like when we lived near each other in the city. I'm single, now." Megan motioned to the candle in the center of the table. "I *am* enjoying a nice dinner out." Megan reached for Julie's hand. "With my dearest friend."

Julie wiped a stray tear from her cheek. "And that's enough?"

"God makes it enough."

Julie dabbed her napkin at her nose. "You talk like that to Wellbourne?"

Megan laughed. "All the time."

Julie's face brightened. "You're good for each other."

Megan looked at Julie quizzically. "I guess so."

Julie opened a packet of sweetener and flicked the powder into her tea. "Yes. Two wonderful people who have lost so much but still have so much to offer." She held up glass up to Megan. "Here's to good, godly friendship."

Megan tapped Julie's glass softly with her own, adding, "And to the lessons we've yet to learn."

Chapter 8

Ron shuffled the papers again and checked his wrist for the fourth time this half-hour. Finally conceding to follow his heart, he paged Teresa. She appeared in his doorway within a few seconds.

"Yes, Mr. Wellbourne?"

"Did I see some pizza coupons in the break room?"

Teresa's expression was almost comical. In the fifteen years, she'd worked for Ron, he'd never ordered a pizza. Ron always ate alone. And he never ate pizza. He had dazed and confused the poor woman. He tried to snap her back to reality by shuffling some papers on his desk. Finally, the older woman looked at Ron.

"Yes. Do you want them?"

"If you don't mind, bring me one from the best place you've found." Ron stopped straightening his desk and hesitated only a moment before asking, "How many slices are in a pizza?"

Teresa shrugged, "Depends on the size. How many people are you feeding?"

Ron knew her question was asked innocently; Teresa

would never pry. His guard went up, however. He wasn't up to something secret, but Ron would prefer no one in his office know that he was taking pizza to Megan and her children. That included his secretary. He'd been in business for almost two decades without, to his knowledge, becoming the subject of office gossip. He planned to keep it that way. "Oh, about a half dozen, I guess," he muttered indifferently.

Ron saw Teresa open her mouth to ask a question then stop herself. Finally, she answered, "Two large pizzas should do it." Teresa bit her upper lip before taking a deep breath and adding, "Unless, of course, most of those eating are small children. Then, two mediums would do." With that, Teresa turned and left Ron's office, closing the door behind her.

"Well, what did you expect?" Ron asked himself. He'd spent his entire adult life alone in his office. Suddenly, over the past few weeks, sunny afternoons pulled him from his desk to the café downtown for leisurely conversation and the occasional stroll by shop windows. He guessed correctly that this had not gone unnoticed by his secretary.

So there. It was out. Ron was seeking deeper meaning in life and he happened to be under the tutelage of an attractive young widow. Let them talk! Ron knew his motives were pure. Megan had told him that she was not interested in romance and he had accepted that. Finding happiness and friendship were timeless objectives for any human.

In fact, that was his reasoning behind asking Megan if he could drop by her house with pizza. He had some sensitive questions he wanted to ask her but had not wanted to put her on the spot in public. He figured she'd be more comfortable

Finally Time to Dance

in her own environment when asked her to help him dig a little deeper in his quest for peace in his life.

Teresa's return snapped Ron to attention. She was holding out a glossy red and blue card with several pictures of pizza and other fast-food Italian dishes on it. "These guys have the best and they deliver. Do you want me to place the order?"

Ron shook his head. "No, thanks. I'll get to it." He took the card she held out and thanked her.

Once he was alone again, Ron ventured to look at his phone. He had written Megan's number on a note and stuck it near the phone, so there was no need putting off calling to ask if he could come over with the pizza. Something still didn't feel right about it, though. How would he explain why he wanted to come over? Ron's thoughts turned to the evening he began entertaining the idea of visiting Megan at home.

He'd stopped by Todd's house one evening last week and been amazed by the amount of noise, and the number of kids, when Todd opened the door. Ron's first reaction was to try to make his excuses and leave, but Todd coaxed him in. Several tiny people immediately came running.

"Who's here, Daddy?" Heston, disguised as a green and purple superhero, was flanked by four other masked crusaders. Ron was struggling to identify the children under the costumes when he saw Krissy Hardin on Todd's hip.

"It's Uncle Ron. He's come to rescue Daddy," Todd answered his older son before shooing the whole brood back to the playroom. Turning to Ron, he handed Krissy

Finally Time to Dance

off. "If you'll rock this one, I'll get dinner finished. She fell and scraped her knee and needs a little extra TLC."

Ron clumsily took Krissy from Todd and made his way to a recliner. "Don't you know how to order pizza?" Ron tossed three stuffed animals on the floor to make room in the recliner to sit. "Or call a babysitter?" Ron was relieved to see Krissy nestle easily into his lap and stop crying. Instinctively, he wiped the stray tears from her cheeks. She smiled up at him, her eyes sparkling.

"Tanx you."

Todd came back and snapped a dishtowel at Ron's shoulder. "One of the drawbacks to having your dream home in the country is that the pizza guy won't drive to your house." He picked up the remote control and lowered the volume. "No matter. Chef Todd is in the house. We'll have macc and cheese in a few minutes."

The evening had turned amazingly calm once dinner was on the table and Ron found himself actually enjoying the twists and turns of the conversation. Growing up an only child, such dinners didn't exist. He'd always assumed eight children around a dinner table would be chaotic. In reality, it was rather entertaining. Ron reasoned that he could eat like this more often and wondered if Megan would mind if he came over with pizza sometime and joined her family for dinner.

So, the time had come to ask. He picked up the phone and dialed the Hardin residence.

"Hello?"

"Megan, Ron Wellbourne."

Ron heard Megan's voice brighten, "It's a little late for

coffee," she teased.

"That it is." Ron relaxed and leaned back in his chair. Megan was so easy to talk to. "I was wondering if you'd let me rescue you from kitchen duty tonight. I'd like to bring some pizza over for the kids." Megan didn't answer immediately, so he recanted, "Of course, if you already have plans…"

"Oh, no, it's nothing like that." Megan hesitated again then continued, "It's just that dinner at our house and the hour or so that follow are not for the faint of heart. Unless you plan to drop off dinner and run, you have no idea what you're signing up for." Megan was laughing, but Ron knew she was serious. She honestly didn't think he could handle it.

"I'll have you know that I dined with your children just last week," Ron retorted playfully.

"Ah. But they were not being asked to get ready for bed after dinner." Megan's voice turned serious. "The weather has been so dreary. They haven't been outside, so the boys are in rare form. It's not pretty." Ron understood her point of view. Bringing dinner would not be a favor; it would be an imposition. "That's fine. Maybe some other time. Like when the weather clears up."

"Actually," Ron could hear Megan's contemplative tone, "you haven't already ordered pizza, have you?"

Ron felt like a fool. He put the coupon down and assured her, "No, no, listen, it's fine. I understand."

"Well, if you don't mind shifting the plan a little, I have an idea."

The round booth in the corner accommodated all seven of them nicely. Tonight was "kids eat free" night at Poppy's and they felt fortunate to have found an open table. Megan let Ali take Lily and the boys off to play a few video games after they ordered their drinks. Krissy sat close to the table in a high chair, munching happily on a bread stick. Ron and Megan took turns serving themselves from the buffet.

Ron waited for Megan to return before picking up his fork, but he didn't offer to pray before they ate. She wasn't sure if it was because he just never prayed before a meal or because his thoughts were so far away. She eyed Ron cautiously. He was twirling spaghetti with his fork, obviously in no particular hurry to eat. Megan guessed he wanted to talk. That was likely the reason he'd called and asked to come over earlier. Not one to beat around the bush, she was direct.

"What was her name?"

Ron looked up, alarmed. Megan rushed to defend the Sheldons. "Julie is the soul of discretion. She and Todd have never explained what happened." Megan gave him a wry smile. "Anyone who retreats into seclusion for twenty years has had his heart broken."

"Clare." Ron lowered his gaze back to his plate. "I'm a coward. I watched you get your heart broken and you were able to rebound and find the good in it." Ron put his fork down and picked up his soft drink. "That's when I realized I'd been a coward. The first time I saw you smile at a birthday party after Chris had died."

Touched by his admission, Megan smiled and reached for Ron's hand. "It's not the same thing. Chris didn't choose to leave." Megan drew a deep breath and sat back in the booth. "In fact, about six months after Chris died, I had a dream that he asked me for a divorce." Megan felt a chill go up her arms. She looked directly at Ron. "That felt worse." When Ron didn't respond, she added, "I'm sorry you got hurt."

Ron shrugged, "It happens, I guess." He smiled at Krissy and handed her another bread stick. "Life goes on."

Megan laughed. "That it does." She leaned toward Ron and waited for him to look at her. "It goes on even while you roll over and play dead." Megan weighed her next remarks carefully before continuing in a compassionate tone. "Time marches forward, your friends move on, your parents grow older." Megan saw Ron wince slightly at the mention of his parents. She did not know to what extent he had shut them out, but she knew Stan and Mabel had suffered far more than Ron had through his brooding. "The one thing that never changes is how much God cares about you." Megan considered stopping there but knew it was worth the risk to continue. "He never stopped caring even when you were pretending you didn't care about anyone else. Or about Him."

Ron sniffed softly as he ran his index finger around the rim of his glass. Megan briefly touched his other hand softly across the table in a gesture of empathy before rescuing him from the moment. "When's the last time you played Pac-Man?"

Ron chuckled and looked toward the arcade. "Decades."

Megan smiled mischievously. "Well, enough of that." She slid out of the booth, pulled Krissy out of her high chair, and held out her hand. "Give me some quarters."

Ron quickly obliged and the two adults spent the next half hour dazzling Megan's children with their knowledge of the vintage game. By the time Megan finally beat Ron, they were all breathless with laughter. It was the most fun Megan had had in a long time.

"Thank you."

"No, thank you." Ron's expression was serious, so Megan gave him her full attention once they settled back into the booth. "Amazing how talking about something that hurts you takes the crippling *power out of it.*"

"Agreed. But," Megan added quickly, "you can't keep looking to me for the real answers. I mean, I can offer godly advice, but you're going to have to get back into church if you want to tap into the relationship that can heal your heart." Megan knew Ron was not accustomed to being spoken to so directly, but she knew he needed to hear the truth, not what he wanted to hear.

"I know."

"So, you'll go to church?"

"Yes."

"It's been a long time. You'll backslide easily if you're not careful. You need an accountability partner." Ron raised his eyebrows hopefully. "Oh, no. Not me. A man."

"It can't be my dad."

Megan thought a few moments. "I've gotten to know a wonderful couple. They have children our age, maybe a little younger. Tom and Liz Fairbanks. I bet Tom could offer some guidance." She could see the pain in Ron's face. Megan knew

Ron did not want to draw other people into his struggle, but she wasn't backing down. Ron needed to be discipled and it wasn't Megan's place to do it.

Finally, Ron conceded. "Maybe I can come to Sunday school and bump into him."

Megan decided not to push any further. "That's a great start." Megan smiled, thinking of the entry about Ron in her prayer journal.

"What's so amusing?"

"Oh, nothing. I was just making a note of something I need to write down when I get home."

Chapter 9

Megan tucked her robe under her feet as she curled up more tightly on the mesh chaise lounge. It was still too early in the season to find warmth at this hour, but the sunrise had seduced her out to the patio for her quiet time. All too soon, she'd be seeking the coolness of early morning out here to beat the summer's heat. Megan opened her prayer journal and added two names she remembered from Sunday school and then let her eyes scan the pages of the tattered volume. Her heart grew warm when she saw the dates next to Ron's name. She'd noted the date he asked Tom to keep him accountable along with several other dates since Christmas when she had really sensed that God had penetrated Ron's heart. Megan counted it an honor to pray for a man who had become her first new friend in God's new place for her family.

Megan and Ron still met weekly for coffee and, almost as often, he joined her and the children for pizza at Poppy's. It was a comfortable, safe friendship, and Megan was thankful it had been founded on Ron's search for a restored relationship with the Lord. Ron's new walk gave them countless topics to discuss and debate and even provided

Megan with the occasional challenge that sent her poring over commentaries and Greek and Hebrew dictionaries until she found the answers she needed. Megan was as thankful for the intellectual stimulation as she was for the companionship.

She flipped the page and prayed over the requests that had been shared at the women's Bible study group she had joined. Liz Fairbanks had asked her to join them and Megan was glad she had done so. Their broad range of ages and backgrounds was a comfort to Megan, who often felt like a fish out of water with women her own age who had not experienced the degree of loss that she had.

When she had finished praying, Megan exchanged the journal for her Bible and walked to the edge of the patio. She turned to the book of Ecclesiastes and soaked in a passage from the fourth chapter.

Done with the reading for now, Megan stood motionless for a long time, relishing the quiet moment alone with God. She stroked the cover of her Bible lovingly. Everything about reading His Word brought her joy. The weight of the Bible in her hand, the sound of the crinkled pages as she flipped to a passage, the way the large book fell open to verses she knew God wanted her to see. On some of Megan's darkest days, only God's Word had lit her path. She silently thanked God for leaving so much of Himself to be accessed through His words, every passage holding deep meaning for a believer. Megan pulled her Bible to her chest as she thought of times she had relied solely on what she had read in it to help her make decisions. She smiled as she remembered how easy it was to make an offer to buy this house since God had already told her about it in His Word.

Amazing. Utterly amazing.

Megan walked back to the table and lay the volume next to her favorite mug. She wrapped her hands around the cappuccino and relaxed in the low chair. As she took in her elegant outdoor living area, Megan let her mind wander to Chris.

She wasn't sure what he'd think of her taking on so much square footage with this new house, but Chris would have loved the large, square patio. It sat atop one of the garages below, providing enough height for Megan to gaze out onto the small college campus below. She'd thought of Chris often as she made the space comfortable. She'd asked the decorator to top the railing with evenly spaced fleur de lis as a tribute to their college days when the young, married lovers spent lazy Saturday afternoons hand-in-hand, strolling the French Quarter, sipping café au lait and nibbling beignets from the Café du Monde. Those days seemed like a lifetime ago. Megan felt tears sting her eyes as she almost let herself feel the truth for a moment: it *was* a lifetime ago, Chris's lifetime.

The sound of the back door opening behind her roused Megan from her musings. She turned to see Krissy struggle to balance her bowl of animal crackers in one hand as she held the knob of one French door with the other. When had she gotten so big?

"Here, let Mommy help." Megan covered the space between her chair and the door quickly and rescued the teetering bowl from Krissy's chubby hand.

Finally Time to Dance

"I get it!" Krissy scowled at her mother and held her hands up for her breakfast.

"Shut the door first." Frowning, Krissy turned back and pushed on the door. Megan helped her push it tight and then held the bowl out to her youngest child. "Thank you. Can you carry this over to the table?"

"Mess, mam." Krissy took back her breakfast and settled in to nibble her cookies at the large, low patio table.

When she was certain Krissy was content to sit a few minutes, Megan walked to the rail and looked back out across her gardens. She soaked in the fragrance of the spring scents and smiled as she remembered the Scripture passage that had led her to buy this home. The cedars were most fragrant at this hour and Megan enjoyed watching the squirrels fly from pine to pine across the back of her property. Already the crepe myrtles had their leaves. The cannas were sprouting and daffodils were sprinkled here and there. In a few weeks she would be able to see for certain which shades of pink, purple, and white bloomed where.

Yes, God had made, and kept, His promise. Megan silently thanked Him for giving her the strength to leave the only existence she and Chris had known and obey God's leading.

With her thoughts heavenward and the clock ticking closer and closer to the opening of their school day, Megan pulled herself from the rail and padded over to the table to take a seat opposite Krissy. She flipped the pages of her Bible back to the passage she had chosen to study this morning. The rustling caught Krissy's attention.

"You read?"

Megan kept her head down and answered Krissy, "Yes, Mommy is reading."

"'Bout Jesus?"

Megan looked at her tiny daughter and chuckled, "Yes, 'bout Jesus."

"Jesus love me."

"Yes, He does, sweet girl." Megan smiled as she tried to focus on her reading. She was thrilled that they had plugged into a church that had such dedicated teachers for the children. Krissy had come home singing about the B-I-B-L-E and the Lord's love every Sunday since Christmas.

"Ron tell me dat."

Megan looked up. "What did Ron tell Krissy?"

"Dat Jesus love me."

"Ron? Wellbourne?" Megan blinked in disbelief. Yes, she had seen Ron at church on a regular basis and knew that he was studying with Tom Fairbanks, but when had he had the opportunity to talk to Krissy about Jesus?

"Yep. Ron Wellorn."

"Yes, ma'am." "Mess, mam." Krissy happily went back to munching her cookies, leaving her mother befuddled until Chad interrupted her thoughts.

"Can I have the last Pop Tarts?"

"Is your brother awake?"

Chad frowned. "Yes."

"Then please share. Get each of you a banana to go with them."

Megan's consideration of Ron's tutoring Krissy in preschool

theology would have to wait. Time to start the day.

"Todd Sheldon is here to see you, Mr. Wellbourne." Teresa's voice over the intercom broke Ron's concentration. He tossed his reading glasses onto his desk and placed both palms over his eyes as he leaned back in his chair. "Thank you. Send him in."

Ron collected himself quickly and stood to greet his chum warmly. Ron marveled at how easy it had become in recent weeks to shift from work to personal mode. At the end of each day, it all seemed to balance. In fact, this morning Ron had caught himself praying about whether or not to continue pursuing a client. Three months ago, Ron would have seen prayer as an intrusion to his work. Now, it was becoming a regular part of it. Ron watched Todd take a seat. His friend smiled knowingly.

"Is it time?"

Ron inhaled deeply and let out a long, slow breath. It felt safe talking to Todd about his personal life knowing he wouldn't share their conversations with Julie until Ron gave Todd permission to do so.

He gazed around the room before looking Todd squarely in the eye. "I believe it is." Ron's smile widened and the relief in his face lit up the room.

Todd threw his head back and hooted. "Praise God!" He composed himself quickly when Ron glanced at his office door. "So, what's your plan?"

Ron gave Todd a wry smile. "My plan is to remain calm. I've spent many hours over the last several months conversing with Megan Hardin." Ron became somber. "A new relationship is the last thing on her mind."

Todd shifted in his chair. "Don't be so quick to assume that. A few weeks ago, a relationship wasn't on *your* mind, either. You didn't want a relationship with God or with a woman. God's softened your heart and reshaped it so that you desire His will. If a relationship between you and Megan is in God's will, He'll change her heart, too."

Ron knew Todd was right, but he couldn't help but pray, *God change her heart quickly.* With that, Ron pulled a folder out of his desk drawer and laid it on the desk between them. With a broad smile, Ron told his friend, "Meanwhile, I want to show you a plan I've already been working on."

Chapter 10

"Let's see, that's coffee, black and caramel latte, whipped cream and caramel on top. In to-go cups." The waitress looked up from her order pad. "Will that be all?" the young woman asked Ron.

He smiled. "Yes. Thank you." She nodded and left Ron to wait on his friend.

Any minute, he'd be able to see her walking up the street. Megan would get to the corner of Broadway and Main and look left, right, then left again before crossing the street, just the way she taught her children to do it. Then she'd toss her hair back and pull her leather bag over her shoulder as she walked east on Main, stealing quick glances into stores windows as she passed them.

Ron felt his heart pick up its pace when she crossed the street. He would be forever indebted to this woman for challenging his behavior and pushing him to see the world from God's perspective instead of his own. Her confidence and total dependence on her faith had made Ron take pause and reconsider Godly living for the first time in decades.

When Megan was less than a block from the coffee shop,

Ron picked up their drinks and timed his steps so that he would open the door just as Megan reached for it.

"Excuse me," Megan said without looking directly at Ron as she bumped into him. She had already stepped into the shop and was looking around for Ron before he could get her attention. Megan laughed when she saw Ron standing behind her with the door propped open. "I guess you'd like to stretch your legs this afternoon?"

"It's far too pretty to just walk." Ron motioned with his head for Megan to follow him out of the store. She obliged, though Ron could see her working at not asking more questions. He handed Megan her cup and made a sweeping motion with his free hand. "After you."

Megan narrowed her eyes, a small smile beginning to play at her lips as she took the cup and walked out ahead of Ron. The friends walked side by side further down Main Street. After only a few steps, Ron stepped off the sidewalk and strode to the passenger's door of a tiny convertible parked at the curb. Megan watched him cautiously, but he saw her face light up in full when he opened the door, obviously expecting her to get inside.

"That's beautiful!" Megan marveled, still standing on the sidewalk unable to take her eyes off the classic MGB. After a few seconds, she looked at Ron. "Is it yours?"

Ron laughed out loud. "Yes, it's mine."

It was Megan's turn to laugh. Then in her best "mommy" voice, she inquired, "How long have you owned something this fun and not told me about it?"

Ron winked playfully, "Too long." He nodded at the

passenger's seat, "You gonna get in?"

Megan squealed with delight as she jumped from the curb and almost directly into the seat. Ron handed Megan her seatbelt and waited for her to fasten it before handing her his own cup of coffee. He shut the door and walked around to his side of the car. Once securely inside, Ron offered Megan a tan baseball cap. 'Don't want to muss up your hair."

Megan declined with a broad smile. "I haven't let the wind blow through my hair in a while. I want to *really* feel it." Ron watched her place his coffee in a holder. She sank into the passenger's seat, tucking a few stray hairs behind her left ear. Ron met her glance and the two sat for a few moments in comfortable silence. Megan reached out and touched Ron tenderly on his cheek.

Ron's heart was pounding out of control. He breathed deeply to get his wits about him and was about to reply when the moment was suddenly over. Megan put her hand back in her lap and looked forward. "What are we waiting for?" she asked. Ron wanted to answer honestly. *For you to let me tell you how deeply I care about you.* But he knew the timing was wrong. He'd keep praying for the right moment to come along. With a great deal of effort, he was able to pull himself together and start the ignition.

"Not a thing. Let's see what's blooming in the park."

With that, Megan slipped her sunglasses on and Ron spent the next half-hour completely content. He listened while she talked about her morning teaching the children and asked his advice about a small home repair issue. Ron asked her a few questions about an upcoming retreat at church and let her know about a musical opening this weekend at the college. After they had been around the park several times, Ron exited the large circle, turned south, and headed for the highway. Megan balanced her empty cup on her lap and stretched out her legs. She appeared perfectly relaxed. Ron felt like he could drive this woman around for the rest of life

After almost an hour of leisurely conversation and fresh air, Megan began looking at her watch. "Guess I'd better relieve my sitter. She has a voice lesson this afternoon." She touched Ron's hand on the gearshift, and his heart did a little flip. "Thanks for doing this for me." She looked around the two-seater car and giggled, "It's like a motorcycle with four wheels. Only two people fit in here."

Ron winked and exited the highway to head back to Megan's car. Ron found a small spot to park nearby and worked deftly to set the parking brake and slip out his door and around to Megan's before she could finish unbuckling her seatbelt. When Ron opened the door, Megan held out her hand so he could help her out of the low car. Her small hand was soft in his, almost like silk. Ron considered caressing it.

"Thank you," Megan whispered. Ron watched her look down and breathe deeply before she raised her head and brushed her long hair over her shoulder. She looked into his eyes and smiled tenderly. "I needed that." Megan let out a small chuckle. "I've probably needed that for a while."

Ron let go of her hand and took a step back, still holding her gaze. "You are most welcome, my friend. We'll do it again sometime."

"I'd like that." Megan replied and made her way briskly to her SUV. Ron stood next to her open door, his hand still warm from her touch.

....

Megan softly closed the door to the little girls' room and tiptoed down the stairs. The boys and Ali weren't sleeping yet, but they were settled under their covers enjoying a few minutes with their new library books before turning off their lamps.

Megan retreated to the master bathroom. A smile played at her lips as she tugged her T-shirt over her head. It still smelled of the gasoline fumes she'd picked up in Ron's convertible this afternoon. Wrapped in her thick robe, Megan sat at her vanity and looked into the mirror without seeing herself. She reflected back on this afternoon's adventure.

Four months ago, she never would have imagined that Ron Wellbourne would undergo such transformation. God had answered her prayers for him quickly. Ron was attending church, making friends, talking to his parents more. He was even being kind to widows and small children. At least one particular widow and five very small children. Megan closed her eyes. It was really time to admit that Ron made her feel special. And that he likely did that because she *was* special to him. Megan lowered her head and rubbed the back of her neck. Sitting next to Ron in his car today had made Megan feel...what was the word? *Protected*? Yes, but something else, too. It was more like *safe*. He respected her opinion while challenging her to think "outside the box." Megan could just be herself and Ron still wanted to be with her. Megan wondered briefly if, perhaps, Ron's feelings for her *had* turned romantic, lately. She occasionally saw his caramel-colored eyes scan her with admiration. She'd felt his hand move this afternoon as though he was going to caress hers when he helped her out of the car.

She quickly brushed off the notion, reminding herself that Ron Wellbourne was a confirmed forty-something bachelor. He wasn't looking for love, especially not with a woman with *five* children. Ron wasn't falling in love with her. He was growing more and more like the brother Megan never had. And it felt wonderful.

Megan quickly showered then, wrapped back into her robe and padded into her closet for nightclothes. The master closet had been overwhelming to Megan at first. It measured fifteen by thirty feet. A large island with forty-five drawers sat in the center. As she had overcome the guilt of having such an enormous suite, Megan settled into making the "excess" practical. She gave each child a section of the huge closet, making the sorting and storing of clean laundry a cinch. The kids all had to get dressed in here with her, but there was so much room, no one cared.

"Ouch!" Megan hopped on one foot as she leaned into the island. She'd stubbed her toe on a large chest. She examined the offended toe and found it no worse for the wear, but the pain still darted up her foot. Resigned to the pain for the time being, Megan sunk to the floor and sat against the island to rub her foot, averting her glance so that she wouldn't have to look at the offending chest. She breathed deeply and worked hard to steady her emotions.

Megan had purposely had the chest put in here out of the way. She'd hoped her children would forget about it in here. They'd unfortunately asked about it once. Thankfully, it had been close enough to bedtime that Megan gave orders to brush teeth then herded them upstairs to bed. She laid a quilt over the top of it later that night, making it all but invisible. They never mentioned it again.

When she was confident she wouldn't cry, Megan came to her feet and finished getting dressed for bed. Finally snug under her soft down comforters, Megan reached for Bible on her nightstand. Before she picked it up, she held her index finger softly to her lips and then pressed it on Chris's picture. "I'm so glad you prayed for me while you were still here." She closed her eyes and silently prayed, *Lord, keep my life simple. Very, very simple.*

Chapter 11

"Good morning, Sunshine." Megan cringed at the sing-songy tone of Julie's voice, uninvited, in her bedroom. And before she'd had coffee. Julie was treading on thin ice. Megan pulled the comforter over her head and tried to ignore the intrusion.

When a ray of sun appeared on the pillow above her head, Megan conceded defeat. She tossed back the cover and sat up straight, still not fully opening her eyes.

"Don't you knock?" Megan was rethinking the wisdom of giving Julie a key to her house.

"No, but I deliver."

Megan caught sight of the latte on her nightstand. She was only slightly remorseful for being cross over the intrusion. "Thanks." Megan stretched her legs out under the covers and watched Julie take a seat across the room. She picked up the steaming paper cup and settled back onto her pillows. After several sips of caffeine, Megan's mood began to improve. "To what do I owe the pleasure?"

Julie smiled sheepishly. "I need help."

Megan rolled her eyes in mock disdain. "What now?"

Julie laughed, "I'm in trouble with Todd."

"And I can help you get out of trouble with Todd?"

"Your organizational skills can."

Megan raised an eyebrow as she sipped her drink. "Sounds like work."

"But fun, too." Megan gave Julie a wry smile. Her friend continued her sales pitch, "I've been promising Todd all winter that we'd get the garage cleaned out before Spring Break. Step number one in the process is a garage sale this weekend. We've already put an ad in the paper and signs up at the end of our road. I even arranged to be off all day tomorrow."

"And?"

"A colleague is sick and I need to pinch-hit at a seminar in Tulsa for the next two days. Todd will take the news better if I tell him you're going to get this junk out of our garage."

Megan mulled over the logistics quickly. She would need to be up late getting things ready and up early for the sale. "Can we camp at your house, tonight?"

Julie's eyes lit up. "Oh, that would be fun! You guys haven't slept over since you moved to town. I don't have to leave until tomorrow morning."

Her friend's enthusiasm was contagious. Megan sat up and crossed her legs. "I'll run by the movie store and pick up something on our way out to your place. Do we need to bring anything else?"

"Just your muscles. Todd and I have done some heavy culling. You have our work cut out for you."

"I'll go out there as soon as the kids are done with school.

Ali and Chad can help me put quite a dent in getting things set up."

Julie checked her watch and rose from the large chair. She walked over and gave Megan a long hug. "Thank you. Having you here is such a blessing."

"Blah, blah, blah." Megan returned Julie's hug then pushed the covers off and put her feet on the floor. "Go to work. Daylight's burning."

....

Megan ran the sleeve of her T-shirt across her forehead. It was only March, but the afternoon sun had heated the Sheldon's garage to over ninety degrees. She looked at Ali's red cheeks and ordered some rest for both her two oldest children. "I think you both have earned a water break. Go inside and cool off." Ali and Chad gladly obliged and Megan took her own water bottle, now slightly warm, and sat on a stray lawn chair to survey their progress.

The garage was empty except for a few pieces of bedroom furniture Todd would need to move out when he came home. She was pleased with the progress she and the kids had made this afternoon and thankful for a schedule that permitted her to help her friends on such short notice. The fresh air and change of scenery had provided a welcome reprieve to a week that had become more emotional than Megan would have admitted out loud.

Soon after her ride in Ron's convertible, Megan had gone to her weekly women's Bible study. Liz Fairbanks had sensed

Megan's distraction and asked her if Megan wanted to talk about anything. She'd succeeded at deflecting Liz, but Megan returned home feeling like she was keeping a big secret. As the week wore on, Megan had grown more confused. She enjoyed Ron's company. She had for weeks, months. Why did that suddenly feel wrong?

Just another unanswered question on a list that lengthened every day. Which was why Megan was thankful she was here, staying busy and being useful to Julie and Todd. Staying busy was how Megan had gotten through the first several months after Chris died.

Feeling like she had hit on a solution for sorting out her emotions, Megan stood and walked to her SUV. She opened the door and grabbed a bag from the home improvement store she had visited earlier. Tucked at the bottom of the bag, Megan found several brochures of paint samples. She walked back to her chair in the garage and began trying to determine which palette she'd like to see in her living room. Though the walls were a good color, the paint in that room was not wearing well with five children using it as a den. Megan heard Julie's car pull up and was still looking through the first set of paint chips when she heard footsteps approach the garage. Without looking up, she queried her friend, "I need your opinion."

"Sure. What about?"

Megan jumped from her seat at the sound of Ron's voice. "You're not Julie."

Ron laughed, "Hardly." He had his hand on Megan's shoulder and was trying to look into her face. Megan was so surprised to see him that her heart was racing and she was, quite frankly, a little miffed. He'd scared her to death!

"You might mention that next time." Megan looked at Ron's amused expression incredulously. "It's not funny." She regretted her tone the second the words were out of her mouth. Ron looked at her apologetically.

"I could see you when I pulled up, so I assumed you saw my Jeep. I'm really sorry I scared you." Ron gave her shoulder a small squeeze then let go and took half a step back.

Megan felt horrible. Poor Ron had no idea that Megan had had little sleep, and even less to eat, since she'd last seen him. She looked at his concerned expression and worked to put his mind at ease. "It's ok. I was just...never mind." She held out her hand and started their conversation over, "Good afternoon, Ron. And how are you?"

Ron grinned and took her hand. "I'm well. You?"

Megan laughed. "Obviously distracted." She held up the paint samples. "I was sitting here pondering a new color for my living room." Megan motioned to the back of the garage. "Of course, now that you're here, I can get back to work. Can you help me move these big pieces?"

Ron frowned. "Todd and I can get those when he gets home."

"I'm perfectly capable..."

Ron cut her off, "Yes, you are perfectly capable, but right now I need your help with these." Megan had not noticed the bags in Ron's hands. He held one open and she peered at its contents: hotdogs and shish-kabobs.

"You're cooking dinner?"

"Todd called me earlier to invite me over to help with the heavy lifting. He also invited me to bring dinner. He'll fire up the grill when he gets home." Ron looked at his watch. "And he should be home any minute. If you'll show me where Julie keeps pans and things, I'll see if I can get all of this organized."

"Some friend Todd is," Megan teased. "Your reward for 'heavy lifting' is that you get to shop for and help cook dinner." Megan fell is step with Ron and they made their way into the house. "Remind me to call you the next time I need furniture moved."

Ron laughed at her teasing and handed her a sack of groceries to put away. "How did you enjoy your MG ride the other day?"

Megan felt a twinge of guilt at the mention of their afternoon. But why? Maybe she needed to keep her distance from Ron until she could sort out some of these emotions. The feeling of Ron's hand on her shoulder startled Megan.

"Megan?"

Megan tried to answer Ron's question. What were they talking about? "I'm sorry, you asked me a question?"

Ron chuckled nervously, "I did." He backed away from her and busied himself with dinner preparations. "But you looked a million miles away just now. I figured you didn't hear me."

Megan swallowed hard and worked to breathe normally. She stood up straight and tried to recall what had distracted her. The car! "You asked me about your car."

Ron eyed her suspiciously. "Yes. I asked you how you enjoyed our ride the other afternoon."

Megan could see she had made Ron uncomfortable with her absentmindedness. She concentrated on conversing with him and trying to put him back at ease. "Oh, it was wonderful." That wasn't a lie. It had been a wonderful afternoon. But it ultimately dragged up new emotions that Megan didn't want to deal with yet. She tried to think of a way to keep their dialogue going. "What year did you say it was?" When Ron stated a year in the late seventies, Megan laughed out loud. "It's almost as old as I am!"

Ron winced. "See, I didn't need to know that. I feel old enough already."

Megan seized the opportunity to rib Ron a little harder about his age. "You're not old. Just because you were in junior high when I started kindergarten..."

Ron tossed a package of hotdog buns at Megan and shot her a look of warning. Megan caught the buns easily and egged Ron on mercilessly, "Not bad aim for an old man," Megan laughed. It felt so good to feel this good.

Suddenly it occurred to Megan that this was exactly the way she had been feeling when she and Ron had been together earlier this week. He made her laugh out loud. Ron also made her feel young again. Days had been few, if any, since Chris's death when Megan felt young and carefree. Megan and her children had all their needs, and most of their wants, met but the responsibility of raising five children and running a house alone allowed her precious little opportunity to let her defenses down. Megan vowed to try to not feel guilty anymore about feeling young and happy when she was with Ron. He was God's gift to her as He lightened a dark season of her life. Megan tossed the buns back onto the countertop and returned Ron's huge smile. *Thank you, God, for a companion I didn't even know I needed.*

Chapter 12

Randy and Lily helped their mother blow out the candles. The children were anxious to get Megan's birthday celebration out of the way and get to the business of hunting Easter eggs. Ron watched Megan patiently remind all of them that the hunt would commence as soon as her gifts were opened. He was thankful no April showers were on the horizon. All eight children were ecstatic about hunting eggs in the Sheldon's hay field.

It took the kids far less time to find two hundred eggs than it had taken Ron and Todd to hide them. All too soon, the hunt was over and the chocolate feast had begun. When the crowd thinned from the patio, Ron collected his plate and walked inside to the kitchen.

As he placed the dish in the sink, Ron felt a slight tug on his left leg. He looked down to see Krissy Hardin, flanked by Lily and Jake. He smiled at the cherub with blue eyes craning her neck to see his face. "You give show'ler ride?" Comprehension dawned quickly and Ron stooped down to face the trio on their level.

"You want me to give *all* of you shoulder rides?" When

his question brought giggles from all three children, Ron scooped them up collectively and answered, "Let's see what we can do." He walked into the Sheldon's living room and stood the tots on Julie's sofa, certain it was not a mommy-approved move. No mommies were about and none of the children complained, so Ron continued, "Who's first?"

Six hands went up at once as Krissy, Lily, and Jake squealed, "Me, me, me."

"Jake, buddy, I think there's a 'ladies first' rule we're supposed to follow, here, so let me take one of them first." Ron eased Lily onto his shoulders and began to carefully circle the room, avoiding low-flying ceiling fans and door facings. After almost half an hour of rotating all three through the sport, Ron was relieved to see their mommies come to his rescue.

"What's going on in here?" The question came from Julie, but Megan was close behind, asking the same question with her eyes. Ron wasn't certain either woman approved, but the kids defended him quickly. Lily was their spokesperson.

"Ron was giving shoulder rides. He was really careful and made us hold on tight." This was true. In fact, Jake had held onto his ears. The women giggled and eyed each other knowingly.

"You've started something I hope you're willing to finish, Wellbourne," Megan warned. "You'll be slave to this game every time they see you, now." Ron liked the way Megan said, "every time." It implied he would see Megan and her children more. And lately, all he could think about was seeing them more.

When Megan laughed, Ron felt like he had come home. All his adult life, Ron had searched for the feeling he got when Megan smiled at him. He felt like his heart would burst if he didn't tell her that soon. Ron knew the time had come to give Megan his gift. Ron got Julie's attention and motioned for her to follow him to the patio. Megan was still distracted with the giggling children and didn't seem to notice them leave the room.

Once he had Julie's attention outside, Ron got straight to the point. "I need your support on something. Follow my lead?"

Julie narrowed her eyes at her husband's lifelong friend. "What are you up to?" Ron put his hands in his pockets and looked at the concrete in front of his feet. The moment of truth had come. If he wanted to walk in faith, he needed to start talking about it. He took a slow, deep breath and exhaled as he looked up.

With his eyes, he implored Julie to trust him as he confided, "Something I've been praying about a long time."

Understanding dawned quickly, and Julie walked over to Ron. She stood on tiptoe and kissed him gently on the cheek. She rubbed his arm tenderly and whispered, "I've been praying, too." Julie walked back to the patio door and looked back over her shoulder. "I'll back you up whenever you're ready."

Relieved that he and Julie were on the same page, and that Julie didn't seem surprised, Ron nodded his thanks. "I'll be in shortly." Alone with his thoughts, Ron felt relief wash over him as he realized that Megan would know how he felt about her within the hour. For weeks, he'd been planning to show her how he felt. Ron knew her feelings for Chris ran deep, but he also knew that there was a sparkle in Megan's eyes whenever they were together.

Ron made his way inside, keys in hand. Megan and Julie were finishing up the supper dishes and discussing their schedule for the next morning. As nonchalantly as possible, Ron interrupted the two women and looked at Megan. "I have to run home to pick something up for Todd." He nodded at Megan, "Care to ride along?" He watched Megan's face light up and then dim.

"I'd better not. It'll be time for Krissy and Lily's baths, soon."

Julie turned from the sink and waved a hand in Megan's direction. "Oh, as if I can't bathe two little girls. Go on."

A smile played at Megan's lips. She looked sideways at Julie. "You sure?"

"Positive." Julie peeked around the corner at Jake, Lily, and Krissy building a house out of enormous blocks. "They won't even notice you're missing," she assured Megan and walked passed her into the living room, settling the matter.

Thrilled, Megan looked at Ron. "I guess I'm free."

The ride to the Wellbourne's house took less than five minutes. Ron offered a silent prayer as he pulled his Jeep into the driveway. He parked near his bungalow and went over to Megan's side to open her door.

"Thank you, sir," Megan said in her best Southern drawl, daintily taking Ron's hand when he offered it. When she was fully out of the vehicle, Megan let go of Ron's hand and stood in stunned silence. Ron studied her face as she walked around his Jeep until she faced his small home. Megan turned her head to the left and slowly scanned the outside of Ron's cottage.

....

Megan rarely found herself speechless. Nothing could have prepared her for what she saw in front of her. The stark bachelor digs of Ron Wellbourne had bloomed!

The front door had been painted a fetching shade of sage. To the left of the thick, wooden door, yellow roses were beginning to climb. To the right, bright azaleas spilled over a rustic clay pot. A small replica of Ron's cottage sat under the large oak tree, replete with curtains in its windows and a tiny flowerbox beneath the front window.

When she caught her breath, Megan turned around so that she faced Stan and Mabel's house. To the side of the main driveway sat a new wooden fort with climbing rocks on one side and a slide on the other. A tire swing hung from the massive pecan tree in front of their home. Megan still couldn't speak; so many thoughts and questions were running through her head. Thankfully, Ron rescued her.

"Come inside a moment." Megan regarded Ron carefully as she eased around him and through the front door she had just stood back and admired. He stepped inside. Megan followed his gaze to the corner near his front window. Tears sprang to her eyes.

An elegant arm chair and coordinating ottoman had

been nestled into the corner. With the Roman shade on the window up, whoever sat in the chair had a perfect view of the playhouse and fort. A small shelf was neatly stacked with Christian storybooks, some pre-teen novels, and several stylish decorating magazines.

Megan looked up at Ron with tears slowly streaming down her cheeks. His face was intense with emotion. When their eyes met, Megan knew exactly what to say.

"You love us, don't you?"

Ron's expression softened and he moved closer to Megan. He cupped her face in his hands and lowered his face, brushing her lips slightly with his. He leaned his forehead against hers and sighed deeply, "Yes, Megan Hardin. I love you."

As wonderful as it felt to be told she was loved by this incredible man, Megan put a few inches between them and looked at Ron seriously. "I come in a big package." Megan took both Ron's hands in hers and squeezed them gently. "Do you love them, too?"

Ron laughed at her question. "They are impossible not to love." He touched the tip of her nose with his index finger. "I fell in love with the 'package' a long time ago."

Megan widened her eyes at this admission. "Oh? Just how long ago was this?" She watched Ron blush before he answered.

"The night you beat me playing Pac Man." Megan laughed out loud at Ron's shameless honesty and wrapped her arms around him. A small envelope with 'Megan' written neatly on the front caught her eye. "What's this?" she asked as she made her way over to the shelf where it was propped against a neat stack of magazines. She picked it up and looked at Ron. When he smiled and nodded slightly, she opened the envelope. A hand-written note, dated several weeks earlier, was inside.

Megan,

You've taught me so much about trusting the Lord with matters of little and great importance. This morning, God showed me this passage. I feel like it pertains to a matter of great importance. I pray that I can share this, and so much more, with you very soon.

Love in Christ,

Ron

The tears that had dried up only moments before were back in full force as Megan read the words from Ecclesiastes 4. It was the same passage that had stirred Megan's own heart during the quiet of the morning on her patio weeks ago.

There was a man all alone;
he had neither son nor brother.
There was no end to his toil,
yet his eyes were not content with his wealth…

Two are better than one…

She stared in awe at the passage, not noticing that Ron had come near her and was now looking up at her from his place in front of her on one knee.

Chapter 13

The scents and sights of autumn tickled Megan's senses as she stood on the tiny bridge. The water several feet below bubbled peacefully. Megan knew she should feel as serene as her surroundings, but the morning's activities had left her feeling more harried than she'd hoped to feel today. Not to worry. In a few minutes, she'd be Mrs. Ron Wellbourne.

Megan watched Stan and Mabel take their seats; they fairly beamed with excitement. Megan knew they had waited a long time for this day. She was honored that they trusted her to love their son.

Megan chuckled to herself as she watched Randy try to wrangle Krissy into submission. She wanted to carry her flower basket on her left arm, much to Randy's dismay. Pastor Dave's wife intervened and Megan saw her children line up just as a violin began to play. Randy escorted Krissy, followed by Lily and Chad and then Ali, who would stand as Megan's maid of honor.

Megan peeked through the break in the trees to see Ron and Todd looking very serious. She knew from comments they had made during last night's rehearsal that both men were wary of five children performing in a wedding. Megan assured them that no one would care if things went awry. Friends and family were here to celebrate with them, not be entertained. She smiled as all five children gracefully took their places in front on the congregation.

As the sweet melody of the processional floated up to Megan from the theatre below, a sudden wave of sadness made her choke back unwanted tears. Liz Fairbanks raised her hand to cue Megan to cross the tiny bridge, and the bride wiped a wayward tear from her cheek. When Liz lowered her hand and began to walk toward her, Megan tried to steady her breathing, diverting her gaze when the older woman began fussing over the strand of pearls at Megan's throat.

"God's right beside you. Just take His arm." Megan felt Liz's gentle kiss on her cheek and squeezed her friend's hand in thanks.

With one last deep breath in and then out, Megan swept away one last tear and took her Father's arm and let Him lead where He willed.

....

Ron couldn't remember ever having spent a lovelier day in his life. A woman he did not deserve had vowed her life to him only an hour ago. The elegant reception had Megan's touch all over it. Each round table was set simply with alabaster flowers in crystal vases. Waiters circled the room, discreetly serving their adult guests.

In the center of the room, a long table loaded with lavender arrangements held huge crystal bowls filled to the brim with tiny orange crackers shaped like fish and candy-coated chocolates. Cake pedestals held brightly-decorated cookies and fountains on each end of the table flowed with punch that Ron knew had been carefully chosen so as not to leave noticeable stains on tiny taffeta and satin dresses.

At their table near the front of the room, Stan and Mabel glowed. Mabel hovered, introducing her new grandchildren to distant relatives who had not yet met Ron's family. Ron brushed back a tear and offered a prayer of thanks for his restored relationship with his parents. God had made the Wellbournes a family, again.

Ron scanned the room, stopping when his eyes rested on the object of his affections. He saw Megan surrounded by family and friends who had traveled from the deep South to see their belle at the ball. Jane Osgood was laughing out loud as she related a story from Megan and Jane's teen years in their small hometown. Megan had introduced Jane to Ron when Todd and Julie hosted the couple's engagement party. Jane stayed a few days and Ron had been privy to a sillier side of Megan that week. The two friends looked, and *sounded*, like young girls when they were together. Ron liked seeing a very young Megan come to the surface. He enjoyed the idea of sharing his home, and everything in it, with a woman who was young at heart.

At that, Ron caught Megan's eye and gave her a questioning glance. She excused herself from her company and made her way over to Ron. "Yes, Mr. Wellbourne?"

Ron took a step closer to his bride and whispered, "Would

it be inappropriate for me to say that I think we've been nice long enough and now I want you to myself?"

Megan fluttered her lashes at Ron and pretended to be offended. "Why, Mr. Ron, is that a question you ask a lady?"

Ron bent low and gave Megan's ear a gentle nibble before whispering his answer. Megan smiled and went to change into her traveling clothes.

....

Megan felt Ron squeeze her hand as the plane took flight from Oklahoma City. She saw him stretch his long legs out and heard him breathe deeply as he asked, "Isn't this great?"

Megan gave him a weak smile, though not intentionally. She was trying to be enthusiastic about their adventure to the Caribbean. She reminded herself that Hessie and her mother could hold down the fort with her kids for a few days and that there was really nothing to be anxious about.

Except this morning. The wake-up call had come late and they had to get packed and out the door without the leisurely room-service breakfast they had pre-ordered. Hungry and still drained from yesterday, Megan had commented on being a little tired as she stepped into Ron's Jeep. "Yeah," Ron replied. "I know what you mean. I guess I'm not used to sleeping with someone. I hardly got any rest."

Megan knew his comment had not been intended for harm, but it fell on Megan's tender heart and wounded her more deeply than she cared to admit. She had been trying for the past two hours to shake it off, but it still stung. Megan took a deep breath and tried to relax.

She felt Ron kiss her fingers softly and resigned to keep her chin up. Life could be far worse than having a man who treasured you take you to a tropical paradise.

You have nothing to complain about, Megan. Quit it!

She gave Ron's hand a squeeze as she assured him. "Yes. We're going to have the time of our lives," she told him, wishing with all her heart that she believed what she was saying.

Chapter 14

The hardwood floor creaked under Ron's feet as he tried to creep down the hall. It was easier to slip out before the kids woke up rather than having them wake Megan. But the light streaming out into the hall made him pause. He glanced into the office as he walked past to grab his jacket from the chair in the hall.

Chad was already up and attacking his schoolwork. He was changing the date on the calendar and moving the arrows so that the "today" one was under today's date...the 16th. Already, they'd been married a month. He'd send her some flowers and hope she was receptive to his affections. Why had she become so sad? Hadn't she wanted to get married as much as he?

Yes, she had. He had seen her eyes at the wedding. The afternoon sunlight had not compared to the way her face had glowed that afternoon in the park. They had stood together and vowed to build a family "for better or for worse." He had seen her eyes. Though she stumbled over the part about death and parting, she was genuinely happy when they exchanged their vows. That much he knew for sure.

Finally Time to Dance

But as they pulled out of the driveway to depart for the honeymoon, he had sensed her apprehension. Ron had figured it was because she was concerned about the children. She was leaving them for the first time ever, and Krissy was still so young. *She'll relax once we're on the plane,* he reasoned.

As they boarded the plane for Dallas, she was quiet. Between Dallas and Miami, she pretended to sleep, but he had seen the tears slip down her cheek. She was sad. *I thought having a husband again would ease her pain. What I have done to her? Lord, please help.*

During the layover in Miami, they had found things to talk about. They grabbed an airport lunch and laughed easily. As they boarded the last leg of their flight she took his hand and thanked him for insisting they go on a "real" honeymoon.

St. Thomas had been everything they'd hoped it would be: peaceful, restful, colorful. They'd boarded the plane for home hand-in-hand, thankful for a memorable start to their new life.

Back at home a week later, however, the sadness in her eyes had returned. She was polite and affectionate, an efficient homemaker and a marvelous mother. She tended to all of Ron's needs. Megan cooked breakfast for him when he didn't have to be at work early, made sure all of his laundry was neatly pressed and hung, and was the wife he had longed for once they were alone at night. But her eyes gave her away. As Ron watched her, he could see pain and sadness surfacing that he thought had been put to rest at the months ago.

Ron wondered if Megan had ever fallen in love with him the way he'd fallen in love with her. Maybe Megan had only agreed to accept his affections to make life easier on all of them. She agreed to marry Ron and make a reasonably happy existence for her children. She was no longer a single mother with him under their roof; they were a family again.

A lot of guys have it worse, thought Ron. *Most of the men I work with are on their second or third marriage and have ex-spouses to deal with on both sides. What more could I want? Megan is kind to me, her children respect me, and I have a place to belong. I have a family. Thank you.*

As he shrugged on his coat and turned to go down the basement stairs, he considered going back in to kiss her goodbye. The smell and feel of Megan intoxicated him, and he could never get enough of her. Ron could easily see now that when Clare left for law school, God had been protecting him rather than taking away His blessing. When Megan had stepped into his life, he knew he'd never really been in love. Of course, love may feel differently in your forties than it would in your twenties, but Megan was all Ron had ever dreamed a woman could be, and more. She completed him. Whereas Ron tried to blend into a room and avoid conversation, Megan thrived on showing her feelings and understanding the feelings of others. She was brave when he felt cowardly, adventuresome when he felt like playing it safe. Of course, Ron's strengths complemented Megan's to a tee. He paid attention to detail when she couldn't remember which one of the kids needed his teeth brushed. Ron could balance a pinewood derby car to five ounces perfectly whereas Megan couldn't make one that would roll straight. But opposites had attracted and now he could not imagine a day, even an

Finally Time to Dance

hour, without her in his life.

Oh, how he longed to kiss her now, to tell her he'd miss her today and couldn't wait to come home to her tonight. He wanted to hear her sleepy chuckle as she touched his cheek and said she loved him. *No, I'll let her sleep. Maybe if she feels rested and I send the florist by, she'll seem more like herself.* He opened the door to the basement and to head down the stairs. "Bye, Ron!" shouted Chad as he threw his arms around Ron's waist. "See you later, Chad," Ron smiled as he ran his hand through the boy's hair and he slipped through the door, praying silently that he would not always be in love alone.

……………………..

Megan heard the garage door go up downstairs. They had made it another night. Time to start the day. As she folded back the down comforters, she felt a lump beside her and leaned over to kiss the face under the tousled blonde hair. No pacifier. It was Lily.

Ali was already at the table holding her spoon in midair over her bowl of Captain Crunch while she kept her eyes focused on the Nancy Drew book in her right hand. A twinge of guilt surged through Megan as she thought of Ali in the kitchen alone finding her own breakfast. To redeem herself, she poured Ali a glass of juice and set it in front of her bowl. "Thanks, Mom." Megan gave her a kiss on the forehead before heading to the schoolroom to check on Chad.

She paused for a moment and watched him check off the things he'd already done. The children's checklists had been born out of necessity when there was no time to plan, or even think, once the day began. Funny how she could look back now and see the small, subtle blessings that had come from those dark days. *The fingerprints of God.* As incomprehensible as it was, God knew all along how her marriage to Chris would end. And He had given her the tools she'd need to go on.

So pull it together and stop this moping around. If you trust in the Lord with all your heart, why are you second-guessing where He's put you? Megan resolved to put her best foot forward and get through at least one day without thinking so much about the past...and the future. *We'll just take this one hour at a time.*

"What can I fix you to eat, Bud?"

"A giant omelet! And some toast cut in rectangles." Megan had to smile at his exuberance, even at seven a.m.

"Coming right up. Try to get one more thing done before you come to the kitchen. It might rain this morning, so maybe you should pull the garbage cans out, now. That way you won't have to get the rain coat on to do it later."

"Great idea, Mom." Chad bounded down the basement stairs and Megan heard the door go up before she cracked the first egg. Ali was finished with her cereal and lingering over her book.

"Do I have to wash my hair this morning?" Megan could tell Ali hoped she'd let her out of it, but a quick glance at the calendar reminded her that today would be busy.

"Yes. You have choir this afternoon and we're jam-packed until then. Go ahead and get it done before you get started

Finally Time to Dance

with school." She ignored her daughter's pre-adolescent sigh and returned to the stove.

"Is it ready, yet?" Megan chuckled at the only explanation for the impatience standing beside her: B-O-Y.

It felt good to laugh, even for a few seconds. Tiny glimpses of normal were better than nothing. *Keep moving. Breathe in; breathe out.* Megan cracked another egg and tried to will away the dull ache already creeping into her temples.

"Go ahead and pour yourself a glass of milk." Chad happily obliged and sat down at the breakfast room table to read an Archie comic book. If there was something new or interesting to read in the house, it was on the breakfast room table.

Megan turned from placing Chad's breakfast on the table, to see Krissy padding into the kitchen. "Mommy, I wake!"

Megan kneeled down in front of the youngest Hardin and popped the pacifier out of her mouth. "Yes, you are." Megan gave her a peck on the tip of her nose. "Did you sleep well?"

"Mess, mam." Ah, a happy Krissy. *Thank you, Lord. I needed that.* "I watch Pooh wif my milk." Krissy smiled at her mother hopefully. Megan, much relieved to have a happy "baby" on her hands, poured chocolate milk in a sippy cup and walked Krissy to the living room where she settled the tot into the recliner and handed her the remote control. Pooh was in the DVD player and her three-year-old could take in from there.

"That's three. Only two more to go," Megan said out loud to herself as she rinsed dishes. When she turned to get a fresh towel from the drawer, Lily was standing there, a vision in Spider Man pajamas and fuzzy pink slippers. *Consider it pure joy...* The very sight of this child brought that verse from the book of James to mind every time Megan lay eyes on her.

"And what can I do for you this fine morning?" Megan was watching Lily pull out the cutting board where she would be served. Phooey with the breakfast room. Service was faster in here and you didn't even have to carry your dirty dishes to the kitchen.

"Waffles, please. No butter. And chocolate milk in my Dora cup." Lily knew exactly what she wanted when her head left the pillow. This was a good thing. Megan even took the time to cut the large waffles into nine squares apiece. She sat the colorful plate in front of her resident food critic. Lily beamed and hugged her mommy for not making the frozen waffles brown on the edges when she toasted them. Once she began stabbing the syrupy squares with her tiny fork, Megan left her to enjoy the feast and returned to the schoolroom, circling through the living room on her way.

Tigger was singing and bouncing and Krissy was dozing happily beneath a chenille throw. Megan stood the empty sippy cup upright and walked out the other door on the far end of the room toward the hall.

She heard the "swoosh, swoosh" just before the toy airplane hit her leg. "Good morning, Randy. Throwing toys down the stairs is never a good idea. You might hit someone."

"Sorry, Mom. It slipped." Randy stood halfway down the wooden staircase with two more airplanes in his arsenal.

"Slipped" indeed, thought Megan. But it was hard to be cross with those chubby cheeks and the bare tummy to match.

"Put some clothes on and I'll fix you a bowl of cheese grits." Randy was not picky about food and, since he lacked the ability to make a decision before roughly nine a.m., Megan took the liberty of deciding what he would eat.

Randy reluctantly put his planes where he had been sitting and made it down two steps before he heard Megan remind him to put his toys, including the one that had hit her leg, in their proper place. *Breathe in; breathe out. Keep moving.*

....

"Good morning, Mr. Wellbourne," Teresa chirped cheerfully as Ron walked through the reception area. "Here are this morning's messages. Mr. Bastrop called to say he'll be ten minutes late for his nine-thirty with you, so I pushed back your ten forty-five." Ron stopped in front of her desk and stared at her blankly. "Coffee's on your desk, Sir," she told him as she turned in her chair.

Ron hesitated and cleared his throat. "Thanks. Do you have the number to the Greenhouse there in your Rolodex?"

Teresa turned back to her boss and took a sharpened pencil from the leather holder on her desk. With pencil poised over a sticky note, she replied, "Of course. What would you like to send? And to whom?"

Ron tried to seem nonchalant as he shrugged and held his hand out for the note. "I'll place the call myself."

Teresa stuck the note to the sleeve of his jacket and placed his messages in Ron's hand. "You're going to have to make it quick. Your eight o'clock just got out of his car."

The mention of a client was all Ron needed. He snapped to attention, crossed the reception to his office, and called to his secretary, "Give me five minutes," just before he shut the door. When he was alone, Ron paused long enough to pray, *Father, help me. What can I do or say to make Megan feel better?*

The sound of voices just outside his door reminded him that he'd better make the call to the florist before his day got too busy. He slipped behind his desk and dialed the number. The phone on the other end rang less than one full ring.

"Greenhouse! How can we brighten your day?"

"Well, you could brighten mine by brightening my wife's. Deliver two dozen fresh daisies to twelve ten east fifteenth. No fluff, no bows, crystal vase. Bill it to Ron Wellbourne."

"Get yourself into trouble, already?" Gladys, owner and queen bee of the Greenhouse, had known Ron since before he was born. Ron knew she had monitored his relationship with Megan by keeping track of floral deliveries. Ron knew Gladys couldn't possibly know what kind of turmoil was going on in his heart, but he felt exposed.

"I'm not sure," Ron mumbled, feeling like a nine-year-old.

"Well, if you're not sure, I can't help you. I need to know what kind of card to use." Ron wondered if all florists included free marriage counseling with every order.

"I can help you with that. The card I can tell you needs

to say 'Happy Anniversary.' We've been married one month to the day."

"Congratulations. What do *you* want to say on the card?"

Do you love me? The question came to Ron's mind automatically. He worked to breathe normally and steady his voice. "Just say, 'One month and counting. I love you.'"

"Think you should sign your name?"

Ron laughed at Gladys's tone but declined, "She'll know who they're from. Thanks, Gladys. I'd better get busy before Teresa finds me playing on the phone."

"If it's your anniversary, get her something that sparkles to go with these flowers."

"Nothing sparkles more brilliantly that her eyes…"

"Blah, blah, blah. Stop by Gem's on your lunch break. You'll thank me."

"Yes, ma'am. Have a good day, Gladys."

As he returned the phone to its cradle, Ron reminded himself, "To work, Old Man." He gently touched the photograph of Megan on his desk before buzzing Teresa and asking her to send in his first client.

Chapter 15

The steaming kettle whistled softly as Mabel turned off the burner and poured the hot water into the porcelain pot. The antique tea set had been her mother's. As a small child, Mabel had spent many afternoons pretending to serve her dolls from the ivory pot with hand-painted violets on its belly. She was not expecting company nor were there even any dolls to share her tea this afternoon, but the ritual relaxed the elderly woman. She carried the silver tray into the sunroom, stopping to check her orchids. Too much water, again. Suzie would really need to stop trying to help with her indoor gardening. She would remind her husband's nurse that the plants were Mabel's therapy and should be left in her capable hands.

Small figures running up the driveway caught her eye and the day brightened instantly. *They're here! Oh, how fun this grandmother business is getting to be!*

As the children ran for the tire swing, Mabel watched the tall, slender figure following them. The mother of her five new grandchildren possessed her mother's wedding ring and the heart of her only child, but Mabel feared Megan had taken ownership of both reluctantly. She had never noticed sadness in Megan's eyes in the months she and Ron had spent getting acquainted, but the younger woman had seemed subdued since her honeymoon. The thirty-five-year-old Southern belle was still courteous and charming, but her ability to light up a room simply by entering it had waned. Grief was taking its toll, and the results could be devastating to all of them, especially the children. Mabel returned to the kitchen for another cup. Megan would not be likely to share her heart with her mother-in-law yet, but she was always willing to share a pot of tea.

Mabel had known Megan and Chris Hardin for years. Megan had long ago impressed Mabel Wellbourne with her spunk and tenacity and especially with the way she raised her young children. Many decades had passed since Mabel and Stan had seen a young family so consistent with their manners and respect. They were children, of course, but it was obvious Megan had children because she dearly loved them and was devoting her life to raising them in the nurture and admonition of the Lord.

It was this very admiration of Chris Hardin's young widow that caused Mabel to take pause when she began to sense Ron's interest in Megan. Ron had stopped attending church with his parents eighteen years ago. Stan and Mabel knew there was a reason behind his obstinacy, but he reacted badly to them the one time they tried to offer their support and lend an ear. In an effort to keep peace with their only child, the Wellbournes built a small cottage under a grove of oak trees and gave it to Ron. Instead of placating their son, however, the gesture had enabled Ron withdraw from them emotionally. He began living isolation and resentment and disguised it as workaholism. Ron had eventually turned his computer hobby into an international hardware components supply company, but it had only enabled him to work from home more, have fewer and fewer friends, and build a defensive wall around himself that kept Mabel and Stan at bay.

So once Mabel saw that Ron was serious about pursuing the affections of Chris Hardin's widow, she made a note in her prayer journal, thanking God for showing her how He was beginning to answer a prayer that had been on her daily list for almost twenty years. Then she had made a second entry: Megan Hardin, discernment.

God had been faithful to answer that prayer. Mabel watched as Ron left for church every Sunday morning and had overheard once or twice Megan reminding Ron to let God be in control of his life. Megan Hardin hadn't backed down from her convictions one bit. For this, Mabel would be eternally thankful.

....

Megan took her time walking along the cobblestone path that led to the back door. There were only yellows and reds left in the flowerbeds. These were not Megan's favorite colors, but the late fall sun illuminated them so that the brilliance dazzled her eyes. Mabel was an avid gardener, even seeing to it that the edge of the walk leading back to Ron's cottage was perfectly manicured. Over the months, as Ron and Megan had begun to spend more and more time together, the cottage had become more colorful. This past summer, purple roses had climbed up the front to the right of the narrow, arched door. Groundcover that flowered yellow had replaced the evergreen that had looked so plain before. Megan knew Ron took notice of every detail of her daughters' preferences, and it had touched her heart that he had included flowers that were their favorite colors.

In fact, in the months that Megan had visited Ron at the cottage, he had made several improvements that suited, and enticed, her children. In addition to the chair and bookshelf inside, Ron had put a comfortable swing with a large canopy over it within view of a tire swing hanging from a large oak tree. Ron had also built a tiny version of his cottage under a mimosa that could be seen from the swing and furnished it with a miniature dinette for Lily and Krissy. Just inside his cottage, Ron kept a small library of books Ali could enjoy while she sat on the big swing and a collection of coins and other ancient artifacts that could keep the eight-year-old enthralled for hours.

`Megan appreciated all the effort Ron had put forth to court her children. He had wanted to please them so badly. At the time, she had chosen to overlook the fact that he had seen them as the perfect opportunity to give his parents the grandchildren they always wanted and had simply done what needed to be done to make her children part of their family. Ron did not see the young girl in Megan that Chris had loved and appreciated. To him, Megan had always been a mother, a mother of many children. Megan knew that Ron loved her because he loved the package in which she came. It was more an attitude of respect than affection. She had married him before that had ever changed, so now she would just have to tough it out. Megan sighed and chided herself. *You have no room to complain. You have a beautiful family and a fine home and your children have a male figure, now. You've done what you had to do for them and it's not entirely unpleasant. You could have fared far worse.*

Megan drew a deep breath and checked the tears that threatened to spill over. She missed laughing out loud. She missed giggling late at night and wearing t-shirts to bed. Ron Wellbourne was caring and thoughtful but he was not silly or animated. "Live out loud" was what Megan did before she became Mrs. Wellbourne. Now, lunch needed to be ready at noon, dinner at six p.m. and everything in order in between. She wore matching ensembles and made sure every hair was in place before leaving her vanity to go to bed. It was a small price to pay for what she had gotten, and what her children had gotten, in return. Megan needed to suck it in and be thankful she was treasured if only as the mother of the family her husband had always wanted. *I just don't behave this well all the time. I'm going to screw this up and Ron will see who I really am and start planning his departure.* "Chin up, Meg." She looked around to see that the children were all occupied before heading inside.

Megan opened the back door without knocking. She found her mother-in-law just settling into one of the deep armchairs that faced the window overlooking the cottage and gardens. She had set a tea tray on the ottoman in front of the other chair. Megan kissed her mother-in-law on the cheek and then sank into the softness of the vacant chair and absorbed the aroma of the imported leaves.

"Good afternoon, Mabel. How's your day been?" Megan watched Mabel ponder the question. At seventy-one, Mabel had not even succumbed to gray hair. She kept her auburn locks trimmed short and neatly-coiffed. Though Mabel would likely be home all day, she was dressed in a gray silk pantsuit and matching pumps.

"It's been a good one, dear. Stan made it to the breakfast room for lunch. Suzie is with him, now, getting his afternoon exercises done." Megan watched Mabel's eyes dance as she gazed out the window to watch the children. She smiled at their antics as she continued on about Stan. "It's glorious out. Hopefully, Suzie will get him out to walk before she leaves. He's just so dead-set against it some days that she doesn't pick the battle."

"I'll help her pick it if need be. The fresh air will do him some good. Maybe hearing the kids outside will encourage him." Megan loved seeing Stan with the kids. The youngest two girls would climb onto him in the wheelchair while Ali, Chad, and Randy took turns trying to make Stan pop wheelies. If Stan's face was any indication after he'd played with the kids, laughter really was good medicine.

"You kids staying out of trouble?" Mabel's question was harmless enough, but Megan wondered if the older woman could sense her gloomy mood. Megan forced back the urge to disclose her fears and smiled warmly.

"It's been busy, but I think we're on the winning end of things. Thankfully, the cool nights are keeping the grass manageable. It's just about time to winterize the lawn and retire the mower for the season. I guess we'll gear up for Christmas next."

Mabel reached for a note pad on the marble table between their chairs. "That reminds me. I need ideas for Christmas gifts for these young ones."

Megan's defenses were instantly engaged. She checked her emotion, but she could tell by the confusion on Mabel's face that she had not done so quickly enough. Megan tried to sound disinterested when she said, "Oh, there's no need to make a big fuss. Maybe a subscription to Highlights Magazine or something else they could all share. I really try to keep things to a minimum so we can focus on the real Birthday Boy." Megan had spent the past several Christmases trying to lower the children's expectations. Chris had died less than a month before Christmas almost three years ago and their church family and Chris's students from the high school had turned out in full force to make it the "best Christmas ever" for the children. It was because these people loved them and wanted to take away their pain, Megan realized, but all the material gifts had created pandemonium and temporary gratification where she had been trying to create calm and peace with lasting Truth. In the end, the four children old enough to appreciate the gifts had pushed aside all the gifts they had gotten in December and returned to playing with the gifts she and Chris had carefully chosen when they had celebrated their last Christmas together October 25th.

It was the most amazing celebration. On October 24th, they had skipped Wednesday night service to read the Christmas story together near the tiny tree next to Chris's hospice bed in the master bedroom. The children were already in their pajamas and excitedly planning how early they would get up on "Christmas" morning when they were interrupted by the sound of the doorbell. Megan peeked out the window to see cars parked all the way down the street. She opened the door and then stepped back to let the children look out while she went to get Chris into his wheelchair. As they made their way into the living room, the voices of their dearest Christian brothers and sisters seeped through the glass door. Chris and Megan sat in awed silence as they listened to the chorus of "O Holy Night." All of the carolers, over a hundred and fifty in all, had dressed in mittens and scarves. Some even wore stocking caps in the seventy-degree night air. The Hardins could only stare and wonder how they had ever come to be so blessed. They felt unworthy of being so loved.

"Megan." Mabel's voice pulled her back into the present. "I think your tea may be a little strong. You drifted off on me. I was saying that maybe more than one subscription would suit them all more. They're close in age, but the same thing that interests Krissy might bore Ali. Or the boys might want something different from the girls." Megan could still just barely hear what the older woman was saying. *What's wrong with me?* Megan tried to steady her breathing and fished for something to say that would reassure Mabel.

Before she could answer, however, Mabel touched

Megan's hand and smiled. "Oh well, never mind all this Christmas chatter." Mabel stood and walked to the door. She motioned to the children. "I'll go see if that bunch is ready for a snack."

"Yes. We'll talk about it more another time," Megan finally managed to say. She tried to summon the strength to say more, but all she could do was smile weakly and take another sip of tea. *This isn't worth it. I can't even carry on a conversation anymore.*

Chapter 16

Julie rang twice before letting herself in the front door. She could see the Hardin children on the futon in the basement television room, but Julie opted not to disturb them by tapping on the low window. Megan was likely out of earshot of the doorbell, sorting clothes in the laundry area or folding them in the master closet.

Julie checked the master suite on the main floor first and found her friend busily hanging and folding laundry in the huge closet. "Closet" was actually a misnomer for the large sunroom that had been converted several years before Megan bought the house. From the bedroom, it appeared to be a normal closet, but once you walked through the narrow door you found yourself in an enormous room with an island in the middle where Megan folded and ironed all of their laundry after she brought it up from the basement.

Though she had called to check on her newly wed friend almost every day, it had been over two weeks since Julie had stopped in to visit. She regarded Megan from the doorway before giving away her presence.

At first glance, Megan looked fabulous. Ron had treated

her to a new wardrobe on their way home from the Caribbean, and the colors Megan had chosen brought her emerald eyes to life and dazzled next to her fair skin. This morning she had paired a new silk, sage t-shirt with her favorite faded jeans. Combined with wooden bangles she'd found in Old Town San Juan, Megan was the definition of shabby chic, and Julie loved it. Megan had waited long enough. Chris had made sure she would not have to work outside the home for many years, but Megan had remained frugal and tried to only buy new clothes for the children, and only when hand-me-ups would not fit or had been too worn to pass to the next child. Now, she could finally enjoy a few indulgences. God was blessing Megan for her patience and good stewardship, and Julie was thankful. Life had not always been so kind to her friend.

The shadows around Megan's eyes belied her colorful new wardrobe. A shiver ran up Julie's spine, causing her to shudder as she watched Megan sort and stack with unnecessary determination. Megan's posture and the faraway reflection in her eyes reminded Julie of the night she'd driven over an hour to Chris and Megan's house the night Chris was admitted to the hospital for the last time.

When Julie had walked into her kitchen, she could see that Megan was irritated but not surprised. She sat back on her heels and rubbed her forehead with the back of her hand, dripping soapy water from the sponge she had been using to scrub the floor.

Julie tried humor first, "Oh, yeah. You're gonna be a real treat tomorrow." Megan stuck her tongue out at her uninvited guest. Julie ignored the gesture and concentrated on being thankful the woman on the floor still had some spunk.

Megan went back to scrubbing. "I told you not to come up here and, for your information, this *is* restful to me. In about six hours, God-only-knows-who will be cooking in here and changing my babies' diapers and running my house in general. I won't have them thinking I can't even keep my own house clean."

Julie sat down and drew in a deep breath. From the looks of things, this bender had been going on for a few hours. More than likely, Chris was in intensive care and visiting hours had ended at eight, leaving Megan feeling helpless and alone. Cleaning was her drug of choice, and she was great at it. As an added bonus, it made her look calm and organized to anyone who didn't know her as well as Julie did.

In the weeks and months that followed Julie had watched helplessly as Megan and Chris made the most of their last days together. The miracle of Krissy coming along even though Chris was on chemotherapy had brightened everyone's outlook for the Hardins. Her birth even made it almost possible to believe Megan when she would say, "Krissy's middle name is 'Hope' because Chris and I are reminding ourselves that, as Christians, we're never without hope, even in our darkest days."

Julie had not been able to see Megan on most of the darkest of those days, but she had seen enough to know that it had been harder than Megan would have liked most people, especially her children, to believe.

After Chris's death, her pastor and a counselor had wisely advised Megan to not make any major decisions for a year. Megan and the children had traveled and done some redecorating and landscaping to brighten things up, but, for the most part, they stayed where they were and did the same things for about eighteen months until God moved them to this house.

Then Ron had stepped into the picture. It wasn't long before Julie and Todd could see that their long-time friend was head over heels in love with the vivacious young woman. Megan radiated life and Ron stayed close to her to soak it in.

Megan took things cautiously with Ron, but his commitment to his decision and to her and her family won her over quickly. After she accepted his proposal, she set about planning a small wedding. Since Ron had never been married and had no siblings, Mabel and Stan Wellbourne basked in all the preparations and excitement of the wedding. Julie smiled as she pictured Megan's face on her wedding day. Her friend was happy, again. It was a most precious moment.

But something had happened since the wedding to cloud Megan's expression. Standing there in her closet, Megan looked tired, maybe even defeated. Julie took a deep breath as she stepped into the closet, and Megan turned to the door. Her expression brightened instantly when she saw Julie.

"Hey. I was just looking for an excuse to make a pot of coffee." Megan put down the towel she was folding and walked over to embrace her friend. "You want me to scrounge up some lunch, too?" Julie followed Megan down the hall and into the large kitchen.

"No, thanks. Todd and I met for breakfast after he dropped the kids off at school. There's one good thing about retail: days off during the week," Julie opted to keep the banter light...for now.

Megan held up two bags of gourmet coffee. "Pick one."

Julie rolled her eyes and asked, "Where do you get this stuff? Don't you just have coffee?"

"Just trying to broaden your horizons, that's all," Megan grinned as she put away her fancy stash and pulled out the huge red container of plain ground coffee they both preferred.

"How's Ron adapting to living with people? Todd says he seems to be taking it in stride."

Megan knew Julie had not meant to hurt her and she tried desperately to keep the emotion from her face, but Julie's comment had made her furious. Not that it took much to make her furious these days, but why was it that everyone thought Ron was the only one making adjustments here? Didn't anyone see what she was giving up in order to make this sacrifice for her children? *Mercy!* When was the last time Megan had gotten to watch a movie of her choice late at night or taken her children somewhere by herself like she used to? *Oh, God, please, I want my life back the way it was. Maybe I was lonely sometimes, but I wasn't miserable, was I? I feel like a part of me is dying...all over again.* Megan tossed her hair over her shoulder and straightened her back. She breathed in and out and counted slowly. *One, two, three, four...get hold of yourself. This is not about Chris. This is about how selfish Ron is and how everyone makes him out to be a saint for taking in the poor widow and her children. If she had never married Ron...*

"I think I'm just tired, Jule."

Megan finished putting the coffee to brew and took a deep breath. She couldn't tell Julie how she felt. When her marriage to Ron was exposed for the farce that it was, their closest friends would be devastated. *What the kids and I need is a few days away from here. I need to go where I can think clearly.*

"You look more than tired, Meg. Ron would hire you help in a heartbeat if he realized you were overwhelmed. Just talk to him. If that doesn't work, light a few candles and whisper sweet suggestions in his ear..."

*Don't! Don't tell me I need help. I was fine. WE were fine. I took care of a newborn and four small children ALONE. If I had never depended on Ron to begin with...*Megan tried to stop the fatalistic line of thinking. This struggle had been going on inside her since the wedding night. She tried to look at it as an ongoing conversation she was having with God.

"I'm OK, Julie. You know 'help' would just be in the way." Megan tried to make light of Julie's suggestion, but anger welled up inside her. *Why? Why did You bring him into my life if having a husband was just going to make me weak and needy? I was strong and depended upon You before! Now, look at me! Oh, Father, please make me strong again. I hate being so weak. I love Ron so dearly, but having him here can't possibly be*

Your will for us.

"Megan, being married is hard work, physically and emotionally."

"I know. It's just that at some point, this all made sense."

"What made sense?"

"Ron and I getting married, making a family." The words were out before Megan could stop them and she could see from the alarm in Julie's eyes that the comment had not been lost on her friend.

Julie took her hand gently and softly reminded Megan, "That still makes sense, Megan. God's will didn't suddenly change."

"You're right. The truth never changes. God gave me those verses. That was how I could say "yes" to Ron's proposal so easily." *But maybe I misunderstood it and took matters into my own hands. Maybe I was just so lonely and I wanted to be loved again so badly that I was willing to hear from God only what I wanted to hear.*

Julie put her cup down. "God's Word doesn't change, either. You remember how clear His direction was. You were willing to walk away from your relationship with Ron if you didn't have peace about, and He gave you that peace. Just rest in that promise and try to relax."

Megan tried to look calm on the outside for Julie's sake, but she screamed to herself, *I want out. I want my kids back. I want our home to be like it was before, with just me and the kids here...*

"You're right." Megan forced a smile. "I'll just relax and

Finally Time to Dance

enjoy being Mrs. Ron Wellbourne." But already a plan was forming in Megan's mind.

....

A glance at her nightstand told Megan it was 3:15 a.m. She could hear Ron snoring softly under the covers. She moved gently and quietly. The bed creaked softly as her feet touched the floor. Megan ignored her robe and left the bedroom quickly.

It had been so long since Megan had actually slept soundly that she no longer longed for rest. She moved mechanically down the hall and ascended the stairs to the children's bedrooms. She stopped in the boys' room first.

Megan smiled as she caught the familiar scene in the glow of their night light. Randy was snuggled warmly under his flannel sheet with Teddy tucked tightly under his arm. Chad had made his way over to Randy's bed and was sleeping perpendicular to his brother, on top of his covers. Their faces were so peaceful, a stark contrast to the bundles of mischief they were during their waking hours. Megan stroked their soft skin. If she looked closely enough, she could see the babies she had brought home from the hospital. Once, when Randy was two and Chad was three, Megan had been carrying them both up the stairs to their beds. Chris had called up the stairs after her, "Enjoy that while you can. Someday, they'll both be men and you won't be able to hold them anymore." Megan realized that Chris had meant that both figuratively and literally and that the day was getting closer and closer all the time.

She crossed the hall to the large room Krissy and Lily shared. Megan made her way to Lily's bed, pausing to pick up baby dolls and Barbies along the way. Lillian Joy Hardin was the epitome of her name. As beautiful as an Easter lily in the spring and content just enjoying the world around her every day, she had brightened Megan's world since the day she was born. Even as she slept, Lily smiled. Krissy was curled up in her own twin bed a few feet away. From the day she had been born, Krissy had been Megan's constant companion. Megan marveled at the tiny hands that imitated the work Megan did around the house each day. Megan pulled Krissy's covers more snugly around her before going into Ali's room next door.

Megan closed the cheerleading magazines that lay on the floor and pet the calico cat stretched out across Ali's feet. Her eyes followed Ali's long legs and arms up to her angelic face. This young lady, who was so adult-like all day in an attempt to help her mother rein in her siblings, looked like a very small child when she was asleep. The seriousness was gone from her expression. Megan was relieved to see that, at least in her sleep, Ali relaxed and let God do the worrying for a few hours. It gave Megan hope that perhaps her daughter had not been through too much.

Relieved to see all of her children soundly asleep, Megan made her way back to the hallway. She stopped at the top of the stairs and took it all in. Just a few steps below was a new life, the new beginning in which she had put so much of her faith this past year. Up here was the old life she wanted to cling to with all her strength. Unable to even contemplate how or if the two worlds could ever be reconciled, Megan sat down on the landing and wept.

....

Ron had hoped Megan was heading to the kitchen for a snack, but he heard her steps go up the stairs. His wife rarely ate and slept only fitfully in short spurts. Ron had noticed at bedtime tonight how the fatigue was beginning to take its toll in the looseness of her clothing and the paleness of her complexion. *Please help me know how to help her, Lord. I have no idea what I'm supposed to do.*

Ron pushed back the comforters. He raised his frame from the bed and made his way absently around their bedroom. He realized he was searching for any clue that might help him understand what he should do. If he went upstairs, he risked angering Megan. If he did nothing to let her know he missed her and was worried about her wanderings, he risked coming across as uncaring. "Darned if I do; darned if I don't," he mused, running a hand through his hair.

He noticed her lavender satin robe lying at the foot of their bed. Megan always wore a matching gown and robe set when she came out of the bathroom at bedtime each evening. He had thought most women slept in something more comfortable, but his wife always looked like she had stepped off the pages of a tasteful lingerie catalog. He loved how her long, tan legs peeked out from under the silk or satin as she walked, but he wondered if she might be more relaxed in the t-shirts he saw her knocking around the house in while she was putting the kids to bed. He stroked the robe tenderly and wished he knew how to ease his wife's pain.

The soft creaking from above had stopped, so Ron crept out into the hall to meet Megan and ask how he could help. When she didn't appear after several minutes, he walked slowly toward the stairs. As he turned to go the stairs, Ron summoned his courage and resolved to go upstairs and ask Megan to come back to bed. He stopped after two steps. There, at the top of the wide staircase, sat his beautiful bride, with tear-stained cheeks. Her head was against the wall, and she was fast asleep.

He was relieved and saddened to see her there. Relieved that she was asleep and saddened that she would not sleep with him. He made his way further up and scooped her into his arms. His heart melted as she cupped her hands behind his neck and rested her head on his shoulder.

Ron carried Megan to their bedroom and gently lay her under the covers. He wiped her cheeks and brushed her hair from her face. Then he walked across their room and made himself a bed on the sofa in their sitting area. Though it felt like some part of him was dying with her so far away, if she did not want to sleep with him, he would respect that.

Ron spent the remaining pre-dawn hours listening to Megan's rhythmic breathing and begging God to intervene.

Chapter 17

Megan knocked tentatively before entering the master closet. She heard Ron walk over and open the door. "Hon, why don't you just come in? It's your house, too."

It used to be my house. Now, it's yours. I feel like a visitor here. "I just didn't want to disturb you, that's all."

She watched Ron contemplate his next move for several heartbeats before he walked over to her side of the closet. Megan was stunned to see him coming closer and took two steps back before stopping herself and taking a deep breath.

"What's wrong, Meg? Have I done something wrong? Have I offended you in some way?"

"Of course not. I mean well, I, I...Aren't you late for work?" Megan braced herself. She wasn't going to let him make this better for her. This could *never* be better.

Ron tossed the tie he was holding onto the top of the island. "I'll get there when I get there. Right now, I'd like to talk to you."

She should have just stayed in bed until he was gone. Seeing the distress in his eyes was doing nothing to help her keep her resolve to take a trip with the kids. There was no way she was going to start believing he cared as deeply about her as he was pretending to right now. *Forget it, Ron. Too little, too late. I'm outa here.*

"In case you've forgotten, I have five children to get up, get fed, get dressed, and educate. *My* job doesn't wait. I have to show up on time." A twinge of guilt tugged at Megan's heart as Ron flinched from her harsh words. She pushed back the urge to apologize. Instead, she attacked him a second time.

"You're so arrogant. What do you think I *do* all day?" Megan shook her head and tried to regroup. "We have a busy morning and the faster I get dressed and get out there, the better."

Ron wasn't backing down. "Is there something I can do to help? Maybe I could cook breakfast for them while you take a nice, long shower or go for a walk. Megan, please, tell me what I can do to make this easier for you and I will. I'll call Teresa right now and have her cancel all my appointments so I can give you the day off.

Tears spilled down Megan's cheeks as she heard the desperation in Ron's voice. Why couldn't he just let her be miserable and not care?

Ron reached out and put his hand on Megan's shoulder and continued. "I've been watching you try to adapt the past few weeks, and I think it's just getting worse for you instead of better. I love you, Megan. I don't want to be a burden to you. I want to be your partner."

Oh, good grief! Don't start reading my mind, now! NO! I'm

leaving and that's that. Get out so I can pack and I can have my children back to myself. You're not sticking around and blending in. You'll just be in the way.

"Ron, I'm fine. I'm not some weakling who needs to be rescued." When Ron folded his arms and sighed, Megan cringed again at the pain in his face, pain she was actually causing.

"I have never accused you of being weak. It's been quite the opposite, actually. I've admired your strength and your determination and your ability to get things done for a long time. But something is wrong and I'm here if you need me." Megan saw Ron pause to study her face before he continued. "You don't sleep; you hardly eat. What can I do to make this better? Please let me help." He stepped closer to her and tried to pull her to him. She turned to face the dresser to avoid his embrace.

"I'll try to get more sleep. Really, Ron, I'm OK." Megan was fighting to hold onto her resolve to be angry at Ron. "You're right. I didn't sleep well last night. I'm no fun to be around when I'm tired. I'll get some coffee and we'll ease into our routine and I'll make the best of it. I think it would just be chaotic if you stick around." Megan gave him a weak smile and saw him grasp at her gesture like a life preserver. It took more strength that she felt she could expend to continue her tirade, but she knew Ron had to leave so she could get out of the house for a few days.

Go to work, Ron." Megan choked back tears as the hoarse words came out. Then she coughed and straightened up and stepped around him to leave the closet. Ron grabbed her right arm as she passed him and kissed her head.

"I love you."

"I wish you didn't." Tears spilled out of Megan's eyes as she realized she had verbalized the thought.

Ron shocked her with his reply. "I realize that. What you need to realize is that I did not get into this to get out of it. I'm not going anywhere. I had never taken a wedding vow before because I never thought I could mean it, but I meant every word I said to you at our wedding. And I will love you no matter what. Love's a choice, Meg. I chose you."

Megan blinked, her heart breaking and her mind stuck on the first part of Ron's response. "You realize I want out?"

Ron stuffed both hands in his pockets and looked at the floor. "I realize you're in shock. I saw your eyes on our wedding night. Our intimacy made you sad somehow.' Megan blushed deeply at his words. Ron studied her and took a step closer. He eased his right hand up to her cheek. "Part of you went away the first time we made love and it hasn't ever returned."

Well, God had gone and done it, again. He'd given her a man who could understand her and tame her with his words. Why didn't God understand that she didn't want to love Ron Wellbourne? Why couldn't this all just go away? *God, I'm sorry I dragged so many people into this but you have to let me out. Please!*

Megan dried the last tear on her lavender gown. "I have to go." She looked down at the floor and waited for Ron to step aside.

Instead of moving aside, Ron took another step closer

and put both hands on Megan's shoulders. When she finally looked up, he stroked her chin lovingly. "Just one more thing."

"What?"

Let me take you out, tonight. I'll get a sitter and we'll go somewhere and talk. Please. Or we can go somewhere and not talk. We can just ride around and gaze at the stars." When Megan did not respond, he asked, "Will you at least think about it?"

"That actually sounds nice." Megan regretted conceding the thought, but going out with Ron tonight actually did sound nice.

"I'll bring home pizza so you don't have to cook dinner at all."

Megan struggled to stand firm on her decision to leave before Ron came home. "I'll think about it," she lied.

By the time Megan got to the bathroom, her head was spinning. Was she staying and cracking open this nut with Ron or was she leaving and letting Ron crack open a different one? She sat in front of her vanity and resolved to control the outcome. If she stayed, Ron would just convince her she was grieving for Chris and give her some psychobabble about adjusting and growing into family of their own. No, it was definitely in everyone's best interest for her and the kids to leave. By the time they returned, the seed of dissolving the marriage will have been planted and they could all work on the next phase: undoing this mess.

Megan heard Ron stop in the hallway outside the bathroom. "Bye, Hon."

"Ron?"

Ron slid the door open and slipped inside. "Hey."

Megan looked Ron squarely in the eye and told him simply, "I have to go."

"Megan…"

Megan turned back to her reflection in the vanity mirror and opened a large compact. "We'll be gone when you get home."

In the mirror, she saw Ron swallow hard. He started to say something but looked away. When he turned back to her, Megan could see the muscle in his jaw twitch. He took a deep breath and asked, "How long will you be gone?"

"Not that long. We'll be safe. Just go back to your folks' and enjoy some R&R." Megan watched a tear congruent to her own slowly make its way down Ron's cheek. He took a deep breath, kneeled next to her vanity bench, and took her right hand, "Sweetie, I didn't get into this to get out. I'm not going…"

Megan gathered her resolve one last time and delivered a blow that she hoped would convince Ron to let go of her hand. "Ron, I don't love you. I never did."

Ron's reaction was audible, but Megan saw him keep fighting, "I don't accept that." He wanted to say more. He wanted to tell her how alive he felt when he was with her and how he loved just knowing she was going to be at the end of the drive home from work. He wanted to tell her that he didn't think he could sleep tonight if she wasn't in their bed. He wanted her to stay. But he knew he had said all she would be willing to hear. Her expression had gone cold. She had put a stone wall between them that he was not certain he could ever penetrate.

Ron could not remember standing up and stepping into the hall, but he found himself headed down the stairs to his garage. He took his keys from his pocket automatically.

The first thing that had ever attracted him to Megan Hardin was her ability to do anything she set her mind to. He had told her that once and she had touched his face tenderly as she told him, "I honestly pray that I never use my rigid determination against you, Ron." Her statement had confused him back then, but her thoughts were clear to him, now. Megan was using the resolve the strength he had come to respect and admire in her against him. He was having trouble breathing.

Once safely in his Jeep and out of earshot of everyone in the house, Ron leaned on his steering wheel and sobbed. The pain Megan's words had caused had him doubled over and crying for mercy. *I've waited all my life to share it without someone. Why is this happening? Please make this stop!*

Chapter 18

Megan asked the kids to pack their backpacks and made it out to be a glorious adventure. Only Randy had asked if Ron was coming. Thankfully, it had been out of earshot of the other children, so Megan quietly explained.

"Oh, Sweetie, Ron has to work. He'll probably just go back to his house and stay with Mabel and Stan like he did before." Randy looked deflated. "What's wrong, Buddy?"

"Nothin'. I was just hoping we'd finally get to travel with a dad, again. Sometimes people ask you where your husband is. I want to have Ron with us so people can see we're a family."

Tears welled up in Megan's eyes and she stroked Randy's coarse blonde hair. His round cheeks looked so soft and frail when he was sad. Megan kissed each of them softly then tipped his chin up so his eyes were level with hers. "Oh, Bud, we talk about this kind of thing all the time. We can't care about what other people think. We can only care about what God thinks."

"Doesn't God think Ron should come, too?"

Megan felt as though someone had punched her in the

chest. Now Randy was making sense, too. What was *with* the men in her life? "I'm not sure," she lied.

"You should ask God, Mommy."

Not on your life. "I'll try, Randy."

Randy hugged her and patted her back with his chubby little hand. *What would I ever do without them, Lord?*

Megan stared at the road in front of her as she listened to the music from the cartoon the kids were watching. She seldom sat down and watched these programs with them at home, but they all laughed together when Megan was being held captive in the driver's seat.

They were already into the second leg of their six-hour trip. All five children had played hard in the fast-food restaurant's play area after they ate their burgers. Experience told Megan that soon her children would all drift off for an hour or so and she would be able to show them that they were in Louisiana when they woke up.

The thought of her home state put a knot in Megan's stomach and she worked hard to push back the sadness that was trying desperately to surface. *Chris has been gone for years. Why does it feel like he's died all over again? I'm tired of hurting.* Megan sighed. *I'm tired of being tired.*

"What time will we get there?" Ali's question brought Megan out of her reverie.

"About two or three more hours. Depends on how things go," Megan tried to sound nonchalant, but she was hoping to make good time so they could walk around town a bit and then swim in the hotel's indoor pool all evening. She had packed swimsuits for all of them and lifejackets for Lily and Krissy in the back of the SUV so she could surprise them.

It felt so great to be alone with them for a while. She and the kids needed a respite, some time to reconnect. Megan felt guilty and disconnected from them ever since she'd come back from her honeymoon. Being married again was taking more time and more energy than Megan had anticipated, and she didn't want her children to have to pay the price for her selfishness. If God really had told her to marry Ron, and she doubted that He had, it wasn't their fault. They deserved their mother's attention night and day just like they'd had before.

It was this line of reasoning that kept her guilt at bay. Her guilt over what she had done to Ron was going to eat her alive if she didn't get him out of her mind. She had been truthful. She had told him she was leaving and would be back. After they were apart a few days and she had her children readjusted to just her, her asking him to leave would make sense. By then, he'd be acclimated to single life again and convinced that living with them really wasn't what he'd wanted. He'd long for his tidy cottage and uninterrupted evenings. She had done him a favor by getting away. But the knot in her stomach came back every time she thought about their conversation that morning.

"Say 'Goodbye, Texas.'"

The Hardin children sang, "Goodbye, Texas! Hellooooo,

Louisiana!"

Megan navigated through Shreveport and south onto Interstate 49. The tall pine trees were reminiscent of home. Though the view from the highway didn't offer much detail about what lay beyond, Megan could picture the pecan groves and lazy lowlands of north Louisiana and, by the time she reached Exit eighty-nine at Natchitoches, she was thrilled they would be staying there that night.

The four oldest children hooted with glee as Megan made the exit and turned left onto the highway that led into town. Krissy squinted at the bright sun coming through her window.

Megan found the Holiday Inn on the Highway 1 bypass easily, and they were checked in and unpacked by late afternoon.

"What are we eating for supper, Mom?" Megan smiled at Chad's question. Eight-year-old boys ate and played and slept and ate and played some more.

"Meat pies."

"Mmm...Lasyone's! Thanks, Mom." Ali appreciated the same kind of quaint and unique places that appealed to her mother. And since Lasyone's didn't open for dinner, a late lunch/early dinner was perfect.

"Then can we go walk by the river?" asked Randy. The last time they had come to Natchitoches, they had been fortunate enough to see a mother duck leading her babies into the Cane River just below Front Street. Randy had talked about those ducks often.

Of course, Megan could still see Chris crouched down next

to Randy, helping him count each duckling as they passed by. *Oh, God, is there really no escape from the pain? I know it should be a fond memory, but I hurt for them when they can't have Chris back.*

"I'll do the river if you boys can be patient enough to let me window-shop a few minutes," Megan bargained.

"Deal," shouted Chad. He knew there were vendors near the water in the evenings, and if they were patient enough, they might be able to talk their mom into a cotton candy.

Megan put her purse over her shoulder and pointed at the door, "To the bus, troops!"

Chapter 19

Stuffed to the brim with meat pies and dirty rice, the Hardins opted to walk the few blocks from Lasyone's to downtown. Their leisurely pace gave Megan a chance to look around at how different and how "the same" the historic town looked to her. She and Chris and their friends from the Louisiana School for Math, Science, and the Arts had spent countless sunny afternoons and humid evenings walking down this very sidewalk, looking for what excitement or entertainment teenagers could find afoot and, for the most part, broke.

The state had chosen to plant a residential high school for academically and artistically gifted and talented juniors and seniors from all over the state on the campus of the small university in Natchitoches. The size of the city and the campus made it a perfect choice for a place where parents could send their "babies" with peace of mind while still providing the students access to a university library and arts department. Megan and Chris might never have met were it not for the Louisiana School where, in algebra class, they met.

Oh, Meg, it's all water under the bridge. Grow up and stop wishing you were back in high school. If Megan had realized back on the interstate that she'd have to take this bittersweet walk down memory lane, she may have found an excuse to keep driving. But she had felt God tugging her here. Before she had gotten out of bed this morning, she had asked God to keep her and the children safe from harm and keep her heart focused on His will.

The irony of that prayer was not lost on Megan. Running away from a marriage could not be part of God's perfect will. But she reasoned that God could still use her time away to help her heal and grow. He could also heal them all after the marriage was officially behind her.

Megan had once spoken to a group of women about encouragement and had reminded them that a broken heart was an open heart. God's lessons and love could be put in there before it healed. Megan was beginning to hope that perhaps her heart was the one that was open now and that God would fill it before He healed it. She prayed she would have the strength to take it in.

The sign near the sidewalk caught her eye and Megan slowed her pace. She stared up at the arched wooden door. The children were skipping and chatting and had gotten several feet ahead of her before they noticed she had stopped. "Mom?" Ali turned walked back up the sidewalk and stood next to her mother. "Oh, wow." Ali walked closer to the door. "Isn't that where you and Daddy got married?"

Megan felt her cheeks grow hot. "How do you know that?"

Ali never took her eyes off the door. Her face lit up with

excitement. "Daddy told me. He and I came down this street for donuts. We stopped here, and he took me inside and showed me where you both stood." Ali looked at Megan with innocent glee. "He said it was the happiest day of his life." Megan took Ali's hand and walked up the wide steps. Ali motioned for her brothers and sisters to follow them. She let go of Megan's hand and helped Krissy and Lily up the steps.

Megan drew a deep breath as she stepped through the vestibule and into the sanctuary. The familiar scent of candle wax mixed with flowers filled her senses. Megan felt the years melt away as she remembered the Sunday mornings she and Chris had sat on these pews together as Megan soaked in God's Word for the first time.

Her parents had only used church as a social and professional crutch. They had attended regularly as a family, but only to mingle and network and see and be seen. Megan had ignored the little she had heard between her parents' bickering and the gossiping women behind her. The Bible had been little more than a book of fairy tales told without rhyme or reason. When she first came to school, Megan seldom darkened the doors of the churches her classmates attended. When Chris realized he had feelings for her, he had confronted her gently about her commitment to Christ.

"He was a good man. I think it's great that you get so much from attending church, Chris, but I just don't. I don't see Jesus as someone I know personally and it kind of creeps me out when I hear kids that talk like they do. I just wasn't raised that way."

Finally Time to Dance

Chris's expression had not changed as she talked. He listened thoughtfully. He didn't bring it up again until the last week of November.

"Megan, may I ask you a question about church again?"

"You can ask me anything you want. We see things differently. That doesn't mean we have to avoid the topic."

"Well, the youth group is having a party Thursday night and…"

"A party? I thought you were talking about church."

"I am. That's where the party is. More like a get-together. There will be homemade ice cream and games and a gift exchange. We play "dirty Santa." I have an extra gift, so it wouldn't even cost you anything to go. We could just have fun."

"What's the catch?"

"There's no catch."

"There's always a catch. People at church expect *something* when you go there. Who are you trying to impress by bringing a girl? Did someone dare you to ask me?"

Megan had watched Chris work hard to squelch his red-headed temper. She figured someday her flippant attitude about anything she didn't agree with or understand was going to be his undoing. He paused long enough for her to keep going.

It was then that she had explained how her family had "played" church rather than belonging to it. She helped him see that Megan viewed church as a social club because she'd never truly been part of a fellowship of believers. In the end, he had left the decision to attend up to her, and she had been waiting outside the dorm when the bus pulled up to take them to the party.

"Glad you could come."

"I hope you brought my gift. I wouldn't have depended on you to do that except that I only made up my mind a few minutes ago."

"I'm just glad you're here."

"Me, too."

Megan's hand had been resting on the seat between them and he had gently placed his over hers. The security of his touch was instantaneous. This young man made her feel safe. She trusted him.

Megan had heard the gospel that night and on many, many Sundays as she and Chris attended services together. She had made her decision to accept Christ shortly before they graduated from high school, finally understanding how she could *personally know* Jesus, who was fully God and fully man.

The stark realization came suddenly. Megan worked to see through the tears that were welling up in her eyes. She focused on a lighted candle and watched the flame flicker.

Jesus Himself had known how her life with Chris would turn out even *back then* as she sat here falling in love with Chris's Savior. God had known all long how many hairs would be on the head of each of Chris's children. God had also known that somewhere a man living a dark and lonely existence would be there to pick up the broken pieces and help her put them back together again.

But Ron didn't deserve that kind of hard, messy work. She wanted to present herself whole and healed to Ron and she had not been able to do that. She hadn't healed long enough to be married, yet. It had all happened too soon. Ron was getting short-changed and he would soon figure that out.

Megan sighed. The mixture of emotions was unfamiliar and unsettling.

Ron would be walking into their empty house any minute now. She wanted to spare him the pain she had seen in his face this morning, but the sooner they went through this pain, the sooner they would get it over with. She had to get out before he saw right through her.

....

Ron parked his Jeep in the basement garage. After the door had lowered, he breathed deeply and relaxed his head against the back of the seat, trying to muster the strength to open the door. Hiding his emotions all day had been draining. He wasn't sure he could make it up the stairs.

Ron could not recall walking up the stairs and into the office, but he was thankful for the respite the soft leather chair gave as he sat alone trying to figure out what on earth he could do to help his wife.

He glanced over at the flowers that the Greenhouse had

delivered earlier in the week. Megan had put them on the credenza behind her desk where she could look up and see them throughout the day.

Sweet, sensuous Megan. Where was his wife? He wanted to hold her and tell her everything was going to work out. They would make it through the initial adjustment and have a routine and feel more like a family in just a few more weeks. They both just needed to relax and give it time.

He pulled his cell phone out and scrolled down to "Megan Cell." Ron prayed as he punched the green button. *Please answer the phone. Talk to me, Meg.*

"Hi, you've reached Megan and the gang and our cell phone. If you've gotten this message, we're probably crawling around the house or truck looking for the phone, so let us know why you called and we'll call you back. Bye."

Ron chuckled at Megan's words. He had watched them crawl around the floorboard of Megan's SUV looking for the phone. Sometimes she even sent the kids down to hunt while she called it from the house phone. He loved that woman.

"Megan, hi. It's Ron. Call me. I'd just like to know that you're alright."

Ron pressed the red button and closed his eyes. The message had come on before it even rang. She had turned off the phone completely.

He told himself that Megan just needed some time and some room to try to suppress the anger that was mounting.

"Wreckless abandon," Ron said the words out loud as he recalled a heated conversation he and Megan had had about her freer, more passionate approach to life.

"Me not taking three weeks to answer a question does not make me 'wreckless,' Wellbourne! I asked you literally three weeks ago if you wanted me to get the tickets. You're just answering me today?"

"I was thinking about it. The tickets are eighty dollars each. That's not something you do rashly. I've thought about it and now I think it's a good idea. So, buy them." He tried to change the incredulous expression on her face by adding, "Please."

"I asked you and you did not answer me. At all. I assumed that meant you thought it was a bad idea, so I let it go. If you were thinking about it, I needed to know that. That way I could have told you that they would likely be sold out that afternoon."

Ron winced at the realization that he had missed the opportunity to see the concert he had spent the past three weeks getting excited about. To top it off, he had reserved adjacent hotel rooms for him and for Megan and the children and arranged for her friend in Oklahoma City to sit with the kids while he and Megan enjoyed the concert and a late dinner. He had made countless phone calls, ordering flowers, making dinner reservations, renting a limousine, and arranging for childcare. He had waited until everything was perfect before telling Megan he'd love it if she got them tickets so they could enjoy the group they both remembered from college.

He was still lamenting and looking for a way to redeem himself when she tossed the newspaper in front of him and said, "Well, I guess you get to buy the tickets, then. Scalpers have them in the classifieds for one twenty." She leaned down and looked him in the eye, "Sometimes it's not 'wreckless abandon' when you jump at an opportunity. We girls call it 'seizing the moment.' You think I'm careless; I think you think too much." Megan turned and walked back to where she was cooking dinner. "And, Ron?"

"Yeah?" Ron rubbed his temple while he waited for her to continue.

"Make sure they're great seats. Spare no expense." He caught her devious grin as she walked into the pantry. *I love that woman.*

Ron bought the best tickets he could find, and carried out his plan. Megan had been ashamed of her behavior when she reaped the rewards of the plans he had made and knew instinctively that he had made them during that three-week window for which she had chastised him. They laughed at their miscommunication and their polar-opposite personalities as they swayed in their stocking feet to the music from Bricktown that drifted up to the balcony that connected their hotel rooms.

Ron felt a small sense of wreckless abandon himself. He pulled Megan close to him and kissed her deeply. "Megan Hardin, I love you." Ron was relieved that the words were finally out, but he felt exposed and prayed she'd say she felt the same way.

Megan laughed before she leaned close to his ear and whispered, "You know, sometimes we girls call 'wreckless abandon' something else; we call it 'following your heart.'" Megan pulled back and looked into Ron's eyes as she breathed, "I love you, too, Ron. I didn't want to at first, but I have for a while, now."

So, how had it come to this? Had getting married really changed her feelings? Ron's feeling had never changed. He loved Megan more today than he had that magical night. Why had Megan's feelings changed?

He needed to get his family home so they could continue building on what Ron knew to be a solid foundation. But with Megan's resolve and the distance she had put between them, the likelihood of it happening smoothly was slim. Ron hoped God really was still in the miracle business.

Chapter 20

Megan flipped her pillow over and tried once more to get comfortable. Knowing that sleep would not come immediately, she risked waking the kids by turning on the lamp between the two large beds. She retrieved the extra pillows from the closet and plumped them into place behind her back. Megan reached for her Bible and began searching for comfort in the only place that had never disappointed her. She spent the next hour turning to familiar passages in Jeremiah, Philippians, and Proverbs, three books that provided guidance and wisdom in the brightest and darkest days of her life.

Thankful that Chris's pastor had advised her early on not to be hesitant to write in her Bible when God showed her something through His Word, Megan read several of notes and knew that she had been through far harder times than those she was facing right now.

Why I am being so weak and selfish about all of this? And why can't I stop?

She felt the vibration of her phone through the stack of pillows. After the children were asleep, she had indulged herself and turned her cell phone back on to see if Ron would call. Knowing that he was there comforted her. She wished she had the strength to answer it.

Her answer came from God as she found the strength to continue her search. Her eyes fell on the twelfth verse of Philippians chapter four.

I know what it is to be in need, and I know what it is to have plenty. I have learned the secret of being content in any and every situation, whether well fed or hungry, whether living in plenty or in want.

Megan knew what the apostle Paul had written next. She had memorized the next verse, taught it to children in Sunday school, sung songs about it. She considered closing her Bible so that she would not have to be confronted with what was written there.

But God's Word had stood for thousands of years and Its truths were not going anywhere. She couldn't hide. Tears poured onto the page as she read verse thirteen.

I can do everything through Him who gives me strength.

Megan knew what the words meant. If she felt weak, she was calling God weak. If she said she didn't have the strength, she was saying that either God didn't have the strength to give her or she was refusing to tap into it.

Oh, God, no! NO! I never think for a minute that you are weak or that you can't give me strength, but it's just too painful. I don't want to live through this pain. I want the pain to stop. Make this all go away.

Out of nowhere, a quote from a book Megan had read

came to her. It was a book about grief given to her after Chris had died. She had waited almost two years before picking up the volume and reading it, but it contained a lot of facts about death and grief that had comforted her and made Megan feel like she was "normal" to have felt what she did all those months.

But one evening she had been reading it when something struck an uncomfortable chord with her. The author wrote, "You cannot get past the grief unless you go through it." At the time, she had disregarded the uneasiness it caused, but now she suddenly realized that perhaps there was some of the grief she had not yet been through. She had let Chris go physically, but emotionally...

Chris died at home, which meant there was a lot of care giving for Megan to do. On top of that, she'd had a newborn to nurse and four young children to tend to. The last year of Chris's life had been a blur in some respects and when he died, Megan continued to stay busy with the children. Physical intimacy between Megan and Chris had waned gradually, as had verbal communication and other little ways they had shown each other affection. She had said goodbye a little at a time.

Or at least she thought so. Megan never wished Chris back in that frail, sick body, but now she realized that she had never wished him back in his healthy body, either. She had been so busy with the details of their lives and carrying on with the children's activities, that she never had a moment when she let herself wish that Chris could be there with her one more time. She could think of two, possibly three instances when she was overcome with emotion over Ali performing in a musical or Chad singing in church. On such occasions, she had almost let her thoughts wander to Chris and how he would have reacted seeing them do their best.

Any such thoughts, though, were pushed away quickly so she would never have to measure how much of his children's lives Chris would not share with them here on earth. Perhaps she had ignored an important part of the grieving process by turning from these painful musings.

Krissy stirred in the other bed, giving Megan an excuse to close her Bible and turn off the lamp. *Enough pondering for tonight.* Megan forced herself to close her eyes. *Besides, you know what you've got to do and rationalizing some ridiculous solution to it will just weaken your resolve.*

I'm not putting Ron and the kids through all of this. I'll just suck it in and move on from here.

Megan wanted to believe that was the only answer, but she fell asleep with her hand on her vibrating cell phone, thankful Ron cared enough to call.

....

Ron set the cordless phone in its cradle in the office and dropped into the soft leather chair behind the desk. He was not certain if it was physical or emotional exhaustion that left him too tired to move.

He had tried several times to get in bed, but the scent of Megan's perfume on her pillow had driven him from their room looking for answers. Ron opened the desk drawer and removed the small "Bible Promises" book Megan kept there for reference. She often referred to it when one of the children needed a word of encouragement or when she was sending a card to a friend. Megan truly possessed a gift for encouraging others, and Ron knew it was because she always got her strength and words from the true Source, the Word of God.

Most of the gold trim on the edges of the pages was gone. The book was worn and many of the passages had notes scribbled next to them. Megan apparently kept an informal record in the book of when she had used the verses and to whom she had sent them.

Seeing her handwriting comforted him. He could almost hear her voice as he "listened" to the exclamation marks and smiley faces she had used to accent her notes.

Ron tugged the faded green ribbon that was attached to the book as a bookmark and flipped to the page it marked. The heading at the top of the page was "hope" and Megan had circled it. Ron read what she wrote, "We gave Krissy the middle name 'Hope' because, even in our darkest days, we were never without hope since we had Christ in our lives."

Ron's breath caught in his throat. How would Megan ever have the same magnitude of bond with him that she'd had with Chris? The Hardins had claimed scripture together, prayed together, been through the very intimate experience of sickness and death together.

Who was he trying to fool? He had no business trying to be Megan Hardin's husband. This champion of faith needed a far stronger man to be her confidante and partner. Ron had strayed from God long ago and had only recently returned. He simply did not possess the tools to be the husband Megan needed him to be.

Ron tried to close the book, but he let his eyes rest on the page once more. He read Megan's neat printing, "We put this on Krissy's birth announcement."

The passage was from Paul's letter to the Romans, chapter five, verses three, four, and five. Ron closed his eyes and sighed deeply. He wanted to close the book before he caught any more private glimpses of Megan's life with Chris. They had had babies together, written their birth announcements, and shared the news with friends Ron likely did not even know. What was written here was none of his business.

But his eyes fell on the words next to her entry.

We also rejoice in our sufferings, because we know that suffering produces perseverance; perseverance character; and character, hope. And hope does not disappoint us, because God has poured out His love into our hearts by the Holy Spirit, Whom He has given us.

The words stunned Ron. Two people had been trying to celebrate the birth of a baby girl, knowing that one of them would not live to see her smile or walk or talk. They had joined together in that adversity and claimed promises on which they would choose to stand. They had shown strength to everyone around them, strength Ron had never felt or experienced.

But it was strength Ron had seen. In fact, he had seen it in Megan first-hand. Still unbeknownst to her, Ron had gone to Chris's funeral. He had known that Julie and Todd would have invited him to sit with them near the front if they had known he was coming, so he said nothing to them about attending. Ron wasn't trying to hide from them, but his own private nature had caused him to arrive almost late and take an inconspicuous seat in the back pew.

He had fully intended to catch up with them after the service, but once he saw the young Hardin family, Ron left the church and drove home to be alone. What he took in that afternoon unnerved him. It left him with an eerie mix of awe and insult.

He was awed by Megan Hardin's strength, and insulted that she'd had the audacity to celebrate her husband's life while she was supposed to be mourning.

When the funeral director asked everyone to stand, Ali entered first, carrying three-month-old Krissy in her arms. Chad was close behind her, followed by Megan, who was carrying Lily on her left hip and holding Randy's hand on her right. Ron had seen her face from only a few feet away and it was unmistakable: she was filled with peace and tranquility.

Ever the cynic, Ron had wondered if some doctor had medicated the new widow so that she could survive the day, but he knew with certainty that what was keeping Megan at peace was not chemical. The source was deep within her and radiated from her like glowing embers on a cold night.

She got up to speak. Megan teased Chris's students and made her own children laugh. The joy within her had not been dampened by today's sadness, and it drew Ron to her. He wanted the peace she had. He wanted to know this person better so he could know the source of her calm.

Ron waited over a year before contacting her through Julie. She had not even been aware that Ron knew Chris had died. She certainly had no idea that Ron considered her joy and her hope all those months and wondered how he could claim them in his own life.

Since then, of course, Ron had rededicated his life to Christ and had married Megan fully intending to be the spiritual leader in their home. But if Megan could find hope in the midst of suffering without him and she couldn't even sleep at night with him, what was he doing here?

Where had her peace gone? Had be taken it from her? Was he not the man God had intended for this family?

Ron was distracted enough by these questions to turn off the lamp in the office and make his way to the bedroom. He stretched his long legs under the comforters and eased back into his pillows. He reached for his cell phone to call Megan once more but picked up the small Bible on his nightstand instead. Mabel had given Ron her father's tattered leather Bible when he graduated from college. Ron had seemed so lost at the time that Mabel had felt like any connection to his family, physical or spiritual, might help.

Ron opened the volume to a passage he had marked shortly before he had asked Julie to help him get in touch with Megan. He had only looked back over the passage once since then: the night he had asked Megan to marry him. He turned to the passage in the twenty-ninth chapter of Jeremiah, and read the passage aloud:

Build houses and settle down; plant gardens and eat what

they produce. Marry and have sons and daughters...Also, seek the peace and prosperity of the city to which I have carried you into exile. Pray to the LORD for it, because if it prospers, you too will prosper.

The revelation hit Ron suddenly. Until this moment, Ron had never understood how people he encountered at church could say that God "gave" them scripture or that they were "claiming a promise" God had made them. Those words now had meaning to Ron.

For the first time, he realized that he had been seeking a renewed, deeper relationship with God when he had found the passage and had marked it without really understanding why. He had been looking for a way to find peace spiritually, and God made Ron a promise. God had been encouraging Ron to build a family for himself. Ron must have realized that on some level because he had turned to the passage again the night he had proposed to Megan.

The realization that Ron and God had been on "speaking terms" even back then made Ron's heart soar! Maybe he wasn't completely spiritually inept after all.

Emotionally spent, Ron closed the Bible and placed it on his chest. He held it tightly, knowing that only this book contained the answers he needed. Ron closed his eyes and prayed that God would tell him how to take care of his wife.

Chapter 21

"Can I go get some breakfast?" Ali asked, referring to the do-it-yourself buffet in the hotel lobby.

Megan ran water over her toothbrush and regarded Ali in the mirror. "No. We're having breakfast with Aunt Jane," Megan answered as she pulled on a plain white t-shirt. Ali sighed.

"What's wrong? I thought you'd be excited about seeing Jane. She's always got such neat surprises for you." Jane was Megan's best friend from high school and college. Jane and her husband, Darrin, had met at the Louisiana School just like Megan and Chris. The couples had spent countless weekends together before the Hardins had gotten busy with their family.

Even then, Jane made it a point to spoil Megan's children whenever they were around. Opting not to have a family of her own, Jane managed a cosmetics counter of a large upscale department store. She always had samples and goodies that had kept Ali entertained since she could hold a lipstick tube.

Ali wrinkled her nose, "I know. It just feels weird being here, I guess." She looked at Megan, "Have you talked to

Ron since we left?"

Megan swallowed hard. She knew Ali saw her hesitation. Megan turned her back before she said, "He called last night." Megan grabbed a ponytail holder and searched her bag for a brush. Ali handed it to her from the counter. *Steady, Meg. Breathe.*

"Mom?"

Megan walked up to the mirror and began to run the brush through her long mane. "What is it, honey?"

"Are you alright? Did Ron do something to make you mad?"

Oh, my. Now she was worrying a ten-year-old. Megan looked at Ali standing beside her in the mirror. Megan knew better than to lie to a child. She considered leveling with Ali completely, but her head ached. She just needed Ali to stop asking her questions. Finally Megan smiled and said, "Oh, Sweetie, of course not. Now, check the bathroom to be sure we've got everything. I told Jane we'd be there by nine."

"When will we go to Grandma's?"

"After we visit Jane a couple of hours, we'll head that way. It's about three hours south of here. Just about enough time to watch a movie." Megan kissed Ali on the forehead then addressed all five children, "And if you guys fight over whose turn it is to choose, I'll unplug the tv. Got it?"

"Yes, ma'am," came in unenthusiastic chorus.

"Thank you, sweet children. Let's get going." Megan rubbed her throbbing temples. Krissy toddled up to her.

"Does yours head hurt?"

"A little." "I kiss it."

Megan leaned down and let Krissy kiss her forehead. "Thank you. Mommy needed a kiss." At that, the other four siblings charged at their mother. Megan steadied herself, and absorbed all the love they were offering her. "Thank you, babies. Mommy loves you." She kissed each of them before standing back up and herding them to the parking lot, back packs in tow.

It was only a short drive to the Osgood's home from the hotel. Megan took her time driving there, taking in every tree, every sidewalk, every memory, along the way.

Megan had been green with envy for a week after Jane called to say they were going to get to settle in Natchitoches. It had always been Megan's dream to return there with Chris and their children, but God had never opened any doors for jobs there for the Hardins.

Megan had put her jealousy to rest and happily helped Jane plan their move from Cincinnati, where Darrin had done his residency. Jane had seen him through medical school and the long three-years in Ohio without ever complaining. Jane had simply worked hard and been supportive of Darrin's work. God had rewarded her by letting them settle in the small historical community where their romance had begun.

Initially, they had bought a modest home and done a little work here and there over the course of about four or five years. When they felt confident that they would stay in Natchitoches indefinitely, they bought a larger, historic home that had already been restored. Megan laughed out loud as she remembered the Osgood's first night in the large home.

Chris and a very pregnant Megan, along with Ali and

Finally Time to Dance

Chad had helped them move and joined them their first night. Every stick of furniture the Osgood's owned could have fit in one of the living areas, leaving the house very sparsely furnished, so they had decided to have a slumber party in the basement romp room. The adults were exhausted. Ali and Chad kept insisting they could hear funny noises from their makeshift beds near the fireplace, but Megan insisted they go to sleep with no more complaining. Pregnant, tired, and sore from the day's work, she had felt like she could have slept through a freight train driving through the room.

At 2:30 a.m., however, all four adults sat up simultaneously. High-pitched screeching was coming from the fireplace. Megan came to her feet and scooped up both children. She and Jane bolted from the room, closing the door behind them to contain the problem to the one room. What they had not realized, however, was that Chris and Darrin could not open the door from the inside. They assumed the bumps and banging they heard during their ascent up the basement stairs were their heroes protecting them from what was lurking in the basement fireplace.

The women had tucked the babies into small pallets on the living room floor and were upstairs waiting for the coffee to brew when two wild-haired, red-faced men came lumbering up the basement stairs.

"For better or for worse, huh?" Darrin's question had made both women, punchy and bleary-eyed, shake with stifled giggles. Tears had been rolling down Megan's cheeks when Chris asked her why they did not come back and unlock the door.

~ 178 ~

"We had no idea the door was locked," Megan tried hard to breathe normally, but hysterical laughter was brimming just under the surface.

"You deserted us, unarmed and half-naked, to fight whatever was down there," Chris's voice told of his frustration at Megan's amusement.

That comment, combined with the sight of their unarmed, half-naked protectors, had been their undoing. Jane and Megan were literally doubled over hooting with laughter before the men knew what hit them. There sat their brides, unable to speak because they were laughing at having endangered both their lives.

Chris motioned for Darrin to follow him. The men were halfway to the master bedroom before Jane managed, "So, what's down there?"

"Baby raccoons," Darrin closed the door a little harder than necessary after he answered.

"Awwww," crooned the girls in unison. They looked at each other, smiled, and raced to the basement room. Oblivious to the danger of the mother raccoon, Jane and Megan had opened the fireplace up to gaze at the tiny creatures. Jane had even gone for her camera and they had taken pictures before closing the doors and going to beg their husbands to let them in the bedroom.

Megan mused at how she often looked at Jane's "wildlife photography" and soaked in the fun memory. It was a bookmark in time that Megan liked to flip to occasionally. They had all been so young and carefree. Chris had been in remission. The four friends had been willing to believe that God had spared his life and that the four of them would grow old together with visits like that one as bookmarks over the decades.

Megan found Jane's house easily and Chad was on the porch and ringing the doorbell before Megan had gathered Krissy and her purse and started up the long sidewalk.

Megan had forgotten how the southern sunshine made the flowers and foliage plush even in November. Jane's yard was still bursting with fall color, whereas Megan's had already gone to sleep for the winter. *Maybe I should have moved here.* This new doubt surfaced as Megan approached the door. *Why didn't I wait longer for more direction from God before buying another house in Oklahoma?*

Oh, God, forgive me. I've made so many mistakes. How will I ever get out of the mess I've made of everything?

Jane squealed when she opened the door. All five children charged her at once. The six of them made a loud, happy bouquet of hugs in the entry hall. Megan stepped around them, thankful she could count on Jane for enthusiasm when she had none of her own. When the children let Jane up for air, she beamed at Megan, "Thank you for sharing. I love being adored. This is wonderful."

"Sorry you didn't get to see them more last month. It was so hectic at the wedding."

Jane heard more than saw the tension in Megan. Something was wrong. Megan would only be here a couple of hours. They needed to talk, and it needed to be now. She ruffled Randy's hair. "Do you know the best thing about November in the south?"

"The flowers?" Randy guessed.

"No. That's more like the second-best thing. The *best* thing is that you can play in the grass without putting bug spray on your legs." Jane looked at all five children and suggested, "Why don't you guys head out? We'll eat outside, today!" In unanimous agreement for dining al fresco, all five children stampeded to the French doors along the back wall of the living room. They were out the doors, across the porch, down the wide steps, and into Jane's garden before Megan knew what hit her. It wasn't like Jane to shoo the children out. Megan wondered if Jane could tell something was wrong.

Jane saw Megan strain to see her children from the living room. "Go on to the porch if you need to keep an eye on them. I'll get our juice and come out there." Megan gave Jane a thankful smile and went outside.

The wide veranda stretched across the length of the old home. Not much for travel or expensive toys, the Osgoods spent most of their spare time and money making their home comfortable and appealing. It was obvious they had spent more time and money on the backyard than Megan had realized. It was breathtaking.

Megan sank into the low wicker chair closest to the back door and took in the view. No longer just a yard, Jane had turned the space into several outdoor "rooms" where she and Darrin could entertain and relax. A conversation area here, a bench there. It was perhaps the most inviting garden Megan had ever seen.

She wished she hadn't told the kids they'd be going to her mother's. Megan suddenly felt very tired and wanted to sleep for several days, wake up to this view, and pretend the past few months had never happened.

"Here we are. We'll start with drinks. Our main dish has a few minutes to go." Jane had come back out, tray in hand, to serve her dearest friend. She set the tray on the low table beside Megan and stretched out on the lavender cushion of the wicker swing perpendicular to Megan's chair. Megan picked up her glass and took a long, slow sip of the cold drink. Megan gave Jane a knowing smile, "I thought we were having plain orange juice."

"I thought you could use one of my house specialties." Jane winked at her friend.

"Thanks." Megan hadn't had Jane's fresh-squeezed raspberry orange juice over crushed ice since she was pregnant with Lily. Megan had come here for a weekend retreat in the heat of the summer and had spent the entire visit propped in this chair sipping Jane's concoctions. Megan stretched her legs on the ottoman in front of her and set her glass back on the table. "Well, at least I'm not pregnant this time."

"You sure? You look tired, May."

Megan rolled her eyes in not-so-mock exasperation. She really didn't want to talk about this. Jane was not the person who was going to give her permission to walk away from a commitment, much less a marriage. "I'm ok."

"I talked to Ron this morning."

Megan was certain her heart had stopped beating. She took two slow breaths and waited for her temples to pulse before speaking. "So, I guess he told you I was a coward and ran away?"

"No." Jane swung her legs around and reclined on the swing. "I was lying. I didn't really talk to Ron." Megan threw a bead-fringed pillow at Jane. "Hey, watch it. You could hurt someone."

"You lie to me again and I will hurt you." Megan sat up in righteous indignation.

Jane was nonplussed. "It's was justifiable homicide. And turnabout. You said there was nothing wrong." Jane put the pillow under her head rolled onto her side and snuggled into the satin. "Now, tell me the truth."

Megan plowed right into her defense. "It's not working out between me and Ron, Jay. He's miserable; I'm miserable. We have to get out of this before we do any more damage."

"What do you mean 'before we do any more damage'?"

"You know, before the kids really start to depend on him, before he gets all his stuff moved in, before the kids start calling his parents grandparent names, before we get in any deeper than we already are."

"Wow. You don't honestly believe that crap, do you?"

"Excuse me?" Megan was in no mood for Jane's attack. The denial she'd been in for the past twenty-four hours had been bliss. How dare she muddy the water with clear thinking?

"The kids aren't attached to him, he hasn't already moved in, Stan and Mabel don't consider them their grandchildren, and you're not in this too deep to get out. Have you lost your mind?"

Megan gave up trying to defend herself. "I think that may be a distinct possibility." She could feel Jane watching as a tear rolled unchecked down Megan's cheek. "And even if I was sane, you still couldn't convince me that he's going to stick around." Megan wiped her cheek with the sleeve of her t-shirt. "He's miserable. We're not what he wanted."

Jane sat up and put her hand on Megan's knee. "Did he say that?"

"No. But it's only a matter of time before he figures it out. It's going to hit him like a ton of bricks when we all least expect it. Somebody's going to start throwing up or throwing things and then all heck's gonna break loose.

"Dinner won't be ready on time, his favorite shirt won't be clean, my truck will have a flat, and a pet rodent will die all on the same day and he'll just look at the great big disaster we are and walk out and never come back.

"He's still on the honeymoon. He's going to come to his senses. I think the solitude of his bachelor pad is already looking pretty good," Megan was sobbing, now.

Jane plucked a tissue out of the box on the table beside Megan and sat on the ottoman. Megan pulled her legs down, put her elbows on her knees, and dabbed her eyes with the tissue. She scanned the yard for her children as she tried to stop her tears and her tirade, hopeful they had not heard her outburst.

"The kids are fine. Stop worrying." Jane prayed silently while she tried to think of what to say to her friend. Surely Megan knew that her fears were normal. She was experiencing fear of abandonment. *God, help me here. This precious woman has been through so much. Give her Your permission to be happy. Touch her so that she feels you. Give me the words to share with her. Come into our presence now and help us in this place.*

"Look at me, May." Megan wiped her eyes again and took several deep breaths in and out. She blew out one final breath before looking Jane square in the eyes.

"What?"

"Ron's not going to die."

Megan's expression grew cold. "I didn't say he would. Do you think that's what I wish?"

"I don't think it's what you *wish*. I think it's what you *fear*." Jane watched Megan collect herself and straighten her clothing.

"I'm not afraid of a husband dying. Been there, done that, remember? What I *am* afraid of, though, is becoming weak and dependent upon a man who has no idea what kind of time and energy it takes to raise five children. The other day, I *asked* him to take the garbage down with him when he went to his car. The next thing you know, I'll *expect* him to take out the garbage and then I'll be disappointed when he doesn't. Then I'll nag and then he'll withdraw and leave. It's really simple." Megan stopped long enough to take a breath. "Why am I the only one who sees what's happening and trying to do something about it?"

"Why don't believe he *wants* to help you? Maybe it makes him feel like part of your family to help you by taking down the garbage. When I was there for the wedding, he showed me the tinting he put on your bedroom windows so you could rest there when you got the beginnings of a migraine. You should have seen him, Megan. He was like a little kid showing me something he did that was helpful to you. He was proud and excited. He likes being what you need."

At these words, Megan was on her feet. "For over three years, I did *fine* without Ron Wellbourne in my life. You know why? Because I depended upon God and God only. I *never dreamed* of asking *anyone* to take my garbage out or stay with my kids while I went to the store. I did it all by myself, and now that he lives there it's like I can't even manage to do that anymore."

Jane didn't react to Megan's words. It was actually a relief to see her expressing some negative emotion. Since Chris's funeral, Megan had been a rock. Leaning on the Rock was good; being an actual rock was not.

"And you ask me why I don't believe he *wants* to help me? It's because of his motives for marrying me. Once the newness of having grandkids for Stan and Mabel wears off, he'll hate helping me. He's just helping me to make my life a little easier so I'll share my family with his."

Jane let out the breath she had been holding. *Aha. She doesn't believe Ron loves her any more than he has to. Oh, she's so mistaken. He's so in love with her.* "Megan, have you actually said that to Ron? Have you accused him of marrying you for your children?"

Megan pulled another tissue from the box. "No, of course not. I don't have to ask him to know the truth."

"So, you are accusing him of something against which he can't even defend himself."

"You're taking his side?"

"We're *all* on the *same* side!"

"Don't yell at me!"

"Goodness, Megan! If you're acting this crazy at home he just might leave you." Jane regretted her words and rose to pace the length of the porch. "I'm sorry, May. What I'm trying to say is that you're not seeing this clearly. You've convinced yourself of things that are not true." Jane came back and tried again, "He's not going to die, Sweetie."

Megan looked up at her friend longingly. She looked like a small, scared child. "You don't know that."

"You didn't know that about Chris, either. It didn't stop you from being happy."

"It would just be easier not to be happy to begin with."

"Too late, my friend. I saw you at the wedding. You were happy." Jane sat down on the arm of Megan's chair. "What happened after the wedding?"

Megan sat back down and looked off to the side. She shook her head back and forth. Jane took her cue and sat back down on the swing. The two women sat without talking until the beep of the kitchen timer broke their silence. Jane got up to check on their quiche. She stopped and touched Megan on the shoulder. "Talk to him, May. He'll understand."

"There are things I just *can't* say to him."

"That's not true."

"It feels like it is."

Jane squeezed Megan's arm slightly before leaving to go into the house.

Megan stood up and wiped her face. She turned to check her reflection in the window. "Get it together, Girl. Time to be a mom and stop worrying about all this marriage and man stuff."

Chapter 22

Megan mulled her conversation with Jane over and over again in her head the entire three hours she drove to her mother's house. Though she had not admitted it to Jane this morning, her best friend had given Megan a lot to think about. They had not had time away from the children again to continue their discussion, but the two women promised to pray about all that had been discussed and let God do some healing and revealing.

Being able to crack a nut open and then part ways without taking out all the meat was a hallmark of their friendship. Time, along with prayer, would bring the answers they needed. God had taught her how to be comfortable with that.

Megan steered her SUV between the white brick pillars as the iron gate eased open. A few hundred feet ahead, she rounded the sharp curve to the left and caught a glimpse of the antebellum estate she had called home as a child. Her grandfather had painstakingly restored his family's home to her nineteenth century grandeur.

Grandfather Harris had always referred to his family

home as a lady. Not a woman, but a lady. One who was respected because of who she was and where she had been, who she had married and how long she had persevered. The old man had not only called this grand dame of southern real estate a lady; he had treated her like one as well. Lawrence Harris had sacrificed all he had ever worked for to make the home livable.

When he and Grandmother Harris had first been married, they had lived in the cook's quarters, just off the kitchen, making an apartment out of the small rooms. He had worked long hours in his small grocery store only to come home every night to sand and paint and peel back the layers of history that revealed the story and majesty of his love. As a tribute to her faithfulness to his family, he had named the home Hannah, after his great-grandmother, who had overseen her building and chosen her original fixtures and décor.

Megan's grandparents had raised her father, Paul, and his sister, Francis, in the small apartment, never quite getting to the point where they could afford to live in the entire house. It had taken all of their income just to keep the square footage above freezing in winter and below scorching in summer.

Paul had told Megan countless stories of a happy existence in the tiny space and how he had spent most of his formative years at his father's side helping him restore the home inch-by-inch. By the time Paul graduated from high school, his only ambition was to find a vocation that would give his parents enough money to live comfortably in the house they had spent their lifetime restoring.

He graduated from Louisiana State University with a

degree in petroleum engineering four years later and was immediately successful in the oil business and ready to make his dream for his parents come true. However, the elder Harrises were content to stay in their tiny apartment. They suggested that he and Francis add a more modern kitchen to the remainder of the house and share it any way they liked.

As the kitchen renovation had neared completion, Francis accepted a marriage proposal. Paul insisted she take the home for her family, reserving a few lower rooms for himself.

Francis Harris' wedding had been the social event of the year for their entire town, if not the entire state. The couple was married in the grand ballroom of *Hannah* in the presence of over five hundred guests. Paul hosted the sit-down reception with his parents. The only mar on the celebration had been Paul's choice of a companion for the evening: a woman of little culture whom both Francis and their mother despised. In order to keep peace, they had suffered through the demands of the socially inept Aimee Devereau, hoping her first social event with the Harris family would be her last.

Aimee Devereau, however, had smelled money that night. The Harrises had less than some but more than many, and Aimee coveted *Hannah* as though the house was already hers. Paul could sense neither the danger nor the damage that his relationship with Aimee would bring.

Three months into Francis' marriage, she conceived a child and miscarried. While she recovered, Aimee became a regular fixture in the home. She initially came under the pretense of helper or nurse for Francis, but it was soon obvious that

Aimee had a more permanent role in mind.

When Francis emerged from the master suite three weeks later, she hardly recognized her home. Aimee had chosen new draperies and wall coverings for the formal dining and living rooms, billing the expense to Paul and claiming that Francis had asked her to take on the task of redecorating. Francis confronted Paul, but he honestly saw Aimee's meddling as helpfulness.

Four months later, Francis miscarried again and, this time, she did not recover. Paul's sister died in the arms of her husband shortly after she lost the baby, before they even celebrated their first anniversary.

Paul's parents both died within a few years, without ever seeing, first-hand, a family grow up in the home they had worked all their lives to preserve.

Unfortunately, Aimee was patient and persistent enough to ride out this stormy season of Paul's life with him and convinced the young heir that she could help him make his parents' dream come true. Aimee told him that they could raise a large family in his home and carry on the legacy his parents had begun. Alone and filled with grief, Paul was willing to believe her and he and Aimee ran away to Las Vegas in July of 1967.

In April of 1968, a baby daughter arrived. From the first time Paul ever laid eyes on Megan, he could see his mother and his sister in her features. He spent every moment of her first week home from the hospital holding Megan and caring for her, hopeful that all of their children would make him feel this complete and happy again. He knew the office

Finally Time to Dance

could survive without him for a week or two and intended to help Aimee as long as possible.

Aimee's reaction to Megan's arrival, however, was a stark contrast. She sent Paul back to work for the large oil firm that kept their income above that of their friends and neighbors and set about finding help for this impossible child who wanted all of her time and attention. Nursery staff came and went for several weeks before Paul stepped in and asked his old friend from high school if she would take the job. Hessie Price had seen the likes of Aimee Harris all her life. The spoiled, irritable housewife was no match for Hessie, who was determined to raise Miss Megan to be a lady, like all Harris women had been before her.

Paul retreated to his rooms in the lower part of the twenty thousand square-foot home. Aimee claimed "female" problems and a "complicated" pregnancy with Megan as her excuse for not bearing any more children for Paul. Aimee Harris used Paul and *Hannah* to climb a small southern social ladder.

Paul spent every spare moment he had with his daughter. He learned to be content with a small family and kept peace with his wife by publicly pretending they were happily married.

Hessie filled the gap by making Megan available to Paul every moment he was home and caring for her when he was away. She guarded the young Miss Harris against her mother as best she could, occasionally making excuses for Megan to stay home instead of being Aimee's trophy in her social circle.

Megan was beautiful enough to be accepted wherever she went with her mother, but Hessie saw the greater good that could come from raising a child to be humble and loving. At Hessie's side, the tiny Miss Megan learned to bake cookies, sew quilts, stitch samplers, and memorize Scripture. As she grew through her teens and into adulthood, Megan became the epitome of feminine class and style, elegant and intelligent on the outside, vivacious and adventuresome on the inside.

Megan Harris' natural affinity for socializing gracefully and helping others willingly made her well-liked by her mother's friends. Megan became the lady Aimee had always wanted to be. The older woman watched as her daughter became truly loved and adored by people from whom she could not even buy affection.

Aimee would have liked to put Megan out of her life once she graduated from high school, but she tolerated Megan's continued presence because it suited her. And because it suited Paul. *Hannah*, combined with Paul's income, had given Aimee the appearance of the life she wanted, so Aimee did what she could to make him happy and convince him that she wanted to be a good mother to Megan.

Paul, of course, saw through his wife's feeble attempts and was thankful that Hessie had been the one with whom Megan had spent most of her childhood. During her trips home throughout college, Megan spent the majority of her time visiting their faithful servant in the kitchen, taking short breaks to spend time with her mother, telling her what she wanted to hear.

Aimee did her best to hide her disappointment when

Finally Time to Dance

Megan agreed to marry the very "common" Chris Hardin. Paul approved of the boy who aspired to be little more than a school teacher, so Aimee pretended he was suitable. Great plans were underway for a grand wedding day at *Hannah* when Megan began hearing rumors from her mother's friends that she was marrying Chris because she "had" to. Without even bothering to confrontAimee, Megan asked Paul for his blessing and the money to elope with Chris. Paul not only gave his daughter his blessing and the money for a wedding trip to Natchitoches; he also set the young Hardins up with a small home in a suburb of Oklahoma City where they could begin their careers and work on their graduate degrees.

Though she missed her home, her father, and Hessie, Megan flourished in her new surroundings. She and Chris plugged into the community, eventually earning their masters degrees. As her family grew, Megan called Hessie frequently for advice or just to chat. Paul visited Megan periodically as her children were each born and as Chris's health deteriorated. Megan was thankful to have two men who both cherished her so much.

Megan's faith was strained and then grew as she watched her husband battle cancer and her father battle his wife. She prayed for the men she loved and learned what she could from them while she had them both close to her. Paul died shortly before Lily was born and Chris died shortly after Krissy came along. Alone with God, Megan had vowed to lean only on Him for advice now, knowing she could visit Hessie at *Hannah* when she needed more tangible renewing.

As Megan slipped from behind the steering wheel and

onto the thick, cool grass, she did not see the mansion and its grandeur. The winding walkways and manicured lawns that framed the enormous home represented the sadness that comes when humans chase what "moth and rust destroy." Her mother finally had all she ever wanted. *Hannah* belonged to Aimee. And she sat in it all alone.

....

"Lord, hep us, now." Hessie pulled an oven mitt and shook her head. "She need to go home." Hessie turned from the window to slide the cookie sheet into the oven.

She came back to the window in time to see Megan scoop Krissy up. The other children followed their mother around to the small picket fence in the back. Chad unlatched the crooked gate and held it open for his mother and siblings, careful to latch it back correctly. He knew about Hessie's rules and "closing whatever you open" was one of them. Ali ran up the small, steep steps and knocked on the screen door as she pressed her face against the screen to see if Hessie was in the kitchen.

"I comin', chil'. You got to give this ole girl a little time to get to the doe." Hessie took her time walking over to the door and unlatching it. Megan saw Hessie's face at the same time she smelled the cookies baking. Megan looked down, ashamed. If Megan guessed right, Ron had called looking for her and Hessie was about to give her a stern lecture about marriage and commitment and send her home to Ron.

Hessie took a moment to size them up. As sure as she

was standing right here, Miss Megan has lost ten pound since the wedding a month ago. From those bags under her eyes, the girl wasn't sleeping, either, and it likely wasn't because she'd been honeymooning. Lord, mercy. If it weren't for that baby on her hip and all these yungins callin' her 'momma,' Miss Megan would look like a six-year-old who had just done wrong and was waiting to be scolded. Hessie sighed, "Well, look at dat. Miss Megan done bro't my kids fo' a visit."

Megan looked up, relieved. She stepped inside and clung to Hessie with all her might.

"Welcome home, Miss Megan." Hessie smiled at Megan smugly. "We has a special surprise for folks show up here without callin' first."

"Oh?" Megan was intrigued.

"Yep." Hessie had gone back to her baking, so Megan could not whether or not she was smiling when said, "You get supper at the club. Miss Aimee's treat." Hessie turned to face Megan. She most definitely was not smiling. "You actin' like her. You just as soon have supper with her."

Megan chided herself. She should have known better than to mess with Hess.

Chapter 23

Ron heard the door to his office open but did not look up. "Yes, Teresa?"

"There's someone here to see you, Mr. Wellbourne. A Mrs. Fairbanks. She says she's a friend of Mrs. Wellbourne," Teresa shifted her feet while she waited for a reply. Mr. Wellbourne had seemed distracted the past couple of days, so she doubted he would visit with the woman.

Thankful for an excuse to stop trying to pretend he was working, Ron tossed his reading glasses onto his desk, "Send her in." He could not immediately recall a Mrs. Fairbanks who was friends with his mother, but surely her face would ring a bell.

Still skeptical, Teresa asked, "Are you certain?"

"Of course," Ron was surprised to hear the terseness in his own voice. Apparently, lack of sleep - and companionship - was beginning to take its toll. He shuffled the papers on his desk and tried again, "I'm kind of stalled out here. A break might be nice."

"Yes, sir."

Ron heard Teresa invite the woman in and offer her

coffee or a cold beverage. He finished tidying his desk just as the woman walked in. Ron greeted her as he took her in. Confident and professional, Mrs. Fairbanks was dressed in khaki slacks and a burgundy blazer. A brooch of old timepieces was attached smartly to her lapel and her blonde hair was fashionably cut. Her warm smile and firm handshake should have put Ron at ease, but this Mrs. Fairbanks was scarcely a day over fifty. This was not an acquaintance of Mrs. Mabel Wellbourne. Ron gained his composure and addressed her, "Good morning. I don't think we've met. Ron Wellbourne. You must be a friend of *Megan's*."

"Yes, I'm Liz. Megan and I attend Bible study together on Tuesday mornings. She's been a great addition to our group." Liz smiled kindly and Ron could see her searching his face. "And I think we may have met. We're in the same Sunday school class."

Ron swallowed hard. He had made little or no effort to get to know the names of his Sunday school classmates. The church directory Megan kept in her desk drawer with everyone's picture in it suddenly had a purpose.

"I'm sorry. Our class is big. I guess I've just not learned who you are." Ron squirmed uncomfortably in his chair. "Can I get you something to drink?"

"Teresa offered. No, thanks. I have coffee in the car." Liz waited before continuing, giving Ron a chance to process why she was here. It was Tuesday and Megan had not been at Bible study. Nor was she answering her home phone or her cell.

Though she had said nothing to their study group, Liz

suspected that the reluctant bride had bolted. She was here to reassure Ron that Megan would be back. And that his job right now was to let her come back on her own. "We missed Megan this morning at Bible study. Is she sick?"

Ron considered lying. He looked up to see Liz Fairbanks half-smiling at him in his misery. Ron regarded her carefully.

He had lied to his mother and to his secretary about Megan's whereabouts. They would just be upset. Particularly, they would be upset with Megan. He had not called Julie because he was too ashamed to tell her that he had run off his new wife in less than five weeks. He needed a female perspective, but that meant admitting the truth. He was running out of options, and out of patience.

He looked Liz straight in the eye and said, "She ran away. Yesterday morning. She wants out of our marriage." Ron looked down and waited for the fallout.

Liz placed her date book on Ron's desk and flipped to this week's schedule. "Well, you'll need a homecooked meal. Tom and I don't have plans tonight. How does seven sound?" Ron was too stunned to respond. He watched Mrs. Fairbanks scribble her cell phone number and address on her business card and hand it to Ron. "We'll see you at seven." Ron noted that she said it more as a statement than a question.

He could feel his heart pounding. The truth was out. At least this stranger had not indicated that the world was coming to an end. But she was a complete stranger and had invited him to her home to have dinner with her and her husband, who was also a complete stranger.

If his world made any less sense… Impossible. It simply couldn't make any less sense. Was the room spinning?

In his confusion, Ron was surprised to recall a line from a movie about a space mission gone terribly wrong. To calm the crew, the commander asked a simple question, "What do we have left on the ship that's good?" Did he have anything left that was good?

Ron walked across the room and closed the door, not bothering to tell Teresa to hold his calls. Surely she'd take the hint.

Good stuff. Dinner plans. That's always a plus. A job. That would only be good if he could regain his concentration and get back to business while he was here. A family. Yes, he still had that. Not only his parents. He had his new family as well. How much longer he would have them was in question, but for now, they were still his.

Ron picked up the receiver on his phone, "Teresa, please get me some coffee. Strong and black." He hung up and grabbed the stack of papers he had set aside when his visitor had arrived. Ron walked over to his planning board, rolled up his sleeves, and got down to business. "Focus, old man. Work with what you've got right here and leave the rest to the Big Guy."

Chapter 24

Ron tugged at his tie one last time before knocking. He took in his surroundings to gather what information he could about his hostess. He would not have guessed that the small, secluded home was where she lived. A mud-caked oilfield truck was parked behind an SUV in the driveway. Nothing outside the home indicated that the woman Ron had met this morning lived here.

Earlier today, Liz Fairbanks had arrived at his office looking like she had stepped off the pages of a Talbot's catalog. She had flipped her daytimer open with French-manicured nails and had carried a designer handbag.

Ron was pulled from his musings when the door opened and light spilled onto the porch. He was relieved to see Liz on the other side of the door. She greeted him warmly.

"Ron! I see you found us. A lot of people pass us up the first try." Liz's throaty chuckle put Ron at ease immediately.

"Well, I found it on my third pass," Ron admitted with a grin. "Thanks for inviting me." He handed Liz a small package of nuts and chocolates. Mabel Wellbourne had seen to her son's social graces. He knew better than to arrive for

Finally Time to Dance

dinner without a hostess gift.

"Aren't you sweet?" Liz took the gift and kissed Ron on the cheek. She introduced the man standing next to her. "This is my husband, Tom. He'll fix you something to drink while I put this away."

With that, the two men were alone. "You have a lovely home." Ron took his time scanning the entrance. This was definitely where the woman he had met in his office this morning lived. Inside, the home was a study in elegance. Sepia-toned photographs lined the gold wall beside the stairs. A half-flight below was a hallway Ron was sure led to bedrooms and other functional areas. He followed Tom up the other half-flight to the small living room, where Liz's love for clocks and luggage made the room interesting and comfortable.

On his way to fix the drinks, Tom motioned to the large leather recliner and Ron took a seat. From there, he could see the kitchen and dining area, both decorated in rustic farmhouse antiques that Liz had blended beautifully with dainty china and silver pieces. The contradiction worked so well. Mrs. Fairbanks dared to combine contrasts and it was very easy on the eyes. Ron sat back and enjoyed the view.

Tom returned with iced tea. Ron noticed his worn jeans and tanned features. He guessed the oilfield truck belonged to Tom. "You must be affiliated with Fairbanks Drilling."

"Yea. The office east of town is mine. My son owns the one to the north. We're just boys, I guess. Neither of us ever could give up playing in the mud." Tom laughed and took a seat in a wide chair opposite Ron.

Liz came into the room and announced that they could serve their plates when they were ready. They would eat in the living room where they could relax and visit for as long as they liked. She stopped to give Tom a peck on the head and rubbed his neck. Ron wondered how long they had been married. Obviously in this case opposites had attracted and everything about the couple and their home told Ron that they had enjoyed celebrating their differences for many years. Tom's eyes twinkled as he kissed her hand before she turned to go back to the kitchen.

Ron enjoyed the meal and the company for over an hour before a pit began forming in his stomach. Megan had been on his mind all evening, but it suddenly occurred to him that Liz might bring up his current situation in front of Tom. He had no desire to get marriage counseling from this couple in their living room. He felt both of them staring at him and was searching for something to say when Tom rescued him.

"Hon, you mind if I show Ron my baby?" He looked at Ron. "With my crazy work schedule, I don't get much time with other boys. I'm going to steal you for a few minutes."

Liz began gathering dishes. "Fine with me. I'll just stack these up and return a call." She winked at Tom. "You can help with these later."

Tom winked back at his wife and led the way down the stairs and into the garage. Liz had put her decorating skills to work even here, where one side was a mecca of dollhouses and comic books for grandchildren and the other half was open for entertaining their adult children's families, save the

'67 Mustang parked in the middle of the room.

"There she is." Tom was as proud as if he was showing Ron his own child. "Rescued her from being scrap metal thirty years ago."

Tom gave Ron a "tour" of the vintage auto, starting under the hood and covering almost every inch before ending by closing the trunk.

"Whatdaya think?" Tom was beaming.

"It's incredible." Ron was caressing the chrome bumper. "I can't even imagine how many hours you must have in this. How did you ever manage? Didn't Liz say you have four children?"

"Five if you count the one we raised for my brother after his wife died." Tom leaned on the driver's door and tucked his hands into his pockets. "Guess it's what kept me sane through all those pregnancies and school plays and teenage drivers.

"It was relaxing just to know this was here and I could make a difference spending a few hours replacing some wires or paintin' the hood. Gave me a good excuse to spend time with my boys, too. I'm not much on fishing or tossing a ball or that sort of thing.

"The boys loved coming down here when they were little and helping or even just watching if I was doing something real delicate." Tom chuckled. "Every now and then, Liz would get mad at all the time I spent here and all the money I spent trying to make it look like something, but we both always knew it was what kept me going. I'll show you pictures sometime of what it looked like when I first dragged it home. Took a lot of faith on Liz's part not to drag it right back to the junkyard."

Ron laughed, "I bet."

Tom stretched and groaned, "I'm stuffed. What say we camp down here a few minutes?" Tom motioned to the sofa in the play area and Ron took a seat. Tom sank into a chair beside the sofa and propped his feet up on the coffee table.

"Liz says you're a bachelor this week." Tom gave Ron a wry smile.

"It's temporary. She'll be back soon." Ron was surprised at how calm his voice sounded. In fact, he even felt calm talking to Tom. The older man didn't make Ron feel threatened or belittled in any way. In fact, he made having a wife run away sound almost par for the course.

Ron took note that Tom had about a gazillion times more experience with a wife than he did and listened carefully when Tom spoke.

"Yes, she will. She won't necessarily be happy or ready to make things right, but she'll be back. She'll probably chew on it a few more weeks. You'll get pretty miserable trying to fix it." Tom took his feet off the table and leaned forward.

"Thing is, she's not going to *want* you to fix it. She's going to *want* you to shut up and listen while she sorts it all out." Tom tossed his hands in the air. "When Lizzy and I first started out, she'd come to me with a problem and I'd have it all figured out and be ready to tell her what to do before she could even get to the end of her whinin'. So, there I'd go and tell her how to fix it and make it sound real simple and then move on to another conversation.

"Man! Would she get hot. She'd accuse me of not listening. And I'd just sit there, dazed. How could the woman think I wasn't listening? I had sat right there and heard every word and even come up with a solution. Did anybody thank me? Noooooo." Ron was laughing at the older man, now, appreciating the wisdom behind the entertainment.

"Then one night, she's rantin' about something while we're getting in bed and I was there waiting for her to finish so I could tell her what she should do, and she stopped in the middle of a sentence and came right over to me."

Tom leaned toward Ron. "She came up real close to me like this, looked me straight in the eye, and she said, 'So help me, Fairbanks, tell me how I should fix this and I'll put you out of this room for a week. I don't want you to *fix* anything! I want you to shut up and *listen!*'"

Tom sat back and smacked his forehead. "It was like a flashing neon sign had lit up right there in the bedroom. It said, 'You're not the fixer; I AM!' It's hard to stay out of the way, but God didn't give Adam and Eve to each other so they could fix things. Bible says God made Eve because it wasn't good for Adam to be *alone*. Same's true for every marriage since."

Ron was stunned by the story that Tom had so easily turned into a lesson in God's truth. He looked at Tom for several heartbeats, wondering what, if anything, he should say.

Had he tried to fix things when Megan talked or had he listened? Truth be told, Megan really hadn't complained about *anything* since they got married. Not even while they had dated. The morning she left, there was obviously something wrong, but she had come to him with the solution and her plan for carrying it out. She hadn't really talked to Ron about what was upsetting her. She had just run away. Maybe if she had talked to him...

"Tom, she didn't complain or tell me what the problem is. She just told me she doesn't expect me to change or do anything and then she left."

"I'm not surprised. Son, listen, she's scared." Tom sniffed. "Actually, she's in shock. But what's going to happen is that she's going to mull all this over while she's gone and come back ready to fight." Tom looked as relaxed as a cat while he talked about Ron's impending doom. "Trust me."

Uh huh. My wife will be combative. I'm supposed to look forward to this? "And that's when I just listen?"

"Not at first. Egg her on a little." Tom chuckled at the look of horror on Ron's face. "Not like that. Just make her keep talking.

"Communication is the key to any healthy relationship. I know that sounds like a marriage conference slogan or something, but it's true. If she doesn't talk, she'll just keep ignoring the real problem and try to get rid of you instead of confronting what's really wrong."

Ron thought about not asking the obvious, but he went for broke. "What's really wrong?"

Tom took a deep breath and lowered his voice. He looked at Ron compassionately. "She misses her husband, Son. She's grieving."

Ron sat back hard like he had been punched in the gut. He had made a point of never trying to compare himself to Chris Hardin or take his place in any way, but by doing so he had missed a crucial need for Megan. She needed to be able to talk to Ron about Chris.

Occasionally, she had done so, but only in passing and it had usually been with regard to the kids. Ron rubbed his temples. This was getting complicated. He needed Megan to come home so he could talk to her. Maybe she would answer her phone if he called.

"And don't go chasing her down or making demands." Ron smiled at Tom's reading his mind. "She'll come back when she's ready. Chances are, she's off seeing an aunt or a girlfriend who'll tell her to get back home and work out her business. Just be ready when she gets there." Tom patted Ron's knee. "I'll be praying."

Ron wiped a tear from his cheek and sniffed softly. "I don't want her hurting. I don't want to cause her any more pain."

"You didn't cause the pain." Tom looked down. "Death caused the pain. It's part of life. Deal with it." The men sat in silence for several minutes.

Ron got up and walked back over to the Mustang. "It's going to be ok, then?"

"In time."

Tom could see Ron had enough to think about for now. He took his leave and told Ron to take his time coming back up to say goodnight to Liz.

When Ron walked into the kitchen Liz gave no indication

that she knew what Tom had said to him downstairs, but on his way out, she pressed a small piece of paper into his hand. "You'll need this. We're praying."

Ron shrugged on his jacket then gave them a small wave. "Goodnight."

Ron stood on the porch and looked up at the full moon. It reminded him of a book he had heard Megan read to Lily last week.

It was a story of a little girl whose parents had gone on vacation. They had come back and told their daughter about all the pretty things they had seen. When the little girl asked what part was the best, the mother told her that the moon had been the best, since it was the same moon her daughter could see from home.

God, wherever she is, tell her I love her. Tell her we're looking at the same moon.

Ron pulled out his cell phone and turned it off. He'd leave her alone for now. "She'll be back soon."

....

Aimee closed the door to her Mercedes and walked around to Megan's side of the car. Her daughter was leaning against the passenger's side door gazing up at the full moon. She watched the beautiful young woman from a few feet away.

Megan had her father's tall, slender build and high cheeks bones. The outline of her face in the moonlight gave Aimee pause. She looked so much like Paul. Megan even had Paul's patient spirit and forgiving heart. Aimee wished she had learned more from them while she'd still had them both.

She took a deep breath. *No regrets, remember?* Sometimes that was so hard when the mistakes were still so obvious.

She approached Megan. "Are you alright, dear?"

Megan looked at Aimee, seeming surprised that she was there. "Sorry, Mom. I was checking out that full moon." Megan's face brightened into a smile. "It reminds me of Lily's favorite book."

Aimee came and stood next to her and gazed up as well. "It's so bright we could almost make do without lights in the parking lot."

"I guess that's true." Megan pulled away from the car and held out her arm. "Shall we?"

Thankful for her daughter's warmth when she knew she didn't deserve it, Aimee smiled and took Megan's arm. "Yes, let's."

Megan strolled across the parking lot with her mother. Her thoughts remained on the moon. The boys loved nights like this when the sky was so clear that Ron could drag the telescope out to the front porch and the three of them could see the moon's craters and then look around for planets and stars. She wondered if the sky was clear at home.

The women reached the door of the club's restaurant and Megan pulled open the door for her mother. Aimee slipped inside.

Megan turned and took one last glance at the bright yellow ball. *God, help him to not be too mad at me.*

And help me know what to do.

Chapter 25

Aimee lowered her menu and looked at Megan. "We have a new chef, you know. He's a master at anything on here with veal, but don't order chicken." Aimee made a face that made Megan giggle.

"I'm not really hungry, Mom. Maybe I'll just have a salad." Not only had her headache scarcely let up all day, but now her stomach was churning as well. Getting sick on the road was never any fun. Megan hoped that whatever was making her feel so out of sorts would pass by morning. She'd have to make a bigger effort to get more sleep.

Maybe Hessie would already have the kids tucked in when she got home and she could head straight to bed. Megan saw the disappointment on Aimee's face at her not trying something more unique. "That way, we'll save room for dessert." Megan winked. "I still love sweets."

This brightened her mother. "Oh, my, yes! Joseph is still the pastry chef. Can you imagine? He's been here over forty years. They'll bring a tray by when we're ready."

Megan conjured up a smile and closed her menu. "Sounds wonderful."

Megan was relieved that Aimee made an effort at conversation during dinner. She asked about each child and how they were doing with their studies given all the changes in their home recently. Megan was able to assure her that all five children had taken the changes in stride and that each day brought them closer to finding their 'new normal.'

It reminded Megan of a similar conversation she'd had with her mother shortly after Chris's funeral. Only at that time, Aimee was campaigning for the children to be sent to a 'real' school so they could 'get on with their lives and stop sitting at home all day.' Megan had not realized that Aimee thought her homeschooling arrangement was temporary or because of Chris's poor health.

Over the past three years, Megan made more of an effort to show Aimee here and there that the children were 'really' in school, even if it was at home. Megan had vowed not to enter into an argument with her mother about it or defend herself in any way. She had just let their skills, accomplishments, and standardized test scores speak for themselves.

Perhaps Aimee was finally coming around. But Megan reminded herself not to go looking for Aimee's approval. She had lived this long and this much without it. No need to start begging for it, now.

They had just begun contemplating their dessert choices when the maitre'd came to their table. Charles was a friend of Megan's from high school who'd made a career out of working here at the country club. Working here was a perfect fit for the boy who married his high school sweetheart and wanted to raise his small family in the same town in which he'd been raised. Megan knew that Charles and his wife, Sharon, lived near his mother's house. When she had the chance to drive by there, Megan was always delighted to see that the couple had made their small house into a charming home and they both seemed happy and contented.

"Mrs. Wellbourne, how nice of you to join us this evening." Megan extended her hand in greeting, trying not to giggle at the clown of her class being so refined in such an elegant setting. She had met Charles's son. If he was any indication, Charles was still a cut-up. But they would play like big kids here in public.

"Good evening, Mr. Scallan."

"How long will you be visiting your mother?"

"Just a day or two. I have to get back pretty quickly. The holidays will be here before you know it." Charles rolled his eyes knowingly.

"Will Mr. Leger be joining you ladies for dessert?" Charles directed this question at Aimee, who tugged at her napkin nervously before placing it back in her lap. The gesture only lasted an instant, but it was not lost on Megan. She was accustomed to seeing Aimee Harris calm and collected at all costs.

Unsure of what to say, Megan turned her eyes toward Charles. He winked at her, trying to hide a smile. Finally, Aimee answered, trying to sound nonchalant, "No, no. I'm enjoying my daughter's company tonight. Good night, Charles."

Megan watched Charles's face break into a full smile and he bid them a "good evening" and walked away.

Finally Time to Dance

Well, this was an exciting development. Aimee Harris had been having dinner here regularly with a *Mr.* Leger. Oh my.

Megan pretended to scan her dessert menu while trying to sneak a peek at her mother's face. She couldn't contain herself any longer! "Mom! You're *blushing*."

Megan covered her mouth with her menu to try to hide some of her amusement, but who could be quiet? Aimee Harris had a boyfriend!

Aside from the color rising in her cheeks, Aimee kept her poker face. "You're creating a scene, dear. Do try and behave yourself." Aimee motioned for the waiter to come take their orders. "We'll have two of tonight's specials." She folded both their menus, handed them to the waiter and dismissed him with a nod. The older woman folded her hands under her chin and rested her elbows in the table. She had not seen their daughter this giddy in years.

Aimee had heard her friends from the club say that Megan's laughter was contagious. It was true. A small giggle erupted from Aimee and before they knew it, both women were wiping tears from their cheeks in an attempt to gain some composure.

Never once in her life had Megan laughed with her mother. It felt incredible to share this moment.

Megan caught her breath first. "So, who is he?"

"Actually, he's an old friend. Someone I knew before I even met your father. Vernon married a girl he met when he went off to school in Texas. They settled there and lived in the Houston area until she passed away two years ago.

"Their children had moved off to different parts of the country and Vernon still had a family home here, so he moved back. We ran into each other about six months ago and we get together and share a meal about twice a week. Having a companion makes me realize how lonely I had become." The laughter was gone from Aimee's face, now. "I spent so many years trying to convince myself that I didn't need anyone. I guess I had started to believe that."

Megan sobered and took a deep breath. This woman had been married to one of the kindest, most loving men on earth for over forty years and she had rejected him. *Now* she saw the need for companionship? She felt the color rise in her cheeks and hoped her mother would not notice.

Their desserts arrived, saving Megan from having to respond right away. She worked hard at stifling the anger that was mounting. Everything that had transpired here tonight was positive. Why let her past frustrations with Aimee dampen that?

Megan took a bite of the creamy cheesecake drizzled with amaretto and closed her eyes. "Mmmm. Tastes like Joseph still has his touch." Megan swallowed the bite and looked at Aimee.

She was waiting for a response from her daughter. Obviously, Aimee needed Megan's blessing, at least on some level. Megan put her hurts aside and summoned some enthusiasm. "Oh, Mom, that's wonderful news. I'm glad you have someone who can keep you company." Megan poked at the dessert with her fork. "I assume he's retired?"

"Yes. From plumbing."

Megan choked on her second bite of cheesecake. Aimee grinned at her reaction. She knew she deserved her daughter's frustration. All Megan's life, Aimee had been chasing money and status. It must seem unreal to her that Aimee was now searching for more fulfilling, less tangible things.

"Sorry. Would you order me another club soda?" Great, now her head, stomach, and throat all hurt. This really had to be gone by morning.

Aimee motioned for the waiter to bring Megan another drink. "I know you must be feeling lots of things right now, darling, not the least of which would be anger. Maybe even some resentment thrown in there.

"I'm sorry I can't change the past. But I was hoping we might look for a better future.

"I've been seeing Vern on Sundays, too. At church." At this, Megan sat back and tried to put her emotions on hold.

"Really?"

"Yes. I've lied to myself long enough, Megan. There's something missing inside me and I need to find out what it is."

Megan couldn't believe it! Megan had prayed for her mother every single day since she had become a Christian. This was it! Her mother was seeking the Lord. "Mom, it's Christ! He can fill that void…"

Aimee held up her hand. "*I* need to find it, Megan. In my own time, my own way."

Megan could accept that. She had seen more promise in her mother's salvation in the past hour than she had seen in the past thirty-five years. She'd just pray and leave the

~ 218 ~

details to God. Was it getting hot in here?

"You look pale, dear. Do you feel well?"

"I'm just tired, Mom. I really haven't slept well in a few days and I think it's catching up with me," Megan answered with more assurance than she felt.

"Let's get you home and in bed. If you plan to drive home in a day or so, you're going to have to get some rest." Aimee winked at her. "We're not as young as we used to be."

"Speak for yourself."

Aimee laughed and called for the check.

....

On the short drive home, Megan checked her cell phone at least three times. Ron had not called all evening.

She felt ashamed that she expected him to call, but she was hurt that he had not. Beyond that, she was angry at herself for ignoring him when all he wanted to do was help her. She held the phone in her hand as she walked into the house, hoping it would ring and wondering if she would answer it.

Aimee kissed her good night and headed up for bed. Megan went to Hessie's apartment in search of her brood.

Randy was laying, face up smack dab on top of Chad, who had fallen asleep with a comic book in his hand. Ali was curled up near the floor lamp where she had likely read Nancy Drew until she could no longer hold her own eyes open. The two little ones were curled up with teddy bears and unicorns, their blonde curls intermingling on the pillow they shared. The first time Ron had seen a scene like this one on Hessie's floor, he had said they looked like a litter of kittens.

It was an accurate description.

Hessie stirred in her recliner. Megan bent down to give her a hug.

"You all have a nice supper?"

Megan sat on the floor in front of the sofa and kicked off her shoes. "Yes, we did." Megan cut to the chase. "What's this about Vernon Leger?"

Hessie hooted, "Oooo, chil'. She done gone and told you ev'rythang."

"Well, I had some help from Charles Scallan. What's the scoop?"

"All I know is that the past six months have been the easiest I've ever had here. I hadn't seen no fits, no lying, no name-callin'."

"I still can't believe you sent me to dinner with her without warning me!"

"Oh, I jus' a sucker fo' surprises, I guess." Hessie's grin was wide. She was proud to have kept a secret so long. "I almost had to call you about two weeks ago, though. It was 3:00 a.m. and they still wasn't back!"

"Three a.m.? My mother came home from a date in the middle of the night?"

"They had gone to Alexandria to see a midnight movie. They came in all giggling like kids who done sneaked somethin' by they parents. Law! They had me worried."

Megan felt so tired. "Aren't they a little old for midnight

movies?"

"Hey, watch it, missy." It was Megan's turn to hoot with laughter.

Hessie's tone got serious. "She's starting to change. You keep praying, you hear?"

Megan nodded. "I will." She leaned her head back onto the sofa. "I'll even pray believing God will actually answer my prayers. I honestly haven't expected to ever see what I saw tonight." Megan rolled her head and smiled at Hessie. "God's still in the miracle business."

"An' don't you forget dat." Hessie leaned up and came to her feet. "Now, ol' Hessie gonna go to bed. Where you sleepin'?"

"I'll crash here on the sofa if that's alright. If one of the little girls needed me, she wouldn't know where to find me if I went upstairs."

"Suit yo'self. See you in the mornin', Sugar."

"Good night, Hess."

Megan slipped into her comfy sweats and made a bed on the sofa. She laid her head on the crocheted throw pillow Hessie had helped her make when she was about eight years old. It felt good to be home.

The only thing that would make it perfect is if…Ron were here? Megan chastised herself for missing him. Wasn't this about missing him less, not more?

And why hadn't he called her tonight? Had she run him off so quickly?

Megan scanned the room. Hessie had been kind enough to haul her bag back down for her once the kids had fallen asleep. She dug in it for her Bible and curled up on the sofa beside the floor lamp. *God, what can I do? Am I so terribly out of Your will that I can't even hear you tell me what to do next?*

Not fully aware of where she was turning, Megan opened to the twenty-third Psalm. Randy was working on this passage in his AWANA handbook, so she had heard the words repeatedly in recent days. She set her Bible on her lap and closed her eyes as the familiar words came to her mind. The first three verses were so comforting and reassuring. Megan could feel God's presence through them. At verse four, however, tears spilled out and rolled down her cheeks. Megan let them fall unchecked.

Even though I walk through the valley of the shadow of death, I will fear no evil, for you are with me; your rod and your staff, they comfort me.

Why couldn't she feel the comfort of His rod and staff right now? *Father, please take away this pain!*

Megan sat up straight and wiped her eyes with her t-shirt. "Girl, get hold of yourself! You're not going to be fit to drive yourself home if you don't get some sleep."

With that, Megan pushed back her cover and walked to the kitchen in search of a drink of water. Her throat was still scratchy, and maybe sitting in the kitchen a few minutes would clear her head. When she flipped on the light, she was surprised to see a familiar figure seated at the table. Shame and embarrassment washed over her.

"Chris? What are you doing here?"

"I heard you moved. I wasn't sure where to find you, so I came here."

"I'm so sorry. I thought you had really died. You've been gone for over three years."

"I know I was sick and taking care of me was a pain, especially with a new baby and all, but you didn't have to ignore me."

"I tried not to ignore you. There were so many things to do. I called hospice in to help." Megan was too stunned to even cry. Her hands were trembling.

"It's OK. Don't worry about it." Chris smiled at her, but his face seemed very different somehow. "Is there room for my stuff in your big, new house?"

Megan considered how much room was left in the closet now that Ron had moved in his clothes... *God, no! What will he say when he finds out about Ron?*

Wait, I have Chris's death certificate. I showed it to them at the courthouse when Ron and I got our marriage license. God, help me!

"Mommy?" Lily was tugging at Megan's afghan. "Mommy, why are you crying?"

Megan sat up and looked around. The lamp was still on and the other four children were still curled up on the floor beside the sofa. She looked toward the kitchen. The light was off and no one was in there. Megan pulled Lily onto her lap. "Mommy was just having a bad dream, Sweet Pea. She's OK."

"But you tell Chad that bad dreams aren't real. If you know that, how come you're so scared?"

Megan tucked Lily's head under her chin and held her close. "Sometimes dreams seem so real they scare you."

Finally Time to Dance

Lily wiggled free and turned around so she could hug her mother. Her tiny hand patted Megan's back softly. "It's OK, Mommy. God's right here with us." Lily looked up with her wide smile. "Isn't He?"

"Yes, He is." *Lord, please, restore my soul.* "Let's go back to sleep. Maybe this time I'll dream about a green pasture."

Lily gave her mom a peck on the cheek and snuggled in beside her.

Chapter 26

Ron poured the contents of his pockets into the silver tray. He sat the tray up on a high shelf so the children could not reach his pocketknife. His heart was heavy again as he realized they would not be home tonight.

Had they been home, he would be upstairs right now hunting for a teddy bear under a bed for Krissy or listening to one last joke from Chad's repertoire. Even Ali waved goodnight from her room, now. He slumped into the chair where he took off his shoes. He was perfectly miserable.

His conversation with Tom had hit him hard. Anger began to mount as he imagined Tom and Liz discussing Ron's inability to understand his wife. He felt helpless and exposed knowing that they knew so much about what was happening in his marriage.

Ron sighed and leaned his head on the closet shelf. If he was so bad at being married that other people noticed, he might have to admit that he wasn't cut out to be a husband after all. The night Ron had asked Megan to marry him, he had felt like God had led him to do it, like God was finally giving him the desire of his heart, giving him a wife.

Maybe he had misunderstood. How could you be sure about God's leading? He certainly had nothing in writing. Had he relied on his own feelings? Or had it been real?

He looked at his cell phone to check for calls, remembering then that he had turned it off. Ron sighed deeply, sat down to take off his shoes, then got up to find his nightclothes. At this point every evening, Megan would select a nightgown and head off to her vanity in the bathroom. It was amazing how quickly he had become accustomed to their routine. Megan always smelled so sweet when she got in bed. He wasn't sure which of the cosmetics on her counter she used or if it was a combination of several, but just the thought of his sensuous wife sinking into her pillow next to his made him light-headed. Every night they spent together, whether they were physically intimate or not, had made Ron more in love with Megan.

On his way out of the closet, Ron paused and touched the nightgown Megan had been wearing the last time she was in his bed.

Bring her back. Show me how I can help her when she gets here.

Ron felt twenty years older than he had when the week began. He tossed his laundry into the chute. Before closing the door, he looked down the dark tunnel. He could not see the bottom from where he stood. It suddenly occurred to him that if Megan had been gone for two days, there may be something down there that needed to be washed or dried or put away. As a bachelor who lived so near his mother and her domestic helpers, Ron had never had to do his own laundry.

What if Megan didn't come home for another week? He'd either have to admit defeat and bring his clothes to his mother or start showing up for work wearing jeans and t-shirts.

Or I could learn to do laundry. Ron contemplated his plight several more seconds before he shut the door to the chute and walked toward the basement stairs. "How hard can this be?"

Laundry tossed into the chute landed conveniently in a large bin next to the washer. Ron did not know this because he had ever seen it; he knew this because he had heard Megan tell several of her friends that she didn't mind carrying clean laundry up the stairs since she never had to collect it and bring it down.

Ron walked into the laundry room and shut the door. He stood in front of the machines, feeling slightly like a prairie cowboy facing off an adversary. With folded arms, he took in the scene for several seconds.

Just above each machine was a sheet of instructions. And not just any instructions. They were written for Ali, Chad, and Randy and came complete with pictures! *Thank you.*

Ron followed the words and diagrams to the letter, careful not to overfill the washer or mix dark colors with light ones. Within a few minutes, the machine was humming and Ron had even sorted the leftovers into the three smaller baskets Megan had neatly labeled in the room.

Ron took his time leaving, scanning the shelves of rubber boots, car wash supplies, and drop cloths he didn't know existed. He wondered if he'd ever need to know where all these things were. Would he and Megan someday wash her truck or paint a bedroom together?

How had she ever gotten all those things done without another adult in the house? Ron wanted desperately to be a helper to Megan. He silently prayed that she would let him.

Still too agitated to settle in for the night, Ron left the laundry room and closed the door behind him. The quiet of the basement stairs was a relief. Ron climbed the stairs and stood in the hallway contemplating what he could do right now to get some answers. Finally, he headed for the bedroom.

Ron glanced down at his Bible. He had tossed it onto the bed before changing his clothes. Megan often sought her Bible out after she tucked the children into bed. She always appeared a little more at ease when she closed it and asked Ron if he was ready for her to turn off the lamp. He doubted that reading Scripture could bring him peace as quickly, but Ron was suddenly too tired to move.

He slid under the covers on Megan's side of the bed instead of walking around to his own. Ron picked up his Bible and held it in both hands. Shame washed over Ron as thought about how cavalier he had been about God's Word. There was power and direction from God in these pages. How could he have ever thought it anything less?

Ron pressed the Bible against his forehead and tried to hold back the tears that were threatening to spill out. He had to admit that he didn't even know where to begin. Megan always opened her Bible confidently, like she knew what she was looking for. Ron hadn't a clue.

He knew he wanted answers, but they wouldn't just magically appear. Ron prayed for direction.

An idea suddenly came to Ron. He put the Bible in his lap and opened it to the middle and then thumbed through Psalms to Proverbs. The last time they had been in Sunday school, a woman had walked up to Megan and thanked her for the suggestion of reading a Proverb a day. Ron remembered then that there were thirty-one chapters in the book of Proverbs, making it easy to read through the entire book in a month by just picking the chapter that matched the day's date. He flipped to the eighteenth chapter.

As he began reading, the search for peace through reading simple words seemed futile to Ron.

How can God talk to me through words I've had read to me all my life?

Then, from somewhere in the recesses of his mind, Ron recalled a verse about "those who earnestly seek Him."

Well, if ever anyone was earnestly seeking You, God, it's me and it's happening right now. Give me something to calm me. Give me some hope.

He read the first several verses before something tugged him back to verse two.

A fool finds no pleasure in understanding but delights in airing his own opinions.

"Now, that's not fair. I didn't give Tom my opinion. And I think I'm trying to understand."

Where had that come from? Who am I talking to?

Ron sat up and threw back the covers, placing his Bible

on the bed in front of him. Recently, Pastor Dave had been teaching about the ways God communicates with us. He listed several ways, but stressed that God most often uses His Word to speak to His people. Ron wanted to believe that. But he also wanted God to take his side, not Megan's or the Fairbanks'.

From the second verse, Ron continued on through the middle of the chapter, where things started to brighten up. He even recognized some of the words as lyrics to hymns they had sung on Sunday mornings. The second half of the passage offered more admonitions and warnings about using discernment and, interestingly enough, guidelines for settling disputes. Ron smiled at the irony.

Then, at verse twenty-two, he picked up the Bible and held it closer. He read the verse again. He looked around the room and breathed deeply.

Was he just seeing what he wanted to see written there or was God making a promise to Ron right now? He read the verse once more.

He who finds a wife finds what is good and receives favor from the LORD.

He was not mistaken. God was speaking to him, right here, alone in his bedroom.

God had given Ron his wife. And it was good.

Relief swept over him like a Caribbean breeze.

Ron and Megan were supposed to be husband and wife. It was only one verse, but Ron had been earnestly seeking an answer to a specific question and God had answered. *Thank you.*

Spent, Ron switched off the lamp and lay back on Megan's pillow. He set his Bible on his own pillow and pulled the comforters over him. He wondered if sleep would come easily or if he'd lay awake speculating about the future of his marriage. Hopeful that he'd sleep, he turned onto his side and closed his eyes.

Beside him on Megan's nightstand, a small red light flashed on the phone, indicating a missed call, but Ron drifted off without noticing.

....

Megan dropped her cell phone back into her bag and slumped to the floor. She'd slipped out from under Lily and left the child dozing peacefully on the sofa.

Oh, God. I've really messed things up, haven't I? Ron's turned off his cell and won't even answer at home. I know I'm just getting what I deserve for ignoring him, but it's not like Ron to play games. I'm the petty one.

I've dragged the poor man down to my level.

Megan cried softly, dabbing her eyes with a napkin she'd found in her purse.

She tried to push the images from her mind, but her dream kept returning. Chris's face was not as clear now that she was awake, but she trembled at the memory of his words. He had wanted to come to live with her and Megan's reaction filled her with shame. When she'd heard his words, she'd been disappointed. Her first reaction was to be upset that he'd be interfering with the new life she was building...with Ron.

Megan grabbed the throw pillow and sobbed into it hard.

I would never have sent Chris away so I could have a new life. You know that, God. I just did what I thought You were telling me to do. I never meant to hurt Chris or shut him out. But he's not here!

"He's not here!" Megan screamed into the room. Ali stirred and looked at Megan then closed her eyes.

Megan got up and walked around the room, trying desperately to stop trembling. After circling Hessie's living room twice, Megan was chilled. She dug around her bag for her OU hoodie and slipped it on over her head. She tucked her cell phone into the front pocket and resumed her pacing. No longer bothering with the wet, wadded-up napkin, she wiped her nose on a thick crimson sleeve.

On her third trip around the room, Megan caught a glimpse of herself in the framed oval mirror Hessie kept near the back door. She paused and stared at her dimly-lit reflection. Streaks ran down both her cheeks and her lips were swollen. Her nose was pink and chapped from wiping it so many times and strands of hair stuck to her wet face. Megan leaned closer to look at her eyes.

Who is this in the mirror? Who am I married to? When did the details get so blurry?

Megan stepped away and walked over to Hessie recliner and sunk into it. She knew she needed to pray, but she didn't have the strength. When Megan was about twelve years old, she had walked into here and found Hessie asleep in this chair with her Bible across her chest. Megan had startled her by calling her name. Hessie had recovered quickly and explained that her "angels" had been busy that evening finishing up her prayers since she had fallen asleep. Megan hadn't given it much thought at the time, but now she wondered if she could count on an angel somewhere to tell God what she wanted to tell Him if she was too tired to pray.

Megan pulled her cell phone out of her pocket and unlocked it. There were no message indicators on the screen, but she checked for voice and text messages just in case.

No messages. How could she call Ron if he didn't want to talk to her? Hessie had been right. Megan had been acting just like her mother and now she was all alone. Alone and scared.

Megan dozed fitfully for an hour or so before Lily called to her from the sofa. Megan went to her and tucked her back in. She stroked Lily's hair a few moments. Megan smiled as she touched her tiny face.

From the moment this child had come into the world, she could make Megan smile. Though she could never put her finger on why, Megan knew that Lily possessed an uncanny ability to brighten a room and make everyone in it feel good about themselves. Ali joked that she was their "family mascot," cheering them on just when they needed it the most.

Last week, for instance, Chris's sister had visited with her children. The Hardin children were ecstatic about seeing their aunt and cousins, but Jay and Michaela were somber when they arrived. Their father had filed for divorce without explaining why, and they were beginning their first holiday season as a "broken" family.

Lily caught on immediately that something was amiss and set about bringing the room to life. Megan thanked God for her child who, without taking on their happiness as her responsibility, could help two hurting children forget their pain for a little while. She had rallied the troops into making cards for the people to whom they would be delivering Meals on Wheels the following week. The visit passed quickly and the cousins had had a memorable, and meaningful, afternoon with a five-year-old leading the festivities.

When Megan was putting her children to bed that evening, Chad asked why his cousins had seemed so sad when they first arrived and Randy asked why Uncle Presley had not come with them. While Megan was still searching for the right words to explain, Ali chimed in with a simple, "He and Aunt Donna got a divorce, remember?"

Chad sighed deeply and responded with, "Well, at least our dad just died."

To Megan's relief, and then horror, all four of his siblings agreed with Chad.

Randy said, "Yeah. Our dad would have stayed if he could have."

Megan watched Ali wipe a tear from under her eye then spoke to Chad. "That's right, Sweetie. As hard as it is to be here without him, he didn't choose to leave us."

Megan had held Ali close as she finished the Berenstein Bear book she was reading. She was thankful her children still felt loved, even though the separation from Chris was very painful.

Megan tried to wriggle out from under the guilt, but it sat there like a dead weight, pushing her down with shame. She could rationalize it any way she liked, but the bottom line was that she was in the midst of planning to put her children through a divorce. She had reasoned for weeks that it would somehow be justifiable since she and Ron had not been married long and since he wasn't their father anyway, but that did not change the truth.

Megan was planning to put her children through yet another loss. And this time it would be intentional.

When Donna first told Chris's family the news of her divorce, Megan had distanced herself from the situation. Megan was very upset with Donna and Presley for walking away so easily and putting their children through something so difficult. Megan had been convinced at the time that there was no problem so big that time and prayer could not fix it.

Until tonight, Megan had not drawn any parallel between her situation and Donna's, but the memory of Chad's comment made her realize that, to her children, it would be exactly the same.

Two people not willing to work things out would walk away from a commitment and, in the end, the children would be abandoned. Again.

But there's so much to work through. Being married to Ron makes me miss Chris. How can I ever explain that to Ron without hurting him? Asking a man to understand both sides of her coin seemed so selfish and wrong.

Megan went to the back door and opened it softly. The screen door creaked as she pushed on it. She left the wooden door ajar and closed the screen door softly. She sat on the back steps and prayed before she dialed. The call connected quickly. One ring, two rings, three… "Hello?"

"Hey."

"Megan?"

"Yeah, it's me." Ron sighed deeply. "Thank you. Are you OK?"

"I'm sorry that getting married was a mistake. The only way to fix it is to undo it, but I don't know how to do that without screwing up everybody's lives." Megan was crying, choking out each word.

"Whoa, whoa. Slow down. You haven't screwed up my life."

"Not yet. But divorce is going to taint all of us."

Ron sat up in the darkness and tried to imagine where Megan was sitting and what she had been thinking the past two days. "Honey, please stop saying that. No one is going through a divorce…"

"Yes. Yes, we are. I know I made a huge mistake but we can undo this. Please, go home before we come back."

Megan heard the comforters rustle. "I *am* home."

Megan waited for Ron to continue. When he hesitated, she put her thumb over the "off" button on her phone.

"Please don't hang up. Talk to me."

Megan took her thumb off the button and tried to talk. Words would not come.

Ron tried to wait patiently. "Are you there?"

"Yes."

Good. She was going to stay with him on the phone, at least for now. Ron had so many questions, but he took Tom's advice and refrained from asking them. He sat up in bed and switched on the lamp. A red light was blinking on the cradle where the cordless phone had been. "Why is this red light blinking on the phone thing?"

"Missed call. You can scroll through caller I.D. and see who called but you have to wait until you're off the phone."

"Will you talk to me, Meg?" When he was tired, Ron's voice was husky and his Okie twang thickened. Megan smiled at his use of the nickname no one else ever called her. She cleared her throat and thought of all the things she needed to say to him, but fear gripped her heart. She knew she was taking the coward's way out, but he could never accept the truth.

"Ron?"

"Yes?"

"It's just not going to work."

"Stop saying that." Ron regretted the admonition. He needed to listen instead of offer a solution. He reached over and picked up his Bible and flipped to the eighteenth chapter of Proverbs.

"What are you doing?"

"Looking something up in my Bible."

Megan sat up straight. He didn't use his Bible when she was there. She wondered if he knew where to find it. What was he looking up? "What are you looking up?"

"The Proverb for today."

Megan raised an eyebrow. She walked down the steps, turned around and rested her rear end on the front bumper of her truck. "Find anything good in there?"

"It says if God gave me my wife, it's a good thing."

"What if He didn't?"

"It doesn't say anything about that."

"Don't you think maybe we were both so lonely that we were willing to believe that God was saying what we wanted to hear? It's possible we don't have God's blessing in all of this."

But He certainly doesn't want us to fix it by doing more harm, Megan! Ron managed to keep quiet until she went on.

"Ron, we're grown-ups. Let's admit defeat and move forward. We'll all recover."

"I just don't think this is the answer. I love being part of this family."

"And you still could be! It's not like we're not friends. I just don't think we should have become..." Megan's voice trailed off.

"Say it."

Megan blew out a deep breath. She couldn't say the word. She couldn't expose herself so blatantly. "I was going to say 'married.'"

Ron doubted that, but he didn't say so.

"I love you, Megan."

Megan felt trapped by his admission. "I think I'm losing my mind." Megan wiped her nose on her sleeve. "I have to go."

"I'll call you tomorrow."

"Goodnight, Ron." Megan pushed the red button. She walked back to the steps and asked God the question she had not yet dared voice.

"Where does Chris end and Ron begin?"

Chapter 27

"Mr. Wellbourne, may I ask you a question?"

Ron tapped his pen several times before lifting his head. For years, he and Teresa had gotten along as executive and administrative assistant without ever crossing the firm line Ron had drawn when he had hired her. His getting married had blurred that line. Having a woman in his life amused his secretary.

Ron was not up to small talk. He tried to keep the irritation out of his voice while he picked up a document to show he was in the middle of something. He looked up at Teresa. "Quickly."

"Are you alright? I know we've never talked about anything personal, but you look awful."

Teresa looked as uncomfortable asking the question as Ron felt in answering it, so he took pity on her and as gently as possible said, "I'm not discussing my health, physical or emotional, in the office. Please respect that."

Teresa looked somewhat relieved. "Yes, Sir. Just know that if I can do anything, I'm at your disposal."

"Thank you." Ron picked up a fax he had just received

and held it out over his desk. "Make four copies of this for my ten o'clock. That should get me to lunchtime." Ron gave his secretary a weak smile. Teresa took the papers then made her way back to the reception area, closing the door behind her.

Ron took off his reading glasses and swiveled his chair so that it faced the window. He chewed absently on the left earpiece while he tried to identify the emotions swirling around in his heart.

A little anger, a lot of frustration, fatigue, some confusion mixed in. Two years ago, this would not have been an issue. His life was as compact as the drive between the Wellbourne's home and this office. He did not wake up sad because he was alone; no one questioned him. It was a simpler existence.

But it had not been enough. Even with all his professional and financial success Ron's life had been hollow until Megan had stepped into it.

Less than five weeks ago, he had gotten his first "Ron's home!" greeting, complete with hugs at the knees and "Look what I made for you!" The moment had made him wonder how he had ever lived alone. His suppertimes had become social events, complete with fresh jokes from the library's repertoire and a straw poll to choose the evening's movie. Having a family was filling a void Ron had ignored for far too long.

And having a wife had filled him to overflowing with all Ron had ever longed for. The sight of that coltish beauty curling her long legs under her as she settled in for their movie each night took Ron's breath away. Seeing her eyes when she laughed at Chad's jokes or smelling her hair as she leaned over him to find a puzzle piece was intoxicating. Long before they married, Ron and Megan had become close friends, happening upon common interests and finding that opposites not only attract but often complement each other.

He'd had a deep respect for the beautiful young mother, but nothing could have prepared him for the bond he'd felt with her now that they had lived as husband and wife. Holding her and touching her had completed him. He never wanted to be alone again.

But alone he was. Their conversation last night had not helped him understand Megan any more clearly. Ron still had no clue when, if ever, Megan intended to come home. He knew enough about her mother and the size of her home to know that Megan could stay gone if she chose, leaving her own home and possessions behind.

If Ron had learned anything about Megan in the past year, it was that she was not attached to material things. Chris's illness had taught her to prioritize, and things money could buy were very close to the bottom of Megan's list of things that were important. She would live in her mother's outhouse if she thought it was in her children's best interest.

Ron rubbed his temples at the thought. Maybe simplicity was best. He certainly never had to sit in his office and worry about his home before he fell in love.

Sadness slowly replaced the small bit of anger that Ron had managed to muster. He didn't want simple; he wanted his family. He hoped Megan would answer if he tried to call her tonight, fighting the urge to call her now.

Finally Time to Dance

More than likely, Megan had the children circled around her, monitoring their lessons and answering their questions. He'd leave his family to their work and get back to his own.

"Mr. Wellbourne?" Ron had ignored Teresa's soft knock. He turned absently toward her. "Here are those copies." Teresa laid the papers on his desk. "What time will you leave for Stratford? Someone called from Galveston wanting to squeeze in a teleconference before you head out."

Ron turned his chair back to face his desk. He placed his glasses back on the end of his nose and gave it some thought. Stratford? Only thirty minutes away. "Set it up. I can eat on the way." Then Ron had an idea. "What's the weather supposed to be like, today?"

"Indian summer. Sunny and seventy degrees."

"Better enjoy it while we can. You know what they say: If you don't like the weather in Oklahoma, give it an hour."

"Yes, Sir. In fact, they're predicting snow by next week."

That settled it. "Make sure we can get the teleconference done by twelve-thirty. I need to stop by my parents' before I head out."

"Anything else?"

Ron gathered the copied faxes and lined up the reports for his ten o'clock meeting. "That should do."

Teresa left to ready the conference room with water and coffee. Mr. Wellbourne was looking more like himself.

....

Ron called Mabel from his Jeep. "Hello?"

"What's for lunch?"

"Well, it depends. Do you want something fresh or leftovers?"

"Whatever's quick. I'm stopping by to get my car. I just have a minute."

Mabel teased playfully, "Taking your new bride to lunch?"

His mother would never have hurt him intentionally, but her words stung Ron. "No, it's business. Listen, if you don't have something ready, it's no big deal. I can come back to town and drive through somewhere."

"Nonsense! I'll have something waiting for you."

Ron wished he had not set himself up to spend time with his parents right now. Tears were threatening to spill over and his frustration was mounting. He took a deep breath as he pulled his Jeep to a stop beside the garage. He turned off the ignition and reclined against his headrest. "Focus, Wellbourne. You have a meeting in forty-five minutes."

He stepped out of his Jeep and walked around to the gray metal door on the side of the garage. The door had remained unlocked when Ron lived a few feet away, but Mabel felt better keeping it locked, now. Ron took out his key ring and unlocked the door.

He lifted the garage door from inside the large, hollow room and squinted in the bright light that streamed in. *Megan would love a drive in the sunshine.*

Finally Time to Dance

Once behind the wheel, Ron cleared the seat beside him to make room for his briefcase. He held Megan's baseball cap in his hand. She used it like a purse, storing her ponytail holder and bubble gum in the hat turned upside down. Ron loved watching her relax beside him. When she leaned back against the seat and closed her eyes with her chin tipped up, Ron felt like he was helping her somehow, providing her a place where she could escape from her responsibilities for a little while. When they were in here, he felt like he was taking care of Megan. In her world, it wasn't that easy.

He took his time starting the car and letting it warm up in the garage before easing it onto the driveway. He parked it in the shade near the back door and made his way to the kitchen for lunch.

"How is he?" Stan was moving his wheelchair back and forth, trying to see around Mabel. She had pulled back the sheer when she'd heard Ron pull up. Mabel had heard from Gladys at the Greenhouse that Megan was out of town. Ron had insisted that Megan and the children were home and doing well when she'd spoken to him about it yesterday morning.

If Ron had lied, he wouldn't be able to keep it up for long. He was cut from better cloth than that. But what really disturbed Mabel was that if he was hiding Megan's sudden departure, there was trouble afoot.

"Hush. He's coming up the walk." Mabel pushed Stan to a more believable angle in the sunroom so they would appear as though they had been coming to the door to greet him.

Finally Time to Dance

"Hey, guys." Ron hugged his mother and then leaned down to embrace Stan. "How are you doing today, Dad?"

"Nothing to complain about here. Come in. Suzie has your lunch ready."

Ron walked into the small dining area and was pleased to see only one place setting. If his parents weren't eating with him, he'd be on his way more quickly. He sat down and took a long drink of the sweet iced tea. Suddenly, Ron didn't feel like eating. *God, please help me. I don't want to break down right here in front of the folks. Help me find something to talk about.*

God rescued Ron with last evening's newspaper. Stan wheeled over to him and held out the folded pages. "Have you seen this?" Ron looked at the headline, "Local Businessman Runs for State Senate." The picture looked only vaguely familiar, but Ron recognized the name.

"Isn't that your buddy from Kiwanas?"

"Yes. Yes, it is. I never thought John would get into politics." Stan continued to chat and flip through the paper pointing out headlines to Ron. Ron enjoyed the conversation and smiled at his dad warmly when he was done with his lunch.

"Thanks, Dad." Ron stood and tugged on his jacket. Mom, lunch was great." Ron patted Stan's hand and gave Mabel a hug. They knew something was wrong.

But his parents were being the same they had always been to him: solid rocks. He loved them for the way they were both desperately trying to stay out the way and let Ron sort this out on his own.

"I've gotta head out, but I'll call you this evening." Ron walked back through the sunroom toward the door.

Mabel checked a tear that threatened to fall. "We're here if you need anything."

Ron turned and looked at them. "You always have been." He slipped out the door and headed to his car.

Chapter 28

"You gonna sleep all day and let these babies teach theyselves school?"

Megan sat up at the familiar voice. From the smell of things, her children had already eaten breakfast, maybe even lunch. "I'm up." Megan slid her feet into her slippers and padded into the kitchen.

"Mommy!" Krissy charged at her mother and hugged her legs tightly. "I go school, too!"

Megan looked around the kitchen. At some point after she'd talked to Ron, Megan had a few lucid moments and came out here to put their school work out. At home, she usually put out a folder for Krissy with coloring sheets or connect-a-dots. Having neither the strength nor the resources to get Krissy's work together, she had just skipped it. Hessie had stood in the gap.

"We doin' home-ec." Hessie was holding the can of baking powder. She pointed to the measuring spoons in Krissy's hand. "Now get back on up here and finish these muffins with ol' Hessie."

Krissy gladly obliged and went back to spooning

ingredients into Hessie's mixing bowl.

"Hi, Mom." Randy gave her a hug. "I already read three pages of reading. Ali helped me with the hard words. I'm almost ready to answer the questions in the workbook."

"Thanks, bud. Keep going." Yikes. They were teaching themselves this morning. Megan walked over to watch Chad attempt a cursive lowercase "f." "Need some help?"

Chad gave her a crooked smile. "It's harder than it looks." Megan borrowed a pencil from Ali's box and slowly wrote one for him. When his face was still uncertain, she made several more until Chad's face finally brightened. "Thanks, Mom!" She loved teaching Chad. He either got it or he didn't and when he did, the whole room knew about it.

Megan smiled and ran her hand through his hair. Ali was enthralled in history, so Megan left her undisturbed. She looked around for Lily.

"That other little one is primpin'. Never seen such fussin' over five-year-ol' hair." Hessie was shaking her head while she showed Krissy how to stir batter without making it slosh over the sides of the mixing bowl.

"Thanks for getting them started." Megan spooned sugar into a mug then poured Hessie's strong coffee over it. She stirred the hot liquid, held the cup up to her nose and breathed in, "There's no place like home; there's no place like home."

Hessie decided not to remind Aimee Jr. that her home was six hundred miles away. Instead, she chuckled at Megan's joke then tried to address the bags under the young woman's eyes.

"That may very well be, but you goin' upstairs tonight. I heard you up all night, back and forth. That ol' sofa's all lumpy. You need to lay in a real bed. No arguin'."

Megan wouldn't dare argue with Hessie. She never had. Nor would she correct her and tell her that the sofa had not kept her awake; Megan's own fears had done that damage. "That's a great idea." Megan looked at Ali and Chad, "When you guys are at a stopping point and ready to brush your teeth and get dressed, we'll move our stuff upstairs. I'll show you where to sleep." Her children looked at Megan like she had three heads. "What?"

"Mom, it's noon. We brushed our teeth four hours ago." Ali looked at Megan with concern.

Megan was embarrassed. And still tired. Oh, good grief. "Well, then I guess it's time for a break. Everyone grab your bag and we'll go up and settle in."

Randy lingered until he was done with his reading and then raced off to pack his bag with Chad. Ali stayed in the kitchen a moment. "Mom?"

Megan could see her hesitating. "Yes? What is it, honey?"

"You look so tired. Again. Does your head hurt?" Megan had had migraines during her pregnancy with Krissy and the memory of her mother having to lie in a dark room to recover still disturbed Ali. Those months had been filled with hospital beds and medications for Chris, too. Seeing her only healthy parent helpless had scared Ali. She didn't want her mom to be sick again. Ever.

Megan tried to calm the fear she saw mounting in Ali's

eyes. "Yes, my head hurts, but it really doesn't feel like a migraine. In fact, I think my throat hurts even worse." Megan tried to clear her throat. Ali's frown deepened. "I'm just tired, Honey. We're moving upstairs to fix that, remember? Come on, let's get to work."

Ali seemed neither satisfied with the explanation nor enthusiastic about moving her belongings up the stairs. Megan tried to balance empathy with discipline. "What is it, Al?"

"Have you talked to Ron?"

Megan was relieved that she was not ashamed of the truth. "Yes, I called him last night." Megan saw Hessie lift and eyebrow and said to both concerned females, "He said he misses us."

Ali's face brightened. "He does? Maybe we can bring him something back from the drugstore in town. Last time we were here, they had lots of souvenirs."

"We'll go for a walk downtown after everyone is done with their schoolwork." Ali squealed over her mother's announcement and ran to gather her books.

"I've only got three things left to do!" She picked up her stack of work and made her way out of the kitchen.

"Where's everybody?" Lily had missed the announcement.

"Heading upstairs with their schoolwork. We'll work on your reading down here before we join them." Megan sat down at the table and opened Lily's reading book to today's lesson. She was going to take advantage of having Lily almost alone while she could.

Finally Time to Dance

"I brushed my teeth. See?" Lily flashed a wide smile and then opened her mouth to show her mother that the back ones were clean as well.

Megan looked down her nose to inspect them carefully under Lily's watchful eye. "Very good." Megan took in all of Lily. "Your hair looks nice, too." Lily had put a small star-shaped barrette over her right ear. It sparkled when she turned her head.

"Thanks. I only used one clippie thing. I saved the other one for Krissy."

"I appreciate that. You're a good big sister." Megan had seen Krissy take barrettes out of Lily's hair. It wasn't pretty.

"I brush my hair!" Krissy was off the kitchen stool and on her way to the bathroom before Hessie knew what hit her. "Now, what about these here muffins?" Hessie's help had abandoned her.

Megan smiled, saying, "Beauty calls."

Hessie laughed. "I guess you right." She began portioning the batter into the muffin tin. Without looking at Megan, she said, "You got some smart, well-mannered kids, Miss Megan." Her voice lowered a little. "Mr. Ron ain't gonna do them no harm. Let him be they daddy."

Megan had honestly thought she was cried out. Obviously she was wrong. Tears streamed down both her cheeks. "It's not that I don't trust him with the kids, Hess…"

"Now, don' try to tell ol' Hessie what she know. You tryin' to protect them. They fine. They just need they momma to accept the blessins' she done got from the Lord." Hessie put both her hands on the counter and tipped her head to the side.

"And lovin' Mr. Ron more don' mean you love Mr. Chris less." Hessie watched Megan fiddle with the corner of Lily's reading book. She looked like a little girl with first day of school jitters, crying and trying to find a way out of having to leave Hessie's safe kitchen. "I know what you done been through been hard, but Mr. Ron loves you.

Hessie walked over to Megan. "And his momma loves your babies. Stop pushin' away all that joy."

Megan wiped away a tear and looked at Lily. "Would you check on Krissy for me? She might need your help with her hair." When Lily was safely out of earshot, Megan told Hessie, "I dreamed about Chris last night. He seemed upset that I wouldn't let Ron move into my new house."

Hessie sat down and pulled Megan into the chair beside her. She began gently, "I know Mr. Chris prayed for you. I heard him myself.

"He prayed for them babies, too. Let God answer the man's prayers."

Megan got up and walked to the small window. "Did you hear what I said? Chris was upset with me for moving without him."

"I heard you." Hessie stood up and went back to her muffins. "That's the devil using his guilt to get you to doubt what you know. And what you know is that God is answering the prayers of a righteous man."

Megan pushed back the crocheted curtain. The day outside was bright and several small finches and wrens were gathered at Hessie's feeder.

"This seems more like your house than Mom's. You're the one who makes it feel like home."

"They say home is where the heart is. I say home is where your family is. Whether you in a mansion or a tent, you make your home when you have your kids and your people with you."

Hessie considered not admonishing the girl, but that's why Megan was still standing here. Miss Megan wanted to know what Hessie thought she should do.

Hessie breathed deeply and opened the oven door. "Your home, your family, is not under this roof. Your family is waiting for you, if you lucky, at your home. Up north.

"Now, get some rest so you have the strength to drive there tomorrow."

Megan let the curtain fall back over the window and turned to see Hessie's peaceful face. Her faithful friend. Megan could count on her mentor to tell her the truth, no matter how hard Hessie knew it would be for Megan to hear.

What Hessie did not realize, however, was that Megan was perfectly willing to go home and dissolve her marriage if she thought it would stop the pain she had felt for the past few weeks. Was that a guarantee? Would she feel better alone with her memories of Chris? Or would those memories haunt her even more?

One thing Megan did know for sure: Ron would never accept Megan sorting through a past life instead of building a new one. The decision would be made for her. Once Ron saw how much Megan still longed for Chris, he'd leave.

Lily and Krissy skipped into the room. Their matching hairdos made Megan smile. If not for the inch and a half difference in their heights, her youngest daughters would look like twins. Megan made her way back to the table. "You two look lovely. You're such big girls to be able to fix your own hair." Lily was beaming. "We'd better get started on reading, Lil. And Krissy, you'd better get those home-ec classes in today." Megan looked at Hessie as she continued, "We have to leave in the morning."

Hessie smiled and she shut the oven door.

Chapter 29

Megan pushed the button on her sun visor and watched the garage door go up. Dread overcame her as she realized Ron might still be awake. It was already dark but not late enough for Ron to have gone to bed. She had not planned to have to face him.

Their conversation last night had not gone as she planned. Megan begged Ron to consider moving back to his cottage for a few weeks to give her space to sort through some of her emotions, none of which she cared to discuss with him right now. She told him how she had prayerfully considered Jane and Hessie's advice and was willing to try harder, but he would have to be willing to let her live alone again, at least for a while.

Ron, however, had been clear about his position in all of this. He would be here when his family came home.

"Megan, I love you. I don't know what's changed suddenly, but I'm going to be here while you work it out."

"But if you just let me work this all out first, I can be a better wife to you." *I can't love both of you at once.*

"You're already a great wife, Meg. *I'll be a better husband* if you let me help you through this."

Ron's reasonable, calm response had angered Megan. "I don't want your help, Ron. I have all the help I need. Get out of my house."

"It's our house. That makes sense to you when you're not tired and angry. We'll talk about this when you've had some rest."

Megan had hung up and tossed her cell phone into her purse. She spent most of the night trying to figure out how to convince Ron he was wrong. Even during the long drive home, Megan had mulled her arguments in her head over and over again. So far, she didn't have anything she could say that would make Ron understand that he'd be better off if he'd move out. Megan would just have to spend the next several days proving her point.

"We're back already!" Chad never ceased to be amazed at how many miles his mom could cover while he slept.

"It's over, Bud. This is our very own garage."

"Home, sweet home," Ali crooned.

The three youngest children were undisturbed by the excitement. Megan would have to carry them up the two flights of stairs to their bedrooms before she brought up all their bags. She was mentally calculating how much Ali and Chad could carry when she heard the back window of her SUV pop open.

Megan caught a glimpse of Ron in her rearview mirror. She grabbed several videos and two empty soda bottles and got out. She met Ron as he was walking into the house with a pillow and her overnight bag.

"I can get these things later. Go back to bed."

"I wasn't in bed," Ron's voice was gentle. "I'll go to bed after you're settled in."

Megan searched for a way to help Ron understand that he already had enough to do without helping her. He was busy enough with work and his parents before he took on the added responsibility of a needy wife. The sooner this was over, the better for all of them.

She looked at her two oldest children and held out an overnight case. "Go up and get your teeth brushed. Your stuff is in here." The two sleepy children obeyed without question.

"Mommy?" Lily was rubbing her eyes.

Megan turned her attention to the bleary child. "Hey, ladybug. We're home."

"Where's Joy?"

Megan scooped up her five-year-old daughter and pointed to the white teddy bear that had fallen on the garage floor. "She's right there looking for you."

Ron handed the bear to Lily. Megan avoided his gaze, but Lily smiled and thanked Ron with, "Thanks, Dad." She held Joy close to her and snuggled back into Megan.

Lily's comment left Ron and Megan both speechless. Megan had not realized Lily had ever considered calling Ron 'Dad.' None of the children had ever called Ron that term of affection. She'd been home three minutes and losing ground every second.

Ron touched Megan's cheek gently, brushing away the

tear that had spilled over. He tried to reason with his wife. "It's too late to call it quits quietly. We made a commitment in front of these children and everyone we know. We won't just be hurting each other. We'll be hurting all of them, too."

Megan cleared her scratchy throat and made sure Ron was looking at her before she answered. "I'm not saying we call it quits right away, but surely you can see that I need some space, Ron. I don't know which way is up."

"Put Lily to bed. I'll take all these things up and we'll talk about this later. Right now, you need some sleep." Ron touched her cheek again. "You feel warm."

Megan had wondered if she was coming down with something, but for now she wouldn't give Ron the satisfaction of being right about anything. "I'm fine," she almost hissed.

"OK. But Lily needs you. Go up. I'll get Krissy and Randy."

Megan tried to figure out how she could argue and tell Ron that she would put her children to bed herself, but the mere thought of climbing the stairs more than once made Megan want to sit down and cry. She had to admit at least temporary defeat. "Thanks."

Forty-five minutes later, all five children were tucked into their beds and the suitcases were lined up in the hall. It was just after eleven.

Megan stretched and yawned as she said, "I guess I'd better get ready for bed." She walked into their bedroom and headed for the closet. Ron followed her. Without commenting, he watched her look for a suitable ensemble for bed. Megan stood in front of the empty rack and folded her arms. "Where are my nightgowns?"

"You don't wear them. Not really. I want you comfortable in your own home, Megan. Wear what you would usually wear to bed before I moved in."

Megan turned and glared at Ron. He couldn't even appreciate the small things she was doing to try to please him. Why was he turning her world upside down? "But I wasn't married then. I at least want to look nice for you."

"You'd look nice to me in a paper bag. You're a gorgeous woman, Megan."

Megan looked away. She did not want his affection. As long as she didn't see his face, Megan could convince herself he didn't mean it. She walked over to her dresser and began opening drawers.

Ron put his hands in his pockets and tried to think of a way to cross the distance between them. "Can I fix you something to drink?"

Megan fished out a t-shirt and gym shorts. Her head was spinning. She felt like there was a cotton ball in her throat. She'd rather have chewed nails than ask for a favor, but her energy was waning fast. "Could you put some ice water on my nightstand?"

"You bet. Anything to eat?"

Megan's stomach lurched at the thought of food. "I'm ok."

Once they were both in bed, Megan closed her eyes and thought back on the past several weeks. The most vivid memory, unfortunately, was the dream about Chris. Megan let her mind wander to the possibility of Chris actually showing up and seeing what she had done.

Had she really done anything to be ashamed of? *God, did I really want Chris to go away? I don't think I did, but maybe You didn't heal him because of my selfishness.*

Megan let the tears fall to her pillow. Ron picked his head up and pushed his own pillow toward Megan. He offered, "Wanna share?"

Megan shook her head slightly without opening her eyes.

"If you change your mind, there's plenty of room for you." Ron stroked Megan's hair and watched her fall asleep.

……………………..

"I made a nine-thirty appointment, but I don't know how long we'll be. With her fever so high, he may want to admit her for a day or two, anyway." Megan wondered whom Ron was talking about. Which one of the girls was sick?

"Don't worry, dear. The children and I will be fine. This old girl can order a pizza if she gets in a jam."

What was Mabel doing here? And which girl was sick? Why had Ron made an appointment without telling Megan? Ron would need Megan's consent to get medical treatment for one of the girls.

Megan tried to sit up so she could set Ron and Mabel straight. The room was dark except for the small lamp next to the sofa. Megan fumbled for the water glass on her nightstand. The sound of breaking glass startled her.

Ron came over and grabbed Megan's hand, moving it away from the nightstand. He whispered, "Lay back down, Meg. Don't try to get up." Ron's voice was louder when he said, "Get another glass of water for her, Mom. Ali can tell you where to find a straw."

"Oh, good. Ali's not sick. Is it Lily or Krissy?"

Ron could barely understand Megan's rambling. "What about Krissy?"

"Is she sick? Or is it Lil?"

"The girls are fine."

Megan was relieved. But who had a fever? Who was going to the doctor?

"Can you hear me, Megan?"

"Yes."

"I'm taking you to see Dr. Nolan. Your temperature is way up."

Megan sat up straight at this announcement. She opened her eyes to show Ron she was serious, but she winced at the pain caused by the dim lamplight. Ron turned off the lamp and said sternly, "Don't try to fight me right now. You have to see a doctor. Mom's here to stay with the kids."

"But Stan..."

Mabel chimed in, "Not to worry, Dear. Suzie has Stan well in hand." Mabel opened the door and spoke to Ron. "Now, shoo. I have to get this dear girl dressed."

"We're married, Mom. I can help you. Grab those clothes on the sofa."

Embarrassment overcame Megan as she realized that Ron and Mabel were discussing getting *her* dressed. Megan swung her feet over the side of the bed and stood up to show them she could fend for herself. The room spun slowly as Megan's ears began to ring. Megan put her hands on the sides of her head in an attempt to squelch the sound. Suddenly, the ringing stopped. Then the room went black.

Chapter 30

The beeping of the IV pump woke Megan. She struggled up out of the low recliner and made her way over to the machine. Tired and disoriented, she tried to remember coming to the hospital. Megan pressed the correct buttons, but the incessant noise continued.

"Looks like they found one you can't fix, huh?" Chris's voice startled Megan. "Why are we back here?"

"I know. Another hospital stay. Don't get so discouraged. I know you thought I had died." Chris sat up and tucked the hospital blankets under his knees. "I couldn't stand the idea of disappointing you, so I told them just to let you believe it was true." Chris reached for Megan's hand. "Kind of a relief, wasn't it?"

"I won't lie and say I wasn't relieved the day it happened. Or should I say the day I *thought* it happened? But I wish you could have seen yourself. You couldn't even talk. Or eat." Megan began breathing rapidly, trying to keep herself from crying. *How can I make him understand?*

"Chris, you're temperature was a hundred and seven. Under your arm!" Megan was sobbing, now. "You turned

Finally Time to Dance

gray, honey. The funeral home people, the nurse, Pastor Mike, everybody. We all assumed you had died."

Megan backed away from Chris and wiped her face with her sleeve. "How could we have all been wrong?"

"It's what you all expected to have happen. You were waiting on it." Chris picked up the remote control and turned on the television.

Frustrated, Megan paced the room several times then stopped at the foot of the bed and stood between Chris and the television. "We did everything we could, baby. We did. All the chemo, all the radiation, all the pain meds." Megan stood taller with resolve. "And we prayed. I never prayed for anything but God's will all those months, all those *years*!" Megan touched Chris's feet and rubbed them gently. They did not feel the same as they used to.

"Chris, look, you did die. I know that." Megan came around the bed and sat on the edge. She took Chris's left hand. She noticed his wedding ring was missing. Of course it was. It was sitting in her jewelry box at home.

God, find the right words for me. Several moments passed before Megan spoke again. "Do you remember the night Dee came by real late?"

"Right after the last diagnosis?"

Megan smiled at Chris. "No, not then. She came again and kept me company all night after you had been in hospice care a few weeks." Megan laughed at the memory. "She pretty much ordered me into the tub and gave me a timer. I wasn't allowed out until I had been in there at least twenty minutes."

"I remember that." Chris laughed and laid his head back on the pillow. "You girls giggled until late. But then didn't the conversation turn serious?"

Megan put Chris's hand under the covers and said, "Yes, it did."

"Remind me what you talked about."

Megan took a deep breath. "We talked about a lot, I guess. But the upshot of it was that I told her that you and I had talked and that we felt so blessed."

"Why?"

"Because we had lived a happy life together." Megan twisted her long hair into a bun. "Because we had no regrets." Megan looked straight at Chris when she said, "Because we had been as happy as two people could be and were going into the home stretch of our marriage knowing that.

"I told her we were content and happy accepting God's will." Tears fell shamelessly down Megan's cheeks.

"That's still true, you know. We still don't have any regrets. We accepted God's will, together."

Megan wiped at one eye with her index finger. "Then why do you keep accusing me of being relieved that you died?"

"Because you need to understand the difference between the kind of relief where you're just thankful I'm dead so you can collect a huge insurance policy, and the kind of relief where you're happy that we made it through the home stretch together and I'm not in pain anymore."

Megan caressed Chris's beard. "You were so sick."

"Not anymore."

"I miss you."

"God's using your new life to heal that, Megan. Let Him do His job."

The door to the hospital room opened and Megan looked up. The room had grown dim and she couldn't make out the figure in the doorway. "Who's there?"

"Well, well, look who's awake. Your husband will be thrilled. I'll go get him as soon as I check your vitals."

Megan looked panicked as she asked, "Who are you?" She looked around for Chris. *And why am I in the bed?*

The nurse just smiled. "My name is Betty. I'll be your 'cruise director' for the rest of your voyage." Betty could still see the confusion in Megan's eyes. She tried explaining more.

"I was trying to make light, Mrs. Wellbourne. You're at Ada General Hospital. Dr. Nolan admitted you yesterday. You have a full-blown case of mono, which is not cause for hospitalization typically, but he says you passed out at home. You were dehydrated."

Betty touched Megan's IV line and punched several buttons on its electronic pump. "We're getting you filled back up with lots of goodies, here. Not much can heal mono except time. Doc Nolan plans to see to it that you have plenty of time and a few medications so that you can recover here."

Megan could see that Betty was doing everything she could to put Megan at ease. For the nurse's sake, Megan tried to relax, but she was angry and confused. No one had her permission to put her in a hospital bed. If she had mono, she should have been sent home to recover. "Where are my children?"

Betty smiled kindly. "Mr. Wellbourne told me that those would be the first words out of your mouth." She took Megan's hand and leaned over the bedrails. "They're fine. Mr. Wellbourne told me to tell you that your mother and Hessie have things well in hand."

The room was spinning and Megan tried to breathe steadily. "My children are with my mother?"

Betty squeezed Megan's hand and laughed, "And Hessie..."

Megan ignored her addendum. "God help us all."

Betty chuckled. "That's my girl."

"He told me you had spunk. It's good to see it coming through already." Betty let go of Megan's hand and picked up her clipboard. She needed to work quickly so Mr. Wellbourne could see his wife. The poor man had not left the floor since his wife had been admitted.

Megan wondered which 'he' thought she had spunk, Ron or Dr. Nolan. Since Ken Nolan was her Sunday school teacher, he was as likely as Ron to have seen Megan's feisty side. Megan refrained from asking. She'd find out soon enough.

Betty looked at her watch. "It's ten o'clock in the morning, Mrs. Wellbourne. I'll be here until three this afternoon. I have orders to cater to your every need and see to it that you rest." Betty handed the call button to Megan. "Please do not move a muscle without this."

Megan groaned at her orders.

"I know you're a nurse, so I'll play fair. I'll let you fend for yourself if you call me and let me be in here when you do it. Deal?"

Megan saw no other choice. Besides, it wasn't Betty's fault she was being imprisoned. Megan would save her wrath for her captors. She took the button from the woman and set it on the bed near her hand. "Deal."

"Thank you." Betty got the blood pressure cuff off the wall and began getting Megan's vitals. "They said you'd be a handful, but you seem pretty nice to me."

Megan rolled her eyes. "Just keep pretending you're not siding with them."

Betty held Megan's wrist between her fingers while she looked at her watch. "Whatever keeps your vitals normal."

"Good girl." Then a thought occurred to Megan. She looked for Betty's nametag. "Are you on staff?"

Betty smiled at her new friend. "You're good." Betty considered lying but opted to earn Megan's trust, instead. "I'm private duty. I get off at three while Mr. Wellbourne takes over or decides that the lovely nurses employed here can do the job. Then I'm back at eleven so he can stay at home with the kids."

Betty touched Megan's hand and leaned closer. She lowered her voice as she said, "I've never seen these kinds of strings pulled. Your husband would not rest until you had your own nurse. The hospital can't even do that in ICU. So, Dr. Nolan finally let him hire me through a private agency."

Betty gathered her stethoscope and clipboard. "I'll go get your husband. Go easy on the man. As far as I can tell, his biggest weakness is how much he loves you." Betty raised her eyebrows at Megan. "It makes a fool out of the man."

Megan wiped a tear from her cheek.

Betty patted her hand and left to go get her boss.

Megan found the right button to adjust the lights in the room. Then she raised the head of her bed and took in her bland surroundings. Her frustration waned as she looked around to see the amount of effort someone had made to make her feel at home.

A fun, funky black and white picture Megan had taken of all five children was propped up on her bedside table in its popsicle stick frame. After a particularly grueling day of home school about six months ago, Megan had taken her gang for a walk through campus. When she had seen all five of them monkeying around in a tree, she'd pulled out her digital camera and snapped the shot. The result was a late afternoon of printing the pictures out at home and then making frames for each child's favorite picture. Megan smiled at the big fun she and her children managed to have with small things.

Several crayon drawings were taped to the wall across the room. Megan couldn't make out the detail of each one, but it was obvious which child's drawing was which. Lily's was a rainbow. Krissy had traced her hand. Randy and Chad had drawn superheroes, and Ali had sketched a design of a fabulous evening gown, complete with matching accessories.

So, they were well. Megan wondered at their reaction to being told their mother had been hospitalized, but it couldn't have been all bad if all five of them had made her pictures.

Finally Time to Dance

Someone had handled it well.

Next, Megan noticed a small glass box. She reached over and picked it up gingerly. She lifted the lid to find the same small mints she kept in her desk drawer at home. The candies were not easy to find. Megan bought them from a small local gift shop that carried the mints only part of the year. She marveled that someone had gone to the trouble to find some for her and put them in the beautiful dish.

Finally, Megan saw what she'd hope to find near her. The one item she never woke without. She tried to pick up her soft, worn Bible, but it was too heavy for her to lift from the bed. Megan laid her hand on the thick volume and closed her eyes. She thanked God she was alive and asked Him to help her remember to be thankful rather than spiteful about her current plight. She thought of several passages within her Bible that told of pruning and growing. Other passages told of trials and valleys. Still others chronicled lessons learned from mistakes and discipline.

But, in the end, the ultimate lesson God taught in His Word was the Good News. His gospels and His promise of return. Because Megan believed the Bible was true from cover to cover, she knew she had never been without hope, without joy, without protection. She prayed she'd have the strength to claim those promises in the days to come. Megan was dozing softly as she meditated on familiar passages when she heard the door click open.

Ron was wearing faded jeans and a t-shirt he'd gotten when he had taken the boys to father-son camp last summer. His face gave away the fact that he had not shaved in at

~ 272 ~

least two days, and his eyes were red from lack of sleep. But somehow he looked peaceful, happy. Relieved. "You're awake." Megan saw Ron move toward her before he hesitated and put his hands in his pockets. He walked over to her bed looked at his wife longingly. "I missed you."

Megan took her hand from her Bible and reached out to him. Ron gratefully held it in both of his. "Did I really sleep for twenty-four hours?"

She saw several tears fall to Ron's cheeks. "Yes. I wound up calling an ambulance and they brought you straight here. Ken met us in the ER."

"I can't believe I put everyone to all this trouble..."

Ron kissed Megan's hand. "I'm just glad you came home when you did."

Megan nodded and then lifted her arm, motioning to the tubes tethering her to the IV pump. "Is all this really necessary?"

Ron's face became stern. "You've lost twelve pounds since we had our marriage license blood tests done. Your blood counts were way up. You needed hydration and we needed to be sure it was *only* mono. When Ken saw you, he was concerned we were dealing with more."

Megan felt her heart race. She tried to keep the alarm from her face. "And?"

"So, far, so good. There are still a few tests out, but it looks like you're just exhausted." Ron stroked her hair. "Meg, you're gonna have to rest, honey."

"So, you put me away at the General Hospital?" Megan tried to sound playful.

Ron used his best Okie accent. "Now, lookie here, ma'am. There's a line of people from here to the next county waiting to get into this spa. I had to pull quite a few strings to get you these accommodations." Ron motioned to the bare walls and small television.

"Ha. You'll never convince me this is what's best." Megan sat up a little more to show Ron she was serious. "I could have had IV therapy *and rest* at home. You could have even brought *Betty* with us." Megan tucked the thin blanket under her knees. "This is conspiracy, plain and simple. And you know it." Megan folded her arms.

Ron leaned toward Megan and put his palms on her bed. He smiled and pressed his nose against hers. "Ah, the fire is back. Nolan said that would be a good sign. Might cut your stay down to a week."

"RON!" Megan pulled back indignantly. "You simply cannot hold me captive here a week!" Megan sat forward and tried to get up, but the room began spinning and a sharp pain shot through her head. She tried to recover, but things went out of control so quickly, Megan cried out in pain.

Ron pressed the call button. "It's ok, hon. I'm here. Come on, lay back." Ron lowered the side rail and repositioned Megan in the bed.

Betty was quickly at his side. "I see our lovely lady isn't convinced she needs to be here."

"I guess we have our work cut out for us."

"I'm still in the room," Megan whined.

Ron lowered his head so that his eyes were level with Megan's. "And to respond to your suggestion that you could rest at home, you'll have to prove that you can rest *here* before we let you go home to your own laundry and housework and school schedule and..."

"I hadn't even thought about the kids' school work. Ron, how are they going to manage? You can't just let them sit there and watch tv all day."

"Thanks for the vote of confidence."

Megan took several deep breaths in an effort to calm her rising temper. "It's not that simple, Ron. They have a routine. We have deadlines that have to be met. They took a few days off for the wedding. They'll get behind if we don't stay on task."

Betty quietly made her exit to give the Wellbournes some privacy.

"The nice thing about your children is that they have a wonderful teacher." Ron searched for a hint of a smile in the teacher's eyes. Seeing he wasn't going to get one, he continued, "We found all your lessons plans and Ali and Chad showed us how to print out their checklists.

"You have a fabulous system. We figured it out in a couple of hours. They're doing their school work right now."

"We?"

Ron drew the line at discussing his decision to let Aimee Harris help. The woman was willing, and able. She was the children's grandmother. It was time she spent more time with them. "We'll save that argument for after lunch."

"Chicken." Megan sunk into her pillow and tried not to look as exhausted as she felt.

She saw Ron smile while he smoothed her covers.

"Yeah."

Megan was drifting back off to sleep. "When can I see the kids?"

"I'll go get them in a few hours."

"Have they already been here?"

"No. I explained to them what happened." Ron lowered himself in the chair next to Megan's bed. "For the first time in my life, I slept with five other people in my bedroom. It was sort of like going to camp."

Megan was amused at the mental picture that conjured up. "You let them sleep in our bed?" Megan opened her eyes and regarded Ron carefully.

"The little ones did. Randy and Chad shared the sofa and Ali dragged her sleeping bag in and slept on the floor."

Megan closed her eyes and asked one more question. "Is my house a mess?"

"Not to me."

Megan snorted, "Great."

"You need sleep."

"Then stop talking to me."

Ron relaxed in his chair and pulled a light blanket over his legs. He reached back over to the bed and dimmed the light. *Thanks. That went better than I expected. But she's going to wake up fighting again. Give me patience. Lots of it.*

Chapter 31

Megan was putting the last of her belongings in her suitcase when Dr. Nolan knocked on her door. She beamed when she saw him.

"Thanks for springing me before Thanksgiving."

"You're most welcome." Ken Nolan bowed slightly. He put her chart under his arm and sat in the low chair next to her bed. "I've had reports of very good behavior from you," he teased.

Megan held up her right hand. "I promised to get rest while I was here, and I did. I also promise to rest when I get home."

The physician's face grew serious. "Megan, as a doctor in a small town, I have to define relationships more carefully than when I practiced medicine in Tulsa. For instance, with you, I have several relationships.

"We are, right now, doctor and patient. At church, we are Sunday school teacher and student. On Main Street, we're simply neighbors. But *always* we are brother and sister in Christ. So, we're going to have two separate conversations before you go, maybe three."

Megan smoothed her jeans and sat on the edge of the bed. "OK. Shoot."

"Let's start with doctor and patient, shall we?" When Megan nodded in the affirmative, he continued, "When you came to the ER five days ago, your physical health was something akin to what we would expect to see in a person who had been without food, water, and shelter for several days. We usually only see that state of shock and dehydration in people who've been in accidents and had to wait for help to come to them. I've seen something similar in a woman who chose to live for a week on the back porch of an abandoned house."

Dr. Nolan leaned forward to make his point to Megan. "No one with food and water and facilities accessible to them should have been in the state of deteriorated health you were in."

Megan held her head high. She would let him make his point. "But I was. What does that mean?"

"It means that you're fighting a losing battle with something. We've run every test imaginable and I have reason to believe the battle you're fighting is not physical. You're emotionally drained as well."

Megan struggled slightly for composure before she smiled at him as though she was accepting what he was saying calmly.

Megan steadied her gaze on Ken and he continued. "And now our conversation will change to that of teacher and student." Megan nodded.

"I know your history, what you've been through

personally, emotionally. You've handled the death of a husband and single motherhood so gracefully that I stand in awe of your faith and determination." Megan was pleased by his comments.

But there was a 'but' coming. This she could tell.

"But, it's time you admitted something." Megan smiled. "What?"

"It's time to grieve." Megan stood up. "That's ridiculous. I grieved. I, I..."

"Please sit or you're not leaving, today."

Megan folded her arms. "We're doctor and patient again?"

"I told you this wasn't easy."

Megan sat back down on the edge of the bed. "Go on."

"The third chapter of Ecclesiastes is familiar to you, correct?"

"Yes, very." Megan had read from that chapter at Chris's funeral, and a friend had given her a framed print of the verses. Megan went over the words in her mind.

There is a time for everything, and a season for every activity under heaven.

A time be born and a time to die,

A time to plant and a time to uproot,

A time to kill and a time to heal,

A time to tear down and a time to build,

A time to weep and a time to laugh,

A time to mourn and a time to dance,

There were more verses in the passage, but Megan was getting tired and they did not immediately come to her.

Her physician and teacher interrupted her thoughts. "I think you favor the parts of that Scripture that tell us there's a time to laugh and a time to dance, so you've spent the past three years dancing and laughing without taking time to cry and mourn."

Megan pondered his words and thought back over the past ten days. "It's funny you should say that. I've been thinking a lot about Chris, lately. Dreaming about him, actually. But I never realized how it was affecting my health."

"We can't discount the viral infection that's been at work in your body for at least fourteen days. That had a lot to do with your physical state, too."

"But it all works together?"

"Yes, you can't be your best emotionally unless your physical and spiritual health are both in order. Same goes for being your best physically and emotionally. The three types of health are closely related." Ken shrugged. "I would argue that they can't really be separated."

"So, my battle isn't just physical? Or just emotional?"

"Nor is it just spiritual." Dr. Nolan stood and walked over to Megan's open suitcase and picked up her Bible. "This is the heaviest thing I want you to lift for the next two weeks. Understood?"

Megan did a bad job of trying to hide her frustration. "I have five children who need me."

"Yes. And if you want to be here to raise them, you're going to follow orders." Ken lowered the Bible back into her suitcase. "Your body can't handle the kind of abuse you've put it through. It's going to have to recover.

"And mono is not a slight thing. You'll be recovering for months."

At this, Megan put her head in her hands. Ken was evidently willing to ignore her body language, as he plunged into another phase of their conversation.

"Which brings me to our brother and sister in Christ relationship."

Megan peeked at him through her fingers, bracing herself to hear more of the sobering truth.

"You're married. To Ron Wellbourne."

Megan picked her head up. She looked at Ken Nolan coldly. "And?"

"That's all." Ken looked at the floor and then back at Megan. "But the implications of that fact get tricky."

Megan swung her feet back onto her bed and lay back on the pillow. "I'm listening."

"He's been busy while you've been here. He's taken charge of your home."

Megan put her right forearm over her eyes. "And I'm supposed to thank him."

She sneaked a peek at Ken and saw a smile playing at his lips. "That may be a bit much to ask at first. Just start with accepting it."

"Oh good grief, Ken."

"Ron has done what he thought needed to be done for his wife and his family. He's the leader in your home, now. So his decisions are the right ones."

Megan processed this revelation. She uncovered her eyes and gave him a look of disdain. Ken continued. "And if you give him a hard time, I'll tell your mother she needs to stay through Christmas." Ken winked slightly.

Megan hooted with laughter. "And I guess the next thing you'll tell me is that if I wouldn't mind if she stayed through Christmas, you'd declare me healthy physically, spiritually, and emotionally."

Ken stood and tapped the bottom of Megan's foot with the chart. "I'll leave that kind of reckoning to God."

....

Ron and Megan had agreed her homecoming should be low-key. No balloons or visitors. No party. Being home would be celebration enough. Aimee had arranged to take the children to the library while Hessie stayed at the Wellbournes' home to help Ron get Megan settled in. By the time the children got home, Megan's bags were unpacked and she was napping peacefully.

Ali knew her mother well enough to ask Ron as soon as they arrived, "Can we wake her up?"

"Yes. She said to let you all in the minute you got in." All five children rejoiced in unison.

"But first," Ron began in a kind but firm voice, "there are a few rules you need to know."

"Like what?" asked Chad, folding his arms.

"Easy there, big guy." Ron rubbed Chad's arm. "Your mom is *very* tired." Ron looked at Ali and touched her shoulder. "She'll recover completely, but it will take a long time. And a lot of cooperation on everyone's part." Ron held up three fingers.

"I've got three simple things for you to remember. First, you can't make loud noises in our bedroom.

"Second, if you get on the bed, you have to be *very* still.

"And, third, don't ask Mommy to get up. She's supposed to stay in bed."

Ron looked at their faces and waited for them to process what he had just said. "Does that make sense?" When all five children nodded in agreement, Ron asked, "Do you promise to follow the rules?" Again, five heads nodded. "OK. In you go. *Quietly.*"

Aimee took in the exchange between Ron and the children then watched them go in to see their mother. Aimee was thrilled for her daughter. To have so many children who loved her so dearly. Heavens knew she had not learned her mothering skills at home. Apparently, God had provided an example somewhere.

Hessie shuffled by with an armload of towels and tossed them into the chute. "Them babies glad they momma home." She patted Aimee on the shoulder.

Hessie had been a large part of Megan's life. Oh, who was she kidding? Hessie had *been* Megan's life. If anyone was to thank for Megan Harris turning into the finest lady Aimee had ever met, Paul and Hessie were. Megan and Hessie likely knew that. Neither woman had ever said that to Aimee, but there was no need to overstate the obvious.

Ron came out the bedroom and shut the door behind him,

Finally Time to Dance

smiling. He put his arm around Aimee as he walked past her. "Let's see what's for dinner."

In her bedroom, Megan was still giving out kisses to her fan club. "I so glad you home, Mommy." Krissy was snuggled under the covers, careful to be very still just like Ron and Grandma had said.

Megan pulled the baby close to her. "Oh, me, too, Krissy. I missed you too much."

Ali was the most reserved of all of the children, but she was still genuinely pleased to see her mother home and looking less pale then when they had driven home from Grandma's house. She watched Megan for several minutes, trying to remind herself that Ron had said her mom would recover completely. "Do you have to go back to the hospital?"

"Not if I do what the doctor says," Megan assured her. Randy piped in with, "What does the doctor say you have to do?"

"Nothing."

Chad laughed, "That sounds easy!"

Megan rubbed his arm. "Yes, it does *sound* easy, but it's kind of hard for moms to do that."

"Why?" Megan wrinkled her nose. "Because we're not real good at it."

Ali smiled at her mother's admission. "But Ron's making it easy."

"Yeah, Mom," Lily giggled. "You don't have to wash dishes or clothes or teach us school or anything."

"I know." Megan regarded their faces carefully. "I heard

Grandma and Hessie are here."

"Oh, it's even better than that," Ali said excitedly. "Ron's got other people coming over, too. Someone to clean the bathrooms and change sheets. Someone else is taking care of your flowerbeds. And this lady comes and gets a list from Hessie or Grandma or Ron and does the shopping."

Megan's head was spinning with all of this information that she was certain Ron wanted to break to her a little at a time. She wanted to scream in protest, but it was no use.

Still, Megan was concerned that all this 'help' would spoil her children. "You're all not letting them do everything, are you?"

Randy answered his mother with a slight frown. "No. Ron makes us show Grandma our list of responsibilities. He even added two to Chad's and Ali's."

Megan wanted to ask what he had added but took Ken Nolan's advice instead. "Well, I'm certain if Ron put it on there, it's important. Obey him. And no complaining." Megan swallowed and worked hard at making it look like she believed what she had just said.

Thanksgiving Day dawned clear and bright. There was a hint of winter in the air and the Hardin children began speculating about when they would have snow.

"I can't wait to sled on the hill next to our house." Anything that involved speed excited Randy.

Ali was skeptical. "But don't we have to have the college's permission to sled on their property?"

"They wouldn't mind, would they, Mom?" Megan could

see that Chad was dying to sled that hill.

"We'll cross that bridge when it snows. Ali, if you'd like you can write down 'call Physical Plant' on that list and we'll see to it that we discuss the hill with the University." Megan was enjoying her little gang, but their combined volume was a little overwhelming this morning. She looked at Chad and mustered a British rogue.

"Oh, Master of the Remote, see if you can find us a parade on the telly." Megan smoothed her comforter. "The rest of you sit still or sit on the floor."

Megan wound up with a bed full of children who happily sat still and watched the huge floats hang over the streets of New York City.

Nurse Betty's services had been retained for Megan even now that she was home. She arrived early and worked around the mob in Megan's bed. A check of her vitals showed that having them close was apparently good for Mrs. Wellbourne. Confident her patient would be in good hands for the day, she left shortly before lunch to be with her own family.

Lunch was a cozy affair. The elder Wellbournes joined them, delighted to get more acquainted with Aimee and Hessie. All of the "mothers" had chipped in to prepare the meal, and it was served on a simply-set table in Ron and Megan's formal dining room.

The children took turns reading their "leaves" of thankfulness off the "Thankful Tree" Mabel had helped them make from a small branch. It was Mabel and Stan's first Thanksgiving as grandparents and they relished every moment.

Megan ate lunch with the family, agreeing to lift only her own fork. Krissy sat next to her mother, nibbling from her plate and chatting happily about Grandma and Mabel both being her grandmothers. The children asked the adults to tell what they would have written on their 'leaves.' When it was Megan's turn, she said, "Family. And around here that's a big deal." The room erupted in laughter and Stan offered a toast to Megan's homecoming.

....

The tap on her bedroom door woke Megan. Certain that Betty had arrived for the night shift, Megan sighed. She tried to be thankful that Ron cared enough to hire help, but good grief! A nurse in the house from eleven to seven was a little extreme. May as well accept it. "Come in." Megan sat up. "Mom?"

"Hello. I just wanted to say goodnight. I didn't want to interrupt earlier when you were reading to the children."

Megan scooted over slightly, making room for Aimee on the edge of her bed. She patted it softly. Aimee perched tentatively next to Megan. "It looks like I woke you."

Megan rubbed her eyes and laughed. "I'm glad. I feel like all I do is sleep."

"You need it, Sweetheart. You're body is trying to get well."

Megan studied her mother's face. It was nice to see a fresh

side of her. Megan wondered if some of her recent exhaustion stemmed from her relationship with Aimee.

Megan had spent most of her life pretending her mother's behavior didn't bother her, but since Paul's death, it had become a struggle to remain numb. Megan broke the not uncomfortable silence. "I'm glad Ron called you. Thanks for coming so quickly."

Aimee squirmed on the bed beside her. Megan saw her almost say something but Aimee stopped herself. Finally, she said, "It feels good to be helpful." Megan did not doubt the sincerity of her mother's comment, but she got the distinct impression that it was not what she had originally intended to say.

Aimee took Megan's hand lightly. "You have a beautiful family, Megan." Megan had to work hard not to deflect the compliment. Aimee had never affirmed her family when Chris was still alive, so her approval now made Megan somewhat sad.

Still, Megan could see the older woman was trying. "Thanks, Mom. I never would have dreamed that I'd have a large family, but it's so much fun." Megan giggled and sat up slightly. After a moment she continued, "I just wish I wasn't so sick. This is going to be hard for them, no matter how many people Ron hires to help."

"Well, I'm actually looking forward to the next couple of weeks. I had Ali direct me around a bit when we went to the library yesterday. She showed me the park. Chad had me drive by something called a 'skate board park.' It's going to be good to spend time with them. Get to know them, finally."

Megan couldn't hide her skepticism. She opted to crack open the nut. "Who are you and what have you done with my mother?" Megan wondered how her mother would respond. Fortunately, Aimee laughed. She held Megan's hand to her cheek.

"I deserve far worse from you." Megan saw tears welling up in Aimee's eyes. She touched her mother's other cheek with her free hand.

"No, you don't. I've kept you at bay long enough." Megan studied the lines in Aimee's face. When had she gotten to be in her seventies? "Friends?" The tears fell down Aimee's cheeks. She nodded her head in agreement.

Megan worded her next comment carefully. "They're smart, Mom. All kids are. They'll know if you're not sincere. Only make promises you can keep."

"I'm done disappointing children."

Megan had no proof that Aimee was capable of change, of loving unconditionally. *I'm going to choose right now to obey You, Father. I will honor this parent. Please protect my children.* "You can do it. They're easy to love."

"So are you, dear."

Aimee kissed Megan on the cheek and quietly made her way out of the room. Megan closed her eyes and went back over their conversation in her head. She wondered what Aimee had wanted to say about Ron calling her. A few moments later, Ron walked in and smiled at his wife.

"See? All tucked in. Not lifting anything. Not dusting or cleaning or checking on my children."

"Yes, you've been a very good patient." Ron kneeled next to the bed and put his head next to Megan.

"You look beat."

Ron's eyes were closed. "Yeah, I'm tired." He picked his head up and looked at Megan, resting his chin on her arm. "But it's a good kind of tired." He grinned. "It's so good to have you back here."

Megan wanted to say that it was good to be back, but she still had not had the time or the strength to sort through her feelings. For now, she was glad she and her children were safe. She'd think about the rest later. Right now, she had some lingering questions about Aimee.

"What did my mom say when you called her? She seemed a little weird when I mentioned it." Ron stared at Megan like she had three heads.

"I didn't call Aimee."

"Did Julie?"

"No." Ron looked concerned.

"Then who?"

Ron got up and sat on the edge of the bed. "No one called her. She and Hessie arrived a few hours after you and the kids. She told me you looked awful and she was worried that you would come home and work yourself to death trying to settle in to your new marriage. She said she figured she'd bring the only person you were likely to accept help from: Hessie." Ron looked thoughtful. "Aimee said she just came along for the ride and to keep Hessie company on the road, but I got the impression that she was the one who wanted to be here for you."

"Yikes." Beyond that, Megan was speechless.

"Don't try to figure it out."

"I won't."

"You sure?"

Megan thought for a few seconds then said, "You know, I am sure. I'm going to start with this one blessing. My mother is here and I am thankful. Period."

Ron looked skeptical. Megan patted his leg and said, "You can be my accountability partner." Ron kissed her forehead and went to closet to change for bed.

Another knock on the door kept Megan from giving the matter much more thought. "Grand Central Station. Come in."

"Oh, we're even spryer than before." Betty waltzed in, stethoscope and medications in hand.

"Hey there," Megan greeted her sleepily. "Sorry. It's been busy."

"We'll have no more of that. It's vitals, meds, then sleep."

Megan groaned, "Is this really necessary?"

"You have a nursing license. Is following doctor's orders absolutely necessary?" Betty worked as she talked, ignoring Megan's protests.

"Nolan's in on this, too? For how long?"

Betty flashed Megan an overly-sweet smile. "Here are your medications, Mrs. Wellbourne." Megan took the small cup and made a face at its contents before putting them in her mouth and rinsing them down with the water Betty held out for her. "Thank you." Betty gathered her supplies and laughed. "Anything else?"

"Are you really sleeping upstairs?"

Betty leaned in close to Megan. "Honey, this is the sweetest job in the world. Don't worry about me."

"What makes a job that takes you away from your family 'sweet'?"

Betty studied Megan a few moments and then began smoothing the covers while she talked. "My family is still in the making." Megan's brow furrowed in confusion.

Betty held out her left hand. "I'm engaged. We're getting married Christmas Eve. God gave me this job." Betty smiled sheepishly then added, "I'm getting the dress of my dreams." Megan's face brightened at that news. "And by late December, you won't need me around the clock, anymore. It's perfect."

Megan took Betty's hand and gazed at her engagement ring. It was a small solitaire set in white gold. It was simple, elegant. "It's beautiful. Congratulations."

"Thank you. I've always prayed for the right man. Since I was a little girl." Betty looked down at the ring. "I found him about a year ago." She looked at Megan. "I just hope he adores me as much as Mr. Wellbourne adores you. The man is crazy about you."

"So you've said." It seemed she was being reminded of that a lot, lately. Reminders were good. "Good night, Betty."

Satisfied that her patient was comfortable and safe, Betty turned off Megan's lamp and left the bedroom.

Ron emerged from the closet and crossed the room. He stretched his long frame under the comforters and sighed deeply. "Happy Thanksgiving, Meg."

Megan wondered at all she had to be thankful for. "Happy Thanksgiving, Ron."

Ron switched off his own lamp and turned on his right side to face Megan. He pulled his pillow over and scooted his head back to make room for Megan. He smiled at her gently.

Megan could not make herself speak or move closer to her husband. Her grief and fatigue still had her emotionally paralyzed. She picked up a magazine and pretended to read. Soon, she heard Ron snoring softly.

Megan watched him for several minutes. When she was sure he was sleeping soundly, she reached over and touched his left cheek. She looked at the amethyst ring on her own hand that Ron had bought for her during a day trip to Tortola on their honeymoon. This man did adore her. Ron had dragged her into several jewelry stores on the U.S. islands they visited, but she drew the line and refused to look at rings when they got to the British island.

"Really, Ron. My engagement ring is beautiful. You've spoiled me enough." They had spent the rest of the early afternoon shopping for the kids and Megan had found a great book on pirates for the boys. They were sipping soft drinks at a sidewalk café when Ron told her he needed to go back to an art gallery to look at a painting for his mother.

That night on the beach in St. Thomas, Ron and Megan were walking in the moonlight when he pulled her close to him and kissed her. He slipped a small box into her hand. "I want you to have this to remember this trip. And the beginning of our life together."

"I thought you went art shopping," Megan teased.

"I did. Mom's print is back in the room." He kissed her again. "But I went shopping for the love of my life, too."

The moment had indeed been magical, with the sliver moonlight reflecting off the Caribbean. They had stayed on the beach for hours before heading back to their room and sleeping with the patio door open so they could hear the ocean breeze. The next morning, they had departed for home. And their new life had gotten...less magical than that moment.

He deserved so much more than she could give.

She laid her hand on the side of his pillow he had offered her and drifted off to sleep.

Megan's soft snoring woke Ron. He kissed her fingers tenderly. *One step at a time. Thank you.*

Chapter 32

"Merry Christmas!" Ron Wellborne handed the festive basket to Liz Fairbanks. Ron had never been one to go all out for the holidays, but this year he felt like he needed to thank some people who had made the past several weeks of transition and uncertainty bearable. Liz and Tom Fairbanks were at the top of his list.

Liz smiled warmly. "And to you." She backed away from the door. "Please, come in."

Ron hesitated and then shook the snow from his trench coat and stomped the ice from his boots. "Thank you."

Liz took his coat and scarf and carried them to the guestroom before escorting Ron up the stairs. "How's your lovely wife feeling?"

Ron laughed. "More like her old self all the time. It's getting harder and harder to keep her in one place." Ron sat in Tom's leather chair. "Thanks for all you ladies have done to keep us afloat." Ron patted his stomach. "We especially appreciate all the goodies you've brought by."

"It's been our pleasure. We're still praying for all of you." Liz stopped near the kitchen. "I have warm cider. Can I get you a cup?"

Ron was still rubbing his hands together. "That's sound wonderful, thank you." He had not planned to sit and visit, but he decided to relax and ask Liz for some advice should the opportunity arise.

Liz came into the living room with two steaming cups of cider. She handed one to Ron and took the other to her chair across from him. "We're hoping you'll let her out long enough for her to come to Bible study next semester. We've missed her insight and encouragement."

Ron nodded and smiled. "We're negotiating her spring schedule. So far, she's made a list and she's trying to prioritize."

Liz returned his smile and then took a more serious tone. "You'll still keep help around the house, won't you?"

Ron lifted an eyebrow. "Yes, but my wife is not thrilled."

"And how are you dealing with that?"

Ron saw his opportunity to fish for that advice. "Quite frankly, Liz, not well."

Liz put down her cup and lifted her own eyebrow. "You're not supposed to play dead. You *can* react."

Ron nodded and stared at his steaming mug. "I do react. I just try to react kindly." Ron squirmed slightly in his chair and worded his next comment carefully. "She talks to me. I talk to her. But it's like we're not saying very much.

"I'm tired of being cordial. I want to confront her and find out what's wrong." Ron laughed as he said, "I can't believe I'm admitting this, but I want to see the fire come back in her eyes."

Liz watched Ron fidget with the arm cover on Tom's chair. He looked unsure about being ready for the spunky Megan to come back into his life. "She's come a long way, Ron. Keep being patient. God's working on her heart."

Ron's expression became even sadder. "She still doesn't have the stamina to go out to dinner and a movie or walk in the park like we use to." Ron gazed out the window. "I miss that. I want to laugh with her again."

"What can I do to help?"

Ron gave Liz a crooked smile. "Pray, listen. All the stuff you're doing already."

Liz thought about the Wellbourne-Hardin home. Ron really had been under a great deal of pressure to hold things together for his new family. Megan was out of her comfort zone, confined to bed and having little control over the care of her home and children.

They had both weathered it well, but it had not been a cake walk. Perhaps it was time for the Wellbournes to play! Liz smiled. "Actually, there may be more I can do. I have an idea…"

....

"MOM!"

Megan jumped at Chad's cry. She rounded the corner in the hall and ran into the screaming, hysterical child. "Honey, what is it? Slow down!"

Chad grabbed his mom's arms and shook her. "Tomorrow

Finally Time to Dance

is *Christmas Eve.*"

"Yes," Megan conceded. What's wrong?" She was looking Chad over for bumps or bleeding or reasons he might be in pain.

"Mom, it's *snowing!*" Megan tried to find Chad's exuberance charming, but she needed him to calm down and tell her why he was so excited.

Megan pulled Chad away from her and looked directly at him. "I know these things. What's *wrong*?"

Chad hugged his mom tightly and buried his head in her shirt. "I'm just so worried, Mom. What if there's no snow left tomorrow? What if it all melts? Or what if there's something wrong with our sleds? Mom! We've waited a *year* for it snow and now it's dark."

Megan looked at the misery on Chad's face. *Why must this child borrow so much trouble?* Megan stooped down and looked Chad in the eye.

"Look, bud, I know you want to get out there in the snow right now, but we've talked about this kind of thing before." Megan brushed Chad's hair from his face and watched him try to contain the tears that wanted to fall. She searched her own heart for a way to console him. "The snow is a blessing you've been waiting for, Chad. Let's spend tonight being thankful. We'll see what tomorrow brings, ok."

"But there's nothing to *do.*"

"Why don't you see if you can get your siblings interested in making Christmas cards until dinner is ready."

His mother could see that Chad was still not convinced, but he conceded, "Yeah, I guess that could be fun."

"And helpful." Megan stood and put her arm around his shoulder. "We still haven't sent a card to Aunt Jane."

Chad's face suddenly brightened. "Mom! That's a great idea!" His raised his voice several decibels and cupped his hands around his mouth as he called to everyone within earshot, "Time to be creative!"

Chad's four siblings came running through the hall, past Megan and into the living room. Hoots of glee and excitement tapered off as they settled in with card-making supplies. There would be a mess later, but that's what houses were for, right?

"I guess snack time is over?" Megan smiled at Ron's new addition to their 'staff.' Lisa Wilson was a college senior who Ron had hired to help Megan with cooking and cleaning over Christmas break. If things worked well between Megan and Lisa, she would stay on part-time after the spring semester started.

Lisa had only been with them a few days, but already Megan could see that she wanted her to stay on after Christmas. Not only was her help desperately needed, she was the most loving and helpful creature Megan had ever met. Megan followed Lisa back into the kitchen and looked at the clock on the microwave. "And soon it will be time for dinner."

"You make it easy. Deciding what to fix would be the hard part." Megan could see that Lisa had already shopped and was beginning to fix their evening meal. Megan planned three weeks' worth of menus when Aimee and Hessie were still here. The food choices were such a big hit that they had continued to prepare meals based on the large chart on the kitchen wall. Calculating the amounts needed and making weekly shopping lists had given Megan a way to feel useful in her own home.

She could see that Lisa could manage without her, so Megan pushed through the swinging door and walked into the formal dining room. The household census had not dipped below eight since Megan had come home from the hospital, so they were in the habit of eating in this room at the larger table. The seven of them could squeeze around the breakfast table, which sat six, but eight wasn't manageable in there. Megan walked across the room and pulled open the drawer of a black bureau-turned-buffet where the linens were kept.

She picked out a damask cloth that was forgiving enough to lie neatly without being ironed. Megan was spreading the ivory cloth on the table when she heard a familiar voice.

Not again! God, please, give me a break.

Megan stood very still, listening closely to the sounds coming from the living room. She wasn't mistaken. Megan pushed the swinging door back toward the kitchen. Lisa smiled at her.

Well, at least I'm not asleep.

Megan let the door swing closed and took a deep breath. She made her way to the living room door and opened it slowly. She could hear Chris coaxing Ali, "Help little brother, Sugar. He's got more way down in the bottom of his stocking." Megan stood mesmerized by the sight, and sound, of Chris with a three-year-old Ali, a one-year-old Chad, and Baby Randy.

Megan felt someone tug her hand, "You come watch 'dis wif, us?"

"Yes, Krissy." Megan bent over and hugged her youngest child. "You want Mommy to hold you?" Krissy held up both arms. Megan gently guided her over to the deep armchair and sat down. Krissy climbed on top of her and settled in to watch more of a little girl who looked just like her, only with red hair.

"That me?"

Megan laughed and answered without taking her eyes off the screen. "No, it's Ali." Megan looked at her oldest daughter. "I never realized how much Krissy looks like you."

"I have. You can really tell in pictures, too."

"I thought you all were making Christmas cards," Megan reminded them. She could see that they had opted to make the cards in the living room and watch a home movie, which they had permission to do without counting it towards tv time.

"We still are," Ali said, smiling.

Megan watched the screen for several more minutes. She tried to remember when she had last watched home movies or perused an old photo album. She could remember seeing a video of their 'pretend' Christmas a month before Chris died and pictures of her and Chris with their children at the Fall Festival that year, but it could be that she'd seen those with Chris while he was still alive.

Had she been avoiding old images of her family with Chris still in it? The thought had never occurred to her. Surely she didn't avoid watching these with the kids.

The children laughed and talked as they watched the home movie. "How many years ago was this, Mom?" The question came from Chad.

Megan had to count. "Well, if Randy was a baby, then it was, hmmm. Oh my. Six years ago."

"Wow. Look how much I grew in just *six* years!"

Megan agreed, "I know. It's hard to believe." *Have I grown that much, Lord. Or am I the same stubborn child I was back then? Have I learned anything in* six *years?*

Megan was trying to calculate how many months this video was filmed before Lily was born when someone sat a goblet of ice water beside her. She smiled and looked up to thank Lisa but almost tipped the glass over when she saw Ron standing over her. He placed one index finger over his lips and waited a few seconds before leaning over to kiss her forehead.

He whispered, "It's OK." He kept his lips pressed against her forehead. "Sshhhh."

Tears fell down Megan's cheeks. Ron walked over to where Lily was perched on the sofa. He picked her up and placed her in his lap so he could watch the movie with them. Megan looked at Ron with frantic eyes.

Ron asked the children, "Who's the little doll with the red curls?"

Ali beamed. "Can you believe how little I was? Listen when I talk. It sounds just like *Krissy*."

Finally Time to Dance

"And Lily, too!" Randy added.

As Ron and the children sat and shared comments and laughs over the memories Megan and Chris had recorded, Megan worried how they would all reconcile Chris being 'in' their home, especially so close to Christmas.

But the more Megan sat and worried, the more she realized that she was the only one worrying. *Calm, me, God. Give me something to cling to!*

As soon as the prayer was thought, Megan remembered the verses she used to share almost every day with Ali when she began her worrying career early into her fourth year of life. Megan had read the verses to her daughter so frequently back then that she even had a hand-written heading above the sixth chapter of Matthew in her Bible that read, "Our Worry Chapter."

Megan knew her own Bible was on her nightstand, but she looked around for one in the living room. Krissy had left her tiny pink New Testament on the coffee table.

Megan whispered into Krissy's ear, "Go get Mommy your Bible."

"Why?" "Because I want to read something in it."

Krissy obeyed and toddled over to the coffee table and returned with the small book. "Here go!"

"Thank you." Megan kissed Krissy on the cheek and turned to the first book. When she found chapter six, she scanned down to the twenty-fifth verse. Megan read the familiar passage. She could have recited it from memory since she and Ali had memorized it together, but Megan had learned long ago that God blessed her effort to open His Word and read, verbatim, even the most familiar Scripture.

Megan made her way through the verses, looking for some answers, some guidance. She stopped after the thirty-fourth verse and read it again.

Therefore do not worry about tomorrow, for tomorrow will worry about itself. Each day has enough trouble of its own.

Megan closed her eyes and meditated on the message the words held for her. *Am I borrowing trouble?* The words echoed the very advice she had just given Chad about worrying about whether or not there would be enough snow for sledding tomorrow.

We'll see what tomorrow brings, bud.

Easier said than done.

Megan had spent most of the past several weeks borrowing trouble not only from tomorrow but from weeks, months, even years ahead.

"Dinner's ready," Lisa called in a sing-songy voice.

Megan watched as her troop made their way to the dining room. Chad stopped the VCR and hit the power button on the television.

Ron made eye contact with his wife and smiled quickly before picking up Lily and filing into the dining room. Krissy scampered off. Chad and Ali were asking Lisa what was for dinner. Seeing all of them appear healed and able to live in these circumstances made Megan sad. She fought back more tears that threatened to fall.

"Do you need some help, Mrs. Wellbourne?" Lisa was standing next to her, waiting for the lady of the house to come to dinner so the meal could be served.

"I'm fine, hon. Go ahead and start without me." Megan picked up her water glass. "I want to drink some of this before I start eating." It was a feeble excuse, but Lisa accepted it and left to get Megan's family's dinner served.

Megan sat up and tried to gain her composure.

Ron had been the picture of grace and patience while Megan sat holding herself prisoner in the worry and doubt that filled her days and nights. Megan need only walk through her home to see what the man had done to make her and her children comfortable and happy. Not a single physical need had gone unmet.

Ron saw to it that Megan had all the supplies and resources she needed to teach the children. Several friends came by each day to offer to run errands or take the children to the park. Megan had so much to be thankful for. She was even thankful that Ron still made a spot on his pillow for her each night. Twice this past week, she had woken up to feel him holding her hand next to his cheek.

It was just still so hard to let that feel safe, secure. Permanent.

The words from Matthew resonated again in her head.

Therefore do not worry about tomorrow, for tomorrow will worry about itself. Each day has enough trouble of its own.

Would she ever be able to let go of the worry?

Megan turned in her chair and stared at Ron's latest contribution to their home. A sparkling tree stood in the front window.

Ron had set it up and retrieved all of the children's Christmas ornaments from the basement. He had watched in amusement as Megan opened each box and the children explained to whom the ornament belonged or who had made it. It had been an exciting two hours for the children while they placed all of their ornaments on the tree. Yet, even the fond memories and bright colors reminded Megan of the confusion and contradictions that plagued her.

The engagement of Megan Hardin to Ron Wellbourne had spawned no less than four bridal showers. An October wedding uniting two adults who had most of the usual household essentials had brought out the creativity in their family and friends. Ron and Megan received at least ten Christmas ornaments that read, "Our First Christmas Together" or had the date of their wedding engraved on them. Though appreciative of the thoughtfulness behind the gifts, Megan had seen them as reminders that she had many other Christmas ornaments that celebrated a wonderful marriage.

She and Chris had collected an ornament to celebrate each Christmas they were married. When Chris was alive, they had put the ornaments on their tree together. After he died, Megan had put them on the tree first before she let the children hang theirs.

Megan dreaded the decision of whether or not to put them on tree this year. Not wanting to face the decision, she came home after the third bridal shower and took the 'Hardin' ornaments out of the large storage containers, intending to replace them with the new ones she and Ron had gotten together. Sitting here now, she realized that she had never gotten around to putting the 'Wellbourne' ornaments where they belonged. Neither set had made it onto the tree, and neither Ron nor the children had noticed.

"Just try to enjoy the tree like it is, Meg," she chastised herself.

Megan heard her family behind her as they sat down to dinner. The room was filled with laughter. She heard Randy ask, "Where's Mom?"

Ali answered, "Thinking again."

Megan waited for someone to ask for clarification of that answer, but the other four children just accepted it and dinner continued. Without Megan.

Megan stood and walked toward the dining room. She paused at the mirror over the fireplace and studied her reflection. Megan tipped her chin up in resolve. She breathed deeply and told herself, "Time to get back in the game, girl."

Chapter 33

"Good night, Mom." Lily leaned over and kissed her mother. Krissy crawled across the bed and threw herself on Megan's lap.

"'Night, Mommy."

"Good night, girls." Megan hugged her two youngest daughters and kissed them both on their noses. Megan loved to hear them giggle when she did that. "Lily, please put this book away for me." Megan held out the large book of puzzle pictures.

"Sure, Mom." Lily grabbed the book and ran off to place it on a bookshelf in the office. Krissy was hot on her heels.

Megan lay back on her pillows and wondered when she had become 'Mom' instead of 'Mommy' to her five-year-old. All of her children were growing so fast. It seemed like only yesterday, Megan was pregnant with Ali. Eleven years ago, she and Chris were gazing at their Christmas tree, wondering if God would give them a boy or a girl. Megan laughed. *He wound up giving us plenty of each.*

Megan picked up her Bible and turned to the passage

she had been reading before dinner. She read the thirty-fourth verse again and thought of the irony of God being as frustrated with her as she was with her own children.

Surely I can do better than that.

Megan mentally tried to measure the worry and frustration that had passed through her heart and mind the past two and a half months. She looked again at the passage of Scripture and Jesus' equating worry to a lack of faith in God to do what He says He's going to do.

Faith. Is that what I lack?

Megan closed her Bible. *All I know is that if I don't get out of this house I'll go nuts.* She considered the likelihood of escaping, and the odds were not in her favor. Megan would need an accomplice to go out in the light snow, but all of her partners in crime were otherwise occupied.

Julie was busy with her own family this close to Christmas. Dee was an hour away. Aimee and Hessie had gone home weeks ago. Betty was in the throes of her wedding rehearsal. Lisa was gone for the evening.

All the friends and family who had helped her escape for brief shopping trips and visits to the hair salon were busy with their own lives. Megan threw back the covers on her bed and walked over to the sofa in her bedroom. She plopped down on the thick cushions and picked up a large stack of magazines and catalogs on the table in front of her. If she was going to be confined to home, Megan would at least make herself useful.

She began making three piles of books, one for throwing out, one for sharing, and the other for keeping, which she desperately wanted to keep to a minimum. When she threw out things, it helped her feel organized inside and out. *Being productive will clear my head and my heart for the holiday. If I don't blow off some steam soon, Christmas is going to be miserable. My children don't deserve that.*

Megan finished her piles. She stood and carried the largest one to the kitchen trash can. Ron was sitting at the breakfast table making notes on a small piece of paper. He smiled at her as she walked past and said something about being just a while longer. Megan felt a small twinge of guilt at not collaborating with him on gifts for the children. He had tried to talk to her about her plans for them and had even suggested he take her to the city so they could do some shopping together. Megan had stubbornly refused and by the next time she had seen her husband, she was armed with the receipts for the gifts she'd bought online, without his input.

The hurt look on his face from that night still haunted her. Ashamed, Megan walked from the room.

There it was again. *Worry.*

Megan pushed theology and Divine guidance aside and walked from the room without acknowledging her husband.

She closed the bedroom door softly and tried to think of something constructive to do. Megan knew there were a million small details she could work on the night before the day before Christmas, but the thought of getting out and, of all things, feeling the wind on her face, kept tugging at her heart.

I want to ride in that little car, Megan groaned inwardly.

For a split second, she considered asking Ron to go to his Mom's house and get his MG. *You've lost your mind! He won't do anything that risky this late. And there's no one to stay with the kids.* Megan sighed and pulled the drawer of her nightstand out. *I'll putter until the urge to play passes.*

"What are you *doing*?"

Megan let out a small scream. She had not heard a knock on the door, and seeing Liz Fairbanks in her bedroom at who-knows-when at night was absurd. She glanced at her bedside clock.

"Liz, it's after ten p.m. What are *you* doing?"

Liz took her bag off her shoulder and made her way to the low sofa. "Well, I'm not cleaning out drawers." Liz settled in with a magazine she pulled from her bag.

"Don't leave that here. I just sorted through a huge stack of magazines and catalogs."

Liz didn't even look at her friend. She apparently recognized 'stir-crazy' when she saw it. "Happy holidays." Liz flipped to the entertainment column and continued to ignore and increasingly agitated Megan Wellbourne.

"I'm not feeling up to company."

Liz smiled. "Oh, honey. I'm not here to visit you. I'm here to get you off your hind end."

Megan stood in miffed silence. Liz read the column without flinching.

"What do you want?" Megan could see a smile playing at the corners of Liz's mouth. She was *enjoying* this! "Liz, I mean it. I'm about to blow. Hit the relief valve or leave me to my sorting and sulking."

Liz closed the magazine and placed it in her lap. "Well, since you're willing to be honest..."

Megan folded her arms in frustration. "Spit it out."

Liz chuckled mischievously. "And your husband thinks you're not feeling well."

Megan had to struggle not to giggle and the ludicrousness of Liz's tone. She held her hands up in the air. "If I had a white flag, I'd wave it. I know better than to tangle with you." Megan lowered her arms and sat on the edge of her bed. "I'm listening."

Liz smiled warmly. "Now, was that so hard?"

Megan laughed.

"I see you're still dressed, so your orders are easy. Your husband is waiting for you in the hall. Go meet him."

Megan looked at Liz in dismay.

"Don't give me that 'et tu, Liz?' look. Just go." Liz went back to her reading. "No need to thank me."

Megan suddenly felt like a small child, chastised and put in time out. She furrowed her brow and looked at the floor. "Why?"

Liz ignored Megan's question. "I can hear the children from here if they need anything. They'll be fine."

Tears spilled onto Megan's cheeks. She wanted to scream at Liz and tell her she didn't know what she was asking and explain how much pain being alone with Ron would cause her, cause everyone. This was *so* unfair!

Megan paced the room twice, looking for a way out. She stopped in front of Liz, who never looked up. Finally, she walked into the closet and shut the door. Angrier than she had been in weeks, Megan pulled on her warmest boots and grabbed the scarf Ali had given her last Christmas. She looked down at the scarf and threw it on the floor.

Last Christmas! When everything still made sense. Megan choked on the sobs that erupted from her throat.

This is *so* wrong! Megan sat on the floor and rested her head against the island. She put her hands on the floor to stop the room from spinning. Megan heard the door open.

"Dr. Nolan told you that your physical recovery would take time. You're going to be back in bed if you keep fighting the inevitable."

Megan couldn't even look at Liz. She was confronting her with the truth and Megan was running from it. It was so simple that Megan was ashamed. After several seconds, Megan managed to ask, "What does he want?"

"Nothing. Absolutely nothing." Megan looked at Liz, doubtful.

Liz elaborated. "He just wants you to go out in the hall." Liz added softly, "With an open mind and an open heart." Liz sighed. "Actually, that last part isn't from him; it's from me. He deserves a few open-minded minutes from you."

"But what if..."

Liz held up one hand. "That's how we Christians always preface worry." Liz shook her head. "Matthew, chapter 6. Do you need a direct quote?"

Megan sniffed and wiped her face with both hands. "No, I was brushing up on that chapter earlier tonight."

Liz's face brightened. "Ah, a God moment. You gotta

love those."

"Hebrews eleven, verse one. Remind me of that one."

Liz smiled and crouched down next to Megan on her closet floor. The older woman took her friend's hand and quoted the Scripture: *"Now, faith is being sure of what we hope for and certain of what we do not see."*

Megan stared at nothing in particular. "I hope for much and see nothing."

"Sounds like He's got you where He wants you."

Megan nodded. "Just go out there? Meet him in the hall?"

Liz rubbed Megan's shoulder. "Like taking a walk in the park."

"If only..."

"Go on. Ron's waited long enough."

....

Ron checked his hair in the bathroom mirror one last time while he went over the list in his head. He hoped he had remembered everything. Tonight was the night. He was going on a date with his wife.

He heard the bedroom door creak open. Megan was standing in the hallway when he turned around. He didn't know quite how to begin. It had been weeks since they had intentionally been alone, and the silence was awkward. Megan rescued him.

"I figured we might be going out, so I dressed warmly." Megan held out her scarf and tipped up her toe to show him her boot.

Ron was grateful. She was trusting him. He reminded himself that this was a good thing. "So, you don't mind going out?"

"Are you kidding? I could kiss you for helping me break out!" Megan blushed at her comment, knowing she really should kiss the poor guy. He had obviously been planning this for a while. "I guess I've started going a little stir-crazy."

Content just to be near his wife and have her talking to him so candidly, Ron didn't solicit the aforementioned kiss. Instead, he held out his left arm and stood beside Megan. "Shall we?"

Megan stood a little taller and giggled, "Yes, let's."

They walked down the basement stairs and into Ron's garage. Ron escorted Megan to the passenger's side door of his Jeep. She hesitated and turned around. "I think I'll grab my coat."

Ron held his ground behind her and coaxed her into the Jeep. "It's all right. You'll be fine." He saw Megan give him a puzzled look but she slid into the seat and took the seat belt when he offered it. Ron breathed deeply and focused on his plan.

The snow had stopped falling, but daytime temperatures in the twenties and low thirties had left everything that had fallen still on the ground. Ron engaged the four-wheel drive before backing out into the driveway. The added traction made the trip down the steep hill in front of their house and around the corner onto Stadium Drive a cinch, even in three inches of snow. Ron saw Megan search his face, looking for a hint about where they were going. Patience was not her long suit, so they were scarcely two blocks from home when she asked, "Where are we going?"

Ron flipped his turn signal on to make a right turn into the stadium parking lot. "Right here."

Megan bit her lip as they made their way across the parking lot. If they were getting out at the stadium, she'd really need her coat. She glanced around, trying not to ask questions, lest she sound ungrateful and accusing.

Ron pulled the Jeep to a stop and gave Megan a wide smile. Still confused, Megan asked, "What?"

Ron nodded to her window. "Look."

When she looked out her window, Megan gasped, "Oh, my." She smiled and turned back to Ron. Her voice was husky when she said, "You really are a fool."

Ron took her hand returned her smile. "Only for you."

With that, Megan pushed open her door and baled out. She slipped slightly on the asphalt, but recovered quickly as she made her way to the MG. Megan was laughing and crying at the same time. She stared at the tiny car in disbelief. This was Ron's pet, his cherished car.

Ron began brushing snow off the ragtop and unhooked the latches. Megan's heart beat faster. "What are you doing?"

Ron walked around to the other side of the car and said, "Putting down the top, of course." As the top went down, Megan saw her coat and gloves sitting on the passenger's seat. A small fleece throw was folded on the floorboard. Megan was beaming.

She understood why he had taken her here to get in the car. The tiny MG would never have made it up or down their steep hill in the snow.

Ron walked back to Megan's side of the car and stood behind her. She could feel his warm breath on her neck as he whispered in her ear, "If we don't go crazy every now and then, we'll both go nuts." Megan felt Ron's lips brush against her neck and ear as he spoke.

She turned and faced Ron, but their eyes met, she felt herself take one step back. Ron moved closer to her and Megan felt an instant of panic before she heard her door click behind her.

Ron's expression lightened as he stepped aside so she could get into the car. "Let's go for a ride, Megan." Megan gave him a grateful smile and got in.

Ron cranked the engine while she struggled into her heavy coat and pulled on her gloves. He helped Megan tuck the throw under her legs before he shifted into reverse. As they left the parking lot and headed away from campus. She leaned her head back and enjoyed the fresh, frigid air on her face as they buzzed along the familiar streets.

The car's heater and the blanket combined to keep Megan quite warm. She chatted easily with Ron as they rode past Christmas lights and snow-covered trees. During a lull in their conversation, she sneaked a glance at Ron's profile. His graying temples stuck out from under his knit hat. His expression was intense as he shifted from one gear to another. Megan wondered at how this handsome, thoughtful creature ever put up with her.

Ron caught her off guard by asking, "You want some ice cream?"

Megan screamed with laughter, "Oh, yes!"

Ron drove carefully into the parking lot of Megan's favorite ice cream store and parked the car. Megan was still trying to find her seatbelt under the layers when Ron came around to her side, opened her door, and held his hand out to her. Her rosy cheeks were framed with the fur on the hood of her coat and a smile was lighting her face. It was the first genuine smile Megan had given Ron since she had left over six weeks ago. Happiness was finally radiating from his wife, again. *Thank you, God.*

....

"I'm frozen solid." Megan was scooping the last of her hot fudge sundae from the small cup. She glanced at Ron. "You're insane."

"Yeah, but you love that about me."

Megan bit her lower lip and then nodded slightly. "Yes, I do. Only an insane person would marry a sad, brooding woman with five children." Megan was surprised by her own candor. She looked at Ron and tried to speak. *Why was telling him the truth so hard?*

After a few seconds, she continued, "I wish I wasn't scared to talk to you."

Ron knew he had to tread lightly. He took her ice cream

cup and set it aside. He held both her hands in his. He felt Megan's hands tense and let them go. *You're afraid of more than talking.* Ron sat back on his side of the booth and spoke in a low voice. "The way I see all of this, Megan, is that we have the rest of our lives to work this out. We'll take it a little at a time."

Though Megan didn't think she had the capacity to speak, the next words came easily. "And the way I see it is that we have to live every day like it's our last and if we're both miserable, we'd better get out and move on."

Ron leaned forward. Megan looked down at the table. Ron said gently, "That's not why you think we shouldn't work at this."

Megan looked up at Ron. Her expression had hardened. "Oh?"

Ron went for broke. "No. You're not afraid that we'll be unhappy for the uncertain number of days we have left together. You're afraid we won't have a lot of days left together."

Megan moved to get out of the booth. Ron grabbed her hand. "Sit down. Please, Megan. Sit down and talk to me." Megan moved her legs back in front of her, but she folded her arms and stared coldly at Ron. He had nothing to lose, so he said, "I don't have cancer, Megan. I'm not going to die."

Megan wiped a tear from her cheek. "You don't know that."

She was right. He didn't know that. "But you don't

know that I do."

"I'd rather not take my chances." Megan looked exhausted. She breathed deeply before adding, "Again."

"It wasn't worth it?"

Anger blazed in Megan's eyes. "You have no right…"

Ron put his hand on her arm and pleaded, "Just let me talk." He looked around at the few other patrons in the restaurant. "If you need to scream at me, save it for when we get home. But right now I deserve a few moments of you listening and me talking." Ron hoped he hadn't sounded too harsh, but he felt his chance to finally get to the bottom of this slipping away.

Megan shook his hand off her arm and sank back. Ron was relieved to hear her say, "Go on."

Ron took out his wallet. Megan's brow furrowed. "What are you doing?"

Ron raised his eyebrows in warning. Megan rolled her own eyes but sat up and tried to pay attention to what Ron was doing. Ron pulled a small picture out of his wallet. He laid it on the table and slid it in front of Megan. Megan stared at the snapshot of her children. Ron spoke softly. "Which one would you have changed if you'd known how things would turn out?"

Megan wanted to argue. She wanted to tell Ron he had no kids of his own and he had no idea what kind of prayer had gone into the conception and birth of each of those precious creatures. She wanted to scream at him and tell him that just because the six of them had survived Chris's death, it hadn't been easy. It had been so hard. *Watching Chris die had been so hard.*

Megan began to tremble. The tears flowed out of control and streamed down her face. She sobbed, "Watching Chris die was so hard."

Ron came over to her side of the booth and put his arm around her. She buried her face in his chest and continued sobbing. Ron was thankful for Megan's sake that their table was secluded. After several minutes, Megan began wiping her face, trying to gain her composure. Megan wiped her nose and glanced at Ron. "Fun date, huh?"

"I wouldn't want to be on a date with anyone else, Meg."

Megan laughed, "Liar."

Ron shook his head. "No. I'm here. I'm not going anywhere." Ron pushed a stray hair out of Megan's face. "You should cry more, talk about Chris more."

"Yeah, right. Just what every man dreams of. Having his wife cry about the one that got away."

Ron turned to face Megan and held her face in his hands. "Everyone you've loved, everything you've experienced, and every moment you've lived has made you who you are, who *I* love. I don't want us to go through the good parts together and have you try to sort out the bad parts alone."

Megan shook her head. "I can't, Ron." Megan picked up her coat and scarf. "It's getting late."

Ron knew that the moment was over. He helped her into her coat and they made their way out to the car.

Ron drove back to the stadium as slowly as he dared. He

wanted her to talk to him more, to trust him more. *I'm trying to be patient, Lord. This isn't easy.*

Though the answer was not audible, Ron heard it resonate in his head and in his heart: *Nothing worth having ever is.*

Chapter 34

Megan set her Bible back on her nightstand and clicked off her lamp. She had been turning to familiar passages, looking for some answers. The initial exhilaration of the car ride, followed by the exhaustion of her conversation with Ron had left her drained. Megan wondered if she and Ron had accomplished anything by getting away together.

She had known all along, if only in the back of her mind, that she had not talked about the 'bad' parts of Chris's illness. Up to now, there had been no point. The details of the weeks spent in their bedroom had been a private matter between Chris and Megan.

What Megan had discovered during those weeks, however, was that holding hands while one of you prepared to go home to be with the Father was truly the most intimate thing a husband and wife could experience together. And that, as precious and unforgettable as it had been, it had been physically and emotionally exhausting beyond anything Megan could have ever imagined.

And not something she ever wanted to take away from Chris and share with Ron.

Finally Time to Dance

Further, she didn't want Ron, or anyone else, to think she was anything less than honored to have been the one to be by Chris's side. Somewhere along the way, however, that reverence for Chris's memory had made Megan feel like she wasn't allowed to complain or even say that it had been that hard, that draining, that frightening.

Megan choked back the sobs in her throat and tried to push aside the line of thoughts that were now flowing so freely. She looked over to where Ron was sleeping.

There he was, steady as a rock. He had extended his 'pillow date' invitation and fallen into peaceful slumber, content to take whatever Megan would offer. Megan admired him more than he'd ever know. He loved her when she was so very unlovely.

She kissed her index finger softly and tenderly laid the kiss on his cheek. "How can I love you both?"

....

Megan turned on the light and gave her eyes time to adjust. She walked to the back corner of the large master bedroom closet where she stored things she did not often use.

Under the bar where she hung her dresses and long coats, Megan kept the cedar chest her father had given her when she went away to boarding school. Its design was simple, which Paul had known would suit Megan perfectly. Anywhere she had lived, Megan had found a place for the special chest. In it, she kept childhood memorabilia, trinkets from when each of her children were born, old photographs, and other pieces of her life that she didn't want to forget. When she had moved to this house, however, she did not display the chest. She felt like the enormous closet was the perfect place for her secret treasures.

Ali had asked her why it was not in the living room where everyone could see it. Megan had placated her oldest daughter by telling her that it didn't match the décor in the living room and really should be kept somewhere else until she decorated a room where it would "fit."

Megan wondered if she'd ever admit the truth to Ali. She kept the chest hidden because she was trying to forget some of the memories it held.

Megan kneeled down and reached behind the wooden chest. She found the tiny door and slid it open. The round key fell into Megan's hand.

Megan worked to steady her hands. She unlocked the chest and opened it slowly. Megan did not take the time to relish in the memories that she uncovered. She worked swiftly and removed everything from the center until a small rectangle at the bottom was visible. She turned the key over and unlocked the small door.

Megan took a deep breath and pulled out the bundle of envelopes and papers. She flipped through them until she found the envelope with the wildlife scene on the corner. She had bought the stationery for Chris, who had loved hunting and fishing when time, money, and his health had permitted. Megan held the envelope up and studied the yellow sticky note on the outside.

This is not to be mailed unless I do not survive surgery one week from today or meet my Heavenly Father at a date not too distant from then and now. Thank you, C. Hardin."

It was dated two weeks after Krissy was born, almost exactly three months before Chris died.

There were two envelopes inside, a larger one and a smaller one. Megan pulled out the smaller one. Their church secretary, Jan, had given her the packet in a stack of cards she delivered to Megan the night before Christmas Eve. The older woman had suspected that some of cards contained gifts that Megan might want to use if she still had shopping to do for the children the next day. Over the course of Chris's illness, Jan and Megan had become friends, and Jan had written her a note about the contents of the envelope.

Megan,

When you read this next letter, I want you to be in a quiet place, kids asleep, and you ready for this. Chris gave this letter to me the night before his last surgery. He said, Give this to Megan for me." I said, "Right now?" He said, "When something happens," and laughed!

After the surgery, I tried to give it back to him. He told me to "give this to Megan when it's the right time." I laughed and said, "When is that?" and he said, "Not immediately – just right."

I've prayed and I believe today is the right time for you to read the letter your very best friend wrote.

Megan let the tears flow freely, shamelessly, down her cheeks and onto her t-shirt. A few tears fell onto the larger envelope as she pulled it out. It was addressed to her at their home in Oklahoma City in Chris's handwriting.

She gingerly pulled out the letter it held. She had only read it once before, the night Jan had given it to her. Megan blinked away tears as she realized that it had been exactly three years ago tonight. She marveled at God's timing and gave her fear and worry to Him as she read the short note on the outside of the folded letter.

For Megan, The Inspiration and Love of my life.

You will never know what you have meant to me and how happy you have made me. THANK YOU!

Megan closed her eyes and cried softly. She could hardly see the paper she unfolded. The tears continued as Megan wiped her eyes and read Chris's words to her.

My Precious Princess,

All of you are sleeping, so I am attempting to write this note to you. I never thought it would come to this —I pray that you will never read this note, but I trust in God's plan completely and am not frightened of what's ahead at all. I am very sad and concerned for you and the kids —I am turning that concern over to God more and more every month.

I could write books to you and never list all of the wonderful things you have brought to my life and all of the joy you give me hourly. Don't ever think that I ever felt neglected or pushed aside. I am just so thankful for you, your love for me and my children, and your precious, caring heart and attitude. I don't know how you do it and I watch you daily and have seen you transform over the years. It is obvious that your true heart's desire is to take care of me and our five children. I pray that God will give you strength and wisdom for years to come. Don't ever doubt yourself or look back and question your motto, "Me and God make a majority." You know our kids better than anyone else in the world. You have to make the best decisions you know how to make for all of you to be able to survive.

I have not given up, nor do I plan to do so, but this is something I wanted to leave you. I hope it is encouraging and reassuring. Thank you for making my life wonderful! I love you with all that I am!

Love always,
Chris

Megan held Chris's note to her chest and tried to steady her breathing. She cherished Chris's words. *I pray that God will give you strength and wisdom for years to come.* Megan knew God was answering Chris's prayers. God was giving her strength and wisdom. But what was Megan doing with it?

Too tired think clearly any more, Megan returned the contents of her cedar chest to its proper place and put the small key back in its hiding place. She shouldn't have been surprised to see Ron standing in the doorway when she turned to leave the closet.

"Coming to bed?" Ron asked.

Megan nodded her head and wiped her eyes with the sleeve of her t-shirt. Ron put his hand around her waist and escorted her to her side of their bed. The candle Liz had lit was still flickering on Megan's nightstand. Megan smoothed her pillow and crawled under the comforters. The tears still would not stop.

Ron settled in and turned on his side to face her. "Megan, I can't say that I know what you're going through. I've never been through, what does the Psalmist call it? The 'valley of the shadow'? Not with someone as close as a spouse or even a parent. You've handled it all so gracefully. I can't imagine how you've done it."

He caressed Megan's face. "If you need someone to listen, I'm here. That's why God put us together. To be a team. To help each other."

Megan turned toward Ron and stared at the wall behind him. She could see her silhouette. Megan lifted one hand and spread her fingers. It cast a huge shadow. "Look how big and scary that is. That shadow. Shadows are dark and scary, Ron."

Ron rolled his head over and looked at the dark, ominous image Megan made with her small, graceful hand. He turned back to her and put her hand in his. Megan saw their hands blend into one shadow on the wall.

Ron watched Megan's face as he spoke to her. "Well, that's the thing about shadows, Meg. We're taught from the time we're little kids that they are big and scary. And to a kid, that's all they are. But as we grow up, we learn a lot more about shadows."

Megan eyed Ron curiously. He brought her hand down and put it between them. "Take that scary shadow you made with your hand, for instance. It's way bigger than your real hand." Megan smiled when Ron kissed her fingers tenderly. "Another thing about that big figure on the wall is that it has no strength on its own. It can't harm you. It doesn't weigh anything. Without your hand, it doesn't even exist."

Ron sat up and scooted closer to Megan. "And the most important thing about a shadow is that wherever there's a shadow, there's light." Ron stroked Megan's hair softly. "You taught me that, Meg. You showed me that the God I had forsaken had never gone anywhere. He's there, even when things look really dark to us."

"I don't deserve you, Ron Wellbourne."

Ron pulled his wife close to him and held her for a few moments. "Sometimes I feel the same way about you, Megan. You're an incredible mother, friend, wife. I'm still in awe that God picked you out for me."

Megan wiped more tears from her face. "Even if I can't stop crying?"

Ron laughed. "Especially when you can't stop crying. That's what makes you so wonderful, Meg. Your tender heart." He pressed his lips to her forehead then tucked her head under his chin. "Stop worrying. We'll sort through all this together."

Ron squeezed Megan's shoulder after a few moments. He asked, "You sleepy?"

"I should be, but not really."

"Come with me." Ron was out of bed and to the bedroom door before Megan could argue. She met him at the door and took his hand when he offered it. "Another adventure?"

"No convertibles, this time."

"Rats."

Ron chuckled and led her to the living room. He motioned

for her to sit on the floor near the tree then pulled a box out from under it. He put the gift on the floor in front of Megan and sat down.

"Let me get one for you." Megan reached under the tree, but Ron stopped her.

"This isn't an 'exchange.' It's more like something I wrapped for both of us." Megan looked at him quizzically. Ron nodded. "Just trust me."

He pushed the box to her. "Open it."

Getting into the spirit, Megan tore at the package with childish enthusiasm. She took the lid off the office supply box and peered inside. Her enthusiasm turned to awe. "And I had just stopped crying."

"Well, we couldn't have that, now could we?" Ron stood up. "Come on. I'll help you hang these."

One by one, Megan began pulling out the Christmas ornaments she and Chris had collected over the years. She instinctively knew that she and Ron's ornaments were further down in the box and they would be able to enjoy each of them as they hung those together. Megan stopped before hanging one that had been special to her and Chris. "Thank you."

Ron looked at the tiny ship in a bottle Megan held in her hand. "Where did you get that one?"

Megan laughed. "Biloxi. We had been married three months when we took our first vacation to the beach. We were still in college and really couldn't afford a hotel room, so Chris packed his old Boy Scout tent and we pitched it on a primitive sight near the sand."

"Sounds like fun."

Megan laughed even louder. "Please! It was awful. It rained and ants infested our tent and a raccoon stole most of our food." Megan looked back at the tiny bottle. "But every year when we hung this up, we laughed together."

"That's what marriage is, isn't it? Finding the good in the bad?"

Megan hung the ornament and then hugged Ron. "Most of the time, yes." She smiled and looked up at him. "But sometimes, when you least expect it, things are just downright good."

Ron tipped Megan's chin up and gently kissed her lips. He held up an ornament Megan recognized from their shower gifts. "Shall we put this one on *our* tree?"

Megan nodded, the swell of emotion leaving her unable to speak. Ron walked to the tree and removed a tiny light from a branch near the top. When he plugged the ornament in where the light had been, a small nativity scene lighted up and *Silent Night* streamed softly through the room.

Ron took Megan's hand and brushed his lips against it. He looked longingly into her eyes. "May I have this dance?"

Megan knew this was the moment. She'd spent months praying for guidance and for strength to move on. God was asking her right now to take a huge step toward living again. Megan looked at Ron and there was really only one answer.

"Yes, you may have this dance."

Ron kissed her softly and stepped closer, putting his hand on the small of her back. He breathed into her ear, "Don't worry if you don't know all the steps. I'll lead." His kissed her again then added, "I'll ask for direction if I lose my way."

Photo by Shawn Freeman

About This Dance

Mamie Thompson is an alumnus of the Louisiana School for Math, Science, and the Arts. She and her late husband, David Daniel, were among some of the first students to walk the halls of Louisiana's only state residential high school for the academically and artistically gifted and talented. They were members of its second graduating class.

Mamie earned her BS in dietetics from Nicholls State University, along the bayous of South Louisiana. She earned her MS in nutritional sciences from the University of Oklahoma's Health Sciences Center in Oklahoma City and is a registered and licensed dietitian.

A dynamic speaker, Mamie found her voice among Christian women by sharing the lessons God taught her through David's illness and death. After several years of sharing her experience and insight, Mamie was inspired to pen a novel about her journey through the valley of the shadow and back into the light as she fell in love once again.

She and her husband, Richard, are the main characters in her first novel, Finally Time to Dance. They live with their six children in Ada, Oklahoma.

You can contact Mamie or find out more about her writing at mamiethompson.com